The Dance of the Muses

Heather Ingman

The Dance of the Muses

A NOVEL ON THE LIFE OF
PIERRE RONSARD

PETER OWEN · LONDON

ISBN 0 7206 0679 9

All Rights Reserved. No part of this publication may be reproduced in any form or by any means without the prior permission of the publishers.

PETER OWEN PUBLISHERS
73 Kenway Road London SW5 0RE

First published in Great Britain 1987
© Heather Ingman 1987

Photoset by Rowland Phototypesetting Ltd
Bury St Edmunds Suffolk
Printed in Great Britain by
St Edmundsbury Press Ltd Bury St Edmunds Suffolk

To my parents, with love

PREFACE

It will be apparent from the start that this book is not intended to be a contribution to the already substantial body of scholarly work on Ronsard. Whilst I am, of course, well acquainted with much of the critical writing on Ronsard and have read or reread many of his classical sources, in *The Dance of the Muses* I have attempted what is essentially a fictional reconstruction of a poet's mind.

Pierre Ronsard (1524–85) was acknowledged by his contemporaries to be the greatest French poet of his century. This fact is more important than it may seem, for Ronsard lived in an age which, unlike our own, placed a high value on poetry. Poets then were capable of swaying the hearts and minds of entire nations; they were respected and listened to, even by kings. They occasionally influenced royal policy.

The novel opens in April 1577 and ends in February 1578 with the publication of the fifth collected edition of Ronsard's poems. This was a period when Ronsard was suffering from ill health and the partial eclipse of his reputation at court, during which one can readily imagine Ronsard looking back over his life, and indeed his poems become arguably more reflective and melancholy around this time.

Although I have tried to adhere to the facts of Ronsard's life as closely as possible, it is above all around Ronsard's own poems that I have woven my fictional re-creation. On occasions, poetry and life part company. For instance, it is possible (how can we ever know for certain?) that Ronsard observed the rule of celibacy incumbent on him as a tonsured clerk of the Church. However, his love poetry tells a different story, and where poetry and life clash, I have chosen to reflect what is expressed in his poems. As one literary historian has remarked, if one suppresses the love element entirely when writing of Ronsard, one risks presenting an emasculated and conventional man. Moreover, it will be readily apparent that the sexual theme is linked closely with the theme of poetical inspiration, as indeed it is in Ronsard's poems. Poetry represents an enlargement of the self or maybe even its replacement by a series of fictional selves. It is with these fictional selves that I am concerned here, that is, not with the literal but the poetic truth, a distinction which Ronsard himself would have recognized.

The *Dance of the Muses* was written, as Rabelais would have said, during the hours normally devoted to eating and drinking. If it encourages more English readers of Ronsard's poetry, it will have achieved its purpose.

CONTENTS

Acknowledgements   x
Prologue   1
Part One: The Soldier   7
Part Two: Scholar's Apprentice   63
Part Three: The Peasant   99
Part Four: Defender of the Faith   123
Part Five: The Courtier   161
Epilogue   191

ACKNOWLEDGEMENTS

I cannot write on Ronsard without acknowledging the guidance and influence of a very fine scholar, Professor Malcolm Smith, who first opened my eyes to the beauties of French Renaissance poetry. He is in no way responsible for the picture of Ronsard presented here and indeed may disagree with it in several respects.

My thanks go also to Dr John Masterson, who read an early draft of the book and laughed at the right parts.

Finally, I should like to thank my husband, Ferdinand von Prondzynski. Were it not for his efforts, the manuscript would still be lying in a drawer.

PROLOGUE

'I'm sorry, I can't seem to . . .'

'It's all right, sir, I don't mind,' replies the girl.

Now King David was old and advanced in years, and though they covered him with clothes, he could not get warm. So they sought throughout all the territory of Israel for a beautiful maiden to lie with him. And they found Abishag the Shunammite and brought her to the King. The maiden was very beautiful and she became the King's nurse and ministered to him; but the King knew her not.

Damn it, I have some years on David, I'll not give up so easily.

'Here, where's your hand?' I say to my Shunammite from the village down the road. 'Rub hard. Here. That's right.'

A pause. Then plaintively, 'My arm is aching, sir.'

'Well then, let's rest a moment. By the way, what is your name, child?'

'Marie, sir.'

I wince. Another slap in the face from fate. Wouldn't my enemies rejoice to see me now, Pierre Ronsard, expert writer of love sonnets, bedded down with a rosy cheeked serving-girl, unable to get it up! But then my penis, like my pen, has always had a life of its own. Perhaps it's no coincidence that at this point both are refusing to work. I glare angrily down at the blue, wrinkled stump.

'I think something's happening, sir.'

I feel a little movement, a stirring in the loins. There is life there still, then. Pity King David!

'Thank God for that.'

I raise her, flushed from her exertions, and turn her over on to her back. I thrust into her and she moans a little, for form's sake perhaps. Her velvety, peach-like softness excites me. Ambitiously, I attempt some circular motions. That's more like it! Things are going fine when – crack! – a burning stab of pain shears down my back and I am stuck. Stuck in the most ridiculous position of all. Plenty of well-respected people have died like this – the Marquis of Mantua's son, the Platonic philosopher Speusippus, even, it is said, Pope John XXII. Is death about to catch me too?

'God forgive me,' I groan, and wrench and pull and tug. Then suddenly the load that has been pressing on me falls away. The veil of sleep lifts. I open one eye warily and look around. There is no girl in my bed. There are no bedclothes either. I must have kicked them off in my efforts to free myself. Yes, there they are, in a heap on the floor. I sink back on to the pillow. It was all a dream, then. My old man's trembling hands reach down for the scarlet wool coverlet and pull it up round my old man's scrawny neck. 'Forgive me, Lord,' I mutter. 'Father of all goodness, give me grace not to offend Thee this day, and preserve me in the religion of my forefathers.' Somewhere in the distance a cock crows.

A dream, yes, but it could so easily have been real. When is a rose still growing and when does it start to fade? At what stage do we stop calling a man young and begin to think of him as old? Where is the turning-point? I have been white-haired for a long time. Why is it only tonight that the realization of my old age has crept up and grabbed me by the leg?

It's a subject I have never cared to think about much, death. Oh, other people's deaths, my father's, Lazare's, Joachim's, Marie's, yes, but never my own. I never really pictured a time when the world would go on without me in it. Now, as I lie shivering beneath the coverlet, the thought of my death steals up on me. It seizes hold of my imagination till all the air around me seems to throb with the stately organ music of death, the moans and sobs of violins.

In the end, however, the chill in my bones and the pain rippling through my muscles (what have I done to my back?) chase away these funereal thoughts. I leave the metaphysical for the physical and concentrate on my cramps.

After an hour or so, Amadis arrives in my room. My

presence has been missed at mass. He touches my forehead and goes away shaking his head. I have a fever again. He summons two of the more trusted monks. They give me an opiate to dull the arthritis in my bones and move me into Amadis's room. He delays his return to court especially in order to tend me. How good he is! The sight of his open, handsome face, his graceful movements, his very presence, soothes me. He used to be my secretary. He turned up on my doorstep one day, a young Endymion kissed by the moon, and I took him on. He was the best secretary I've ever had, but he is a poet in his own right now and the court claims more and more of his time. His poetry is popular there, more popular than my own, I have to admit. The court – that bitch goddess, maker and breaker of men. . . .

Lucky for me that Amadis is here. Naturally rumours of my illness have reached Paris and naturally we are plagued by 'anxious' visitors inquiring after my health. Not that it's my health they are concerned about. No. All they want to know is whether they should polish up the obituaries they have had lying in their drawers for months and whether they should start intriguing for one of the posts that will fall vacant after my death. Amadis deals with their prying questions so skilfully that they go away certain that the tales they have heard of my imminent demise cannot be true.

But despite Amadis's tenderness, as I lie here in bed surrounded by phials and basins, doleful symbols of old age, the gloomy thoughts which seized hold of me that long night keep returning. I believe that ridiculous, humiliating dream has marked my turning-point. It's a warning from the gods that it's time to pass on the torch; I've tasted all the pleasures of life, the emphasis is now on dying. Count me out of the race from henceforth – I've a debt to pay to nature.

The signs have been there for a long time, of course – gout (too much wine and love-making, one always has to pay for it in the end), arthritis (so bad this year that I can hardly stoop to plant my beans). And other, more important things, such as no longer having the King's ear, which in itself is a kind of living death for anyone who would live at court; and seeing my place as national poet usurped by that Philippe Desportes. Yes, the roses are fading rapidly and I realize I am entirely unprepared to face whatever lies beyond, after the last petal has fallen.

Death is perhaps only a matter of months away: it is vital I get some sort of a grip on my life. What kind of a man have I been? Curious, I have never asked myself that question before, at least not in so many words. Start with the poems. Lying in bed, I go over my verses in my head, but as I do so, I begin to lose more and more my sense of self. The poet is always two people: one, the man who lives and, peeping over his shoulder, the other person who writes poetry. Sometimes the two live together in peace, sometimes they clash. In me, the shadow nudging at my shoulders seems to have completely taken over. My poems show me as the lover of Cassandra (which I never was), a dogmatic defender of the Catholic Church (whereas my faith has always been . . . less than it should be), the writer of a much talked of epic poem (best buried and forgotten, that one). My life has been put together from all these different parts. As a poet, these selves hold together, for poetry has the power of seeing hidden connections. But shall I voice my suspicion? When I look upon my life as a man, all these varying selves disintegrate and fall apart. How could I have written love lyrics for a peasant girl at the same time as I was advising kings how to run the country? Did the same man publish a collection of erotica and a volume of philosophical poetry? Is it possible?

No, no, it's ridiculous to look to my poetry to make sense of my life, for poetry is fiction. It comes into being from a single line floating in the air like a will-o'-the-wisp, or from a stray rhythm lurking beneath a tree, and these lines and these rhythms dictate the whole pattern. As I repeat my poems to myself, I no longer know where the fictional self ends and I begin. We poets are professional deceivers and sometimes finish by deceiving ourselves. Death's chill swirls around my heart, filling my lungs with blackness. I shiver. Enough!

I get up from the bed that has been placed in Amadis's room. I put on a woollen robe and sandals and make my way unsteadily down the stone-flagged corridor to my own room. I push open the heavy wooden door. Light streams in at the window, bouncing off the whitewashed walls. The monks have left everything as it was. My old jowls blush with shame to see the narrow bed in the corner with its scarlet wool coverlet tossed and rumpled. I go painfully, for my back is not yet right, over to the table by the window. The scent of hyacinths lightly taps me in the face. I bend over to look out. A lush splash of pink and purple beneath my window. They are coming along nicely.

I stare down at the papers strewn across the table, at the insect trails of black lines staggering over the pages. In Paris, that's all they say I'm fit for now – correcting my own poems. Every morning, I spend two hours going through them, altering a word here and there, cutting, correcting, polishing the lines till they sing. The fifth edition of my collected works is growing and gathering shape, a shape more perfect and more rounded, I hope, than any of the previous editions. They will be surprised, those doubters, when this edition comes out, at how large it is. All the poems written at the command of princes and scattered over France like grain, I have gathered them all up and given them a home. It will be a royal collection and on its success depends my name, my reputation – yes, even my life.

What do those scoffers know? A poem is never finished; it is constantly changing shape, like smoke blown in the wind. Yes, to finish a poem is to kill it. Despite their taunts, I shall go on revising my poems as long as I have breath, till they have no need of my physical presence and can make their own way in the world, singing down the centuries.

And then, the doubts. I pick up a page. Is it true the Muses have finally deserted me, as they say? Have they taken another lover? In Paris they have been whispering for months that Desportes is a better poet. What if they are right and the black-eyed goddesses have left me? A lifelong affair about to end, and as usual the betrayed lover is the last to know. I admit it, above all things I fear neglect. As I stare down at the pages, the lines run up and down before my eyes, confusing me. The only self I have ever been sure of, that of poet, is collapsing and leaving me floundering. The only women I have loved deeply are abandoning me just as my relations with mortal women seem to have come to an abrupt end too, if there is any truth in dreams. I glower over at the scarlet coverlet.

All right, then, let's leave this poetry business. What right has an old man to be writing verse anyway? Poetry should vibrate with the enthusiasm of youth and Apollo's frenzy. It needs hot, eager blood. My laurel leaves are as withered as my member.

I pour out a glass of wine from the jug on the table.

Very well, then, Bacchus will be my god from now on, not Apollo. Bacchus is the god for an old man. He is the only one who can help me transcend this earthly prison, this stinking heap of flesh and bones. If I am to get to heaven, Bacchus must lend me wings. I sip the wine. Over the last few days a project has been gradually taking shape in my head, like an egg forming in the womb. An account of my life set down in prose (that in itself is a sign that the Muses have fled, for who would write prose if their verse were still adequate?).

Yes, yes, I am quite aware of the boldness of my project. I know it is only men of action who are expected to write their autobiographies, men like Julius Caesar and St Augustine, not mere poets. What do we know of Homer's life? Of Virgil or Horace? I shall be thought very odd.

And yet it's time to take stock. I've had one warning. When the next one comes, I want death to find me with my bags packed, ready and waiting to leave. So, let me tear off my poet's mask, let me blow the dust from my memories and travel back into the past. I want to leave behind the court, its ambitions, strivings and lies; forget about impotence, both physical and creative. I want to crawl into a corner and pull the past around me like a warm, protective shell.

Two days later, having persuaded Amadis I am fit again, I sit down at the table in my cleric's black robes, take up a sharpened quill, and with the scent of hyacinths in my nostrils, begin my attempt to recover in prose the self I have lost through writing poetry.

PART ONE

THE SOLDIER

Chapter 1

I tumbled out from between my mother's thighs during the night of 10th September, 1524. I found myself on a huge bed in our château at La Possonnière. Calliope and her eight sisters who had fled the earth after Augustus's time, returned at that moment to sing and dance along the banks of the Loir (but see, see how quickly fiction creeps in, and I promised to stick to the facts).

So, keeping strictly to the facts, let me describe that bed from which I was launched into the world (it was really quite magnificent). Clusters of grapes dangled from its elaborate oak frame and around it hung tapestry curtains embroidered with hunting scenes. Altogether a most suitable bed for the begetting of little Ronsards. It still stands in the bedroom at La Possonnière, though now it has passed into the hands of my nephew Louis. I was the last born of our family and have had to make do with that narrow wooden pallet you see behind me and on which . . . but I think in fairness to myself, the time has come to draw a veil over that little episode.

The only piece of furniture I managed to take with me from the family château is that oak chest standing in the corner. In my mother's time, it was filled with jewellery and linen and gave off a sweet perfume. Now it is crammed with my discarded manuscripts and smells of must. Though sometimes, bending over to search for a stray poem, I fancy the scent of rosemary still lingers there, like a long forgotten melody. How the Ronsards have come down in the world, at least this lopped-off branch!

To get to La Possonnière, you take the south-west road out of Paris and when you have gone over a hundred miles, you come to the little village of Couture at the junction of the Loir and the silvery Braye. A mile to the south lies the white stone château of La Possonnière and, just to fill you in on the situation, four miles from La Possonnière is the monastery of Croixval, where I sit writing this account. Eleven years ago I persuaded Amadis to give it to me in exchange for an annual allowance, partly because of its proximity to the family home, but mostly for the magnificent view it has over two valleys.

The château, as we call it, was only a small manor-house when my father inherited it from my grandfather. But my father had gone on military expeditions to Italy and these had given him ideas; for at that time everything new, everything splendid and beautiful, came from Italy. My father was so impressed by their architecture that he had our rustic family home rebuilt entirely in the Italian style – you know the sort of thing, marble and carved pillars all over the place.

Entering the château through the low, wide gate with its Gothic archway and single storey running across the top, you find yourself in the inner courtyard. If you stand in the middle of the yard, knee-deep most likely in mud and horse-shit, you will see on the north side the living quarters with their huge Italian-style windows. The tower, though, is medieval. This hotchpotch of styles was typical, by the way, of the state of the arts in France at that time with old and new jostling for space, destroying any chance of a distinctive French style.

Over the door of the tower is an inscription dedicating the family home to pleasure and the graces. What's this? Do I see you nodding off? Be patient, these details are necessary if you are to understand my childhood (anyway, I am used to displeasing my public, the vulgar amongst them at least). Well then, the façade of the house is covered with inscriptions warning the visitor to 'look to the end' or reminding him that *veritas filia temporis*: as I am sure you have gathered by now, my father was an educated man. On the wall between two of the windows a certain emblem is painted, a wild rose bush bursting into flames. Our surname is supposed to be derived from this emblem, or so my father said, and he had a particular interest in genealogies.

Turning your eye to the east side of the courtyard, you will see the business part of the house – the laundry, food-cellar, storage-rooms and wine-cellar. There is even a small prison where my mother (never my father) used to lock recalcitrant servants for the day. To the south lie the farm buildings, and in the south-west corner of the yard stands a tiny chapel.

If you step inside the house (making sure to wipe your feet first), you will find yourself in a great hall dominated by an enormous fireplace of carved stone reaching right up to the ceiling. Owing to my father's interest in genealogy, it is decorated with dozens of family crests, including the King's emblem, the salamander, and of course the flaming rose bushes. I suppose this monstrous creation may have encouraged in me some sort of visual sense which was useful later when I had to organize festivals of painting and architecture at court. But its main effect was to instil in me the importance of coats of arms – there is nobody more snobbish than a member of the minor nobility trying to move up in society. I learned early on to share my father's ambitions, for which I think that fireplace is largely to blame.

Tapestries and mildewed family portraits hung on the walls. Muskets and rusty crossbows jostled for space with stags' horns and other assorted hunting trophies. In the middle of the room stood a long oak table, but that was used only for special occasions. Most of the time we huddled for warmth in the kitchen.

It was to this transformed manor of La Possonnière that my father Louis, at the age of forty-five, brought his new wife Jeanne Chaudrier. In a sense this marriage was rather a comedown for my mother. As she frequently reminded us, she came from illustrious stock. In the fourteenth century one of the Chaudriers succeeded in capturing La Rochelle Castle from the English and handed it over, in return for gold, to the King of France. This was a great piece of good luck for the Chaudriers – there is even a street named after them in La Rochelle. Another of my mother's ancestors had been Marshal of France and fought heroically in the battle which finally ended the Hundred Years War in France.

Before such a family tree, my father's ancestors paled into insignificance. They were country people, wardens and gamekeepers of the Gâtine Forest, which roams the hills behind La Possonnière. My grandfather, Olivier, was the first to emerge from the green shade of the forests. He held several posts at court under Louis XI, setting an example for his eldest son, my father, who followed him to court and became a soldier and diplomat.

Was it the dullness of my father's family that deepened the lines of frustration and disappointment around my mother's mouth? She could hardly complain, however, for her reputation was scarcely spotless when my father married her. Aha! That's caught your interest. You like a bit of gossip, don't you? You want to know about it?

Well, then: she had been orphaned at an early age which no doubt had strengthened her character and she was brought up by her grandmother, a lady of similar toughness. When she was still quite young, fifteen at the most, she caught the eye of Jacques de la Rivière, a nobleman with a fondness for pretty women and gambling. He escorted my mother to balls, helped her on with her cloak, held her gloves; in short, performed all the servile tasks necessary to woo a lady of the court. In this case the lady was more than adequately wooed, but her family, having got wind of the Seigneur de la Rivière's reputation, were adamantly opposed. She was forbidden to see him.

However, one night as Jeanne de Chaudrier lay sleeping, there came the light patter of pebbles against her windowpane. The dashing La Rivière had arrived to kidnap her from her grandmother's. Whilst the old lady snored on undisturbed, her granddaughter escaped from the bedchamber with rope thoughtfully provided by her suitor and galloped off into the night with him. Well, the next day there was a terrific fuss. The illustrious Chaudriers, having connections in all the right places and money enough for bribes, soon tracked down the errant couple. Tiring rapidly of his new love now that she was at close quarters, and with an eye on the gaming-table, La Rivière was not slow to seize the opportunity of exchanging my mother to cover his gambling debts. She was returned to her grandmother, if not intact, at least unharmed and with the family fortune safe. To make it entirely secure, the King himself was persuaded to intervene and forbid the marriage (our kings have always been very keen to control their nobles' breeding patterns).

There remained, however, the problem of my mother.

With all the scandal, she had become a considerably less attractive marriage prospect. In the end they found a rather seedy old nobleman, Gui des Roches, who had fallen on hard times and she was married off in haste. My poor mother with that awful old lecher!

The Seigneur des Roches eventually died, exhausted perhaps by his own lust. After a suitable period of mourning, my mother married Louis Ronsard, a minor nobleman back from the wars, but as I have explained, she was hardly in a position to complain.

When I was younger, I thought all poets should have a romantic heritage. It used to worry me dreadfully, my ancestors' lack of glory, until I remembered a story I had heard my father tell of a distant ancestor who had come from the borders of Hungary with a band of noblemen to offer his services to Philippe de Valois against the English. This sounded romantic enough. I carefully cultivated the rumour that my family had originated by the banks of the icy Danube and accounted for my poetic talent by the exotic Hungarian blood which, I said, still flowed in my veins. All poets are born liars anyway.

My mother bore my father six children, of whom a less than average number (two) died in infancy. She was forty-two when I put in an appearance that September night. Forty-two and heartily sick of childbearing. I was a mistake, I think, an afterthought sown on one of my father's trips home from court. I doubt if they slept together after that. Long years at war had accustomed my father to celibacy, and my mother had a horror of becoming pregnant again. Yet she was fond enough of her eldest children – Claude because he was handsome and daring, Charles because he helped around the house and Louise because she was a girl and my mother had ambitions for a good marriage for her. But that's enough about my family. I always say that if you have nothing else to write about a man, then praise his ancestors – and I have plenty of things to tell about myself.

I was sickly and weak, the last of the litter. There's a story that when carrying me across the fields to the church in Couture to be baptized, my nurse stumbled and dropped me amongst the flowers. I don't know whether it is true or not, but in return for a tip the villagers will point out the spot to unsuspecting visitors from Paris. My mother lost patience with this sickly child and sent me down to the village to spend my first years with a wet-nurse. So from the start I was an outcast. Though nowadays it pleases me to think that my first home was amongst the common people.

   I can't remember anything of that time in Couture, except that like Brother John's nurse in *Gargantua* the good woman who suckled me must have had soft breasts, for my nose, instead of being snubbed by their firmness, grew longer and longer, much to my mother's distress.

The gentle slap of leather against the flagstones in the corridor makes me put down my pen. There is a knock at the door. Hurriedly I hide the pages I have been writing on beneath a book. A brown-robed monk stands in the doorway, summoning me to prayers and food. Over the meal, a simple one of peppered stew and home-grown vegetables, we discuss the roof of an outhouse that has blown down during a recent storm. My routine is establishing itself again after my illness. Many priors neglect their priories and their monks. I used to do the same myself, spending most of my time at court promoting my poetry. Now in old age I have returned to the countryside of my childhood and to the company of these simple but kindly men who have been entrusted to my care. I have another priory at St Côme, on the outskirts of Tours. I divide my time between these two, only interrupting country life for the occasional, unavoidable visit to Paris.

   I can see by the monks' expressions that they have need of me. I decide to devote the rest of the day to getting estimates for the roof, overseeing accounts and disciplining the kitchen staff, who have got dreadfully out of hand during my absence.

   In the evening after prayers I retire to my room with a large jug of wine and read over what I have written. It's accurate as far as it goes, but it could just as easily have been written by some historian ferreting through archives of the Ronsard family. Why did I go into such detail about my family? They have little bearing on the rest of the story. The self I am seeking remains as elusive as smoke blown in the wind. I sigh and push the pages aside. Outside my window the moon hangs in the sky like a great white fruit. I am disappointed, I admit it. It isn't working out as I had hoped. Is it worth continuing? I glance up at the huge expanse of velvet blackness. My head reels with the immensity of the heavens and the smallness of one man.

I sleep badly. The arthritis in my joints makes me toss and turn under the scarlet coverlet. Eventually I get up, pull on a robe and go grumbling down the chilly passageway to the kitchens. There I squeeze some poppy-juice and sit down by the glowing embers in the hearth to drink the opiate.

The next two days are taken up with superintending the repairs to the outhouse roof. On the third, I am woken at dawn by a lark making the dew tremble with its song. Rain during the night has scrubbed the earth clean. The world seems altogether a better place, or is it just that I have had a good night's sleep? I feel a sense of purpose again. There are stories to tell – of battles, heroism, love and death. I sit down at the table to continue my account.

Duly weaned, I was brought back to La Possonnière to the company of my mother and sister. Claude and Charles were away at school and my father had gone to Madrid on the King's business. The King of France at that time was the great François I, a civilized, cultured man who was determined to make the half-medieval country that was France into a nation worthy of the period of rebirth in which we were living. By his military exploits and his support for learning, he was attempting to drag his barbaric kingdom screaming into the sixteenth century. He and my father, with his admiration for all that was Italian, got on well.

Unfortunately, the King's plans did not always come off. In the year that I was born, François was captured by the Spanish Emperor Charles V in the disastrous Battle of Pavia. France hung her head in shame. The Emperor agreed to release the King on condition that he sent his two eldest sons to the Spanish court as hostages. My father was chosen to accompany the royal children, François and Henri, into exile. He was a gentle man, well read in the best literature of the day (which, of course, meant Italian). This may have been the reason for his appointment. François did not want his two sons to return from exile savages. My father was with them practically every minute of the day reading to them, comforting them in their homesickness, even sharing a spell in prison with them.

But all this is history. What I am trying to do is trace the slow unfolding of a human life. My earliest memories – moving through a world of smells, candle-smoke, beeswax, musty tapestries and polished leather. Tastes too, bitter and sweet, salt and honey. And sounds – my childhood rang with my mother's shouts: 'You clumsy girl! How dare you burn the bread!' and the slap of her hands as she boxed a kitchen-maid's ears. In my father's absence, she ruled the house and land like a general. She should have gone to war. She would have made a splendid commander – with her in charge, France might even have won Pavia. But of course our customs dictate that women have very few outlets for their energies – my mother poured all hers into tyrannizing the maids and the farm-workers. She knew exactly how many slices could be cut from a side of beef and every evening she would hold a reckoning in the kitchen when servant-girls, trembling at the knees, had to account for every scrap of food, down to the last crust of bread.

Most of the important activities took place in the kitchen. Seated on a three-legged stool, my mother haggled with neighbouring farmers for the best deal in wheat and rye. And they, alternately charmed and bullied by this high-spirited woman, gave in and sold their crops at half the price they had intended. All our meals were eaten in the kitchen, except on feast-days and when Claude and Charles came home from school. On these occasions my mother would order all the floors to be scrubbed and sweet-smelling rushes laid down. The harsh lines around her mouth softened a little as she put on a new gown and selected a gold bracelet from the oak chest.

'Look at me.' Claude danced around on top of the kitchen table, brandishing his new sword. 'I'm going to be a great soldier. I shall ride by the King's side and protect him from the Spanish.'

He was tall and handsome and my mother's eyes shone with pride. He had brought presents for us all, lace, perfume, a purse for Louise and a spinning-top for me. He regularly overspent his allowance, but my mother always found money to give him, even though it meant the rest of us had to eat frugally for the next month. In the corner, plump and solemn, stood Charles. Like most second sons he was destined for a fat benefice in the Church. I did not envy him. There was no glory in being a priest. I had made up my mind long ago to be a soldier like Claude.

'A soldier,' sneered my sister Louise, 'you puny little thing!' And she would pinch me.

It was true I was often sick as a child. My mother, who despised all illness, would shake her head and hand me over like a useless bundle to be cared for by a woman from the village. Not that I hold it against her. Children are a nuisance at the best of times. Anyway, the callous intimacies of family life have never appealed to me: as soon as I was allowed up again, I would race out into the fields far away from my mother's scolding and my sister's taunts. Yes, it was nature who reared me. I was born in a land of sparkling crystal and soft green hills where the streams are streaks of silver through fields of corn. The sweet hum of the honey-bees, the gentle song of the skylark shaking the dew from his wings at dawn, was the first music I knew. From my communion with that land, my poetry was born and spread from that tiny corner of France to all the courts of Europe.

Every morning after chapel I raced out to play by the banks of the slate-coloured river. I discovered all kinds of wild flowers growing in the fields. I learned to distinguish the scent of wallflowers from that of honeysuckle, lilies from roses. Whereas the servant-girls smelled of milk and honey and the stable boys of dung, my mother's scent was amber or musk, perfumes I was to encounter again on ladies of the court. But I must not proceed too fast.

Thanks to my mother's utter lack of interest in me, I was free to roam the countryside, eating the wild strawberries and black cherries that grew around our house, living more like a peasant boy than a nobleman's son. When my mother took Louise visiting neighbours, I was left behind. This suited me fine. I much preferred watching the villagers turn the hay, clip the vines and brand the sheep, to making polite conversation in some nobleman's chilly dining-hall with my mother keeping an eye out for a rich suitor for Louise. Sometimes the villagers let me help. 'Don't tell your mother,' an old man would say, handing me a little fork to toss hay. 'Why not?' I would ask, puzzled. But he would just grin and reveal a mouth full of yellow stumps. I did not know then the rules that separate the nobles who own the land from the peasants who work it.

In the autumn I watched as they crushed nuts for oil or killed pigs and salted the meat to last during the long winter months. I saw clotted milk, white as my mother's skin, drying for cheese-making on mats of rushes. I loved, I still do, the regular rhythms of country life, the rise and fall of the seasons, the hard work punctuated by saints' days. St Gervais was the saint honoured by the good people of Couture. On that day all the village prayed that St Gervais would intercede for their sins and, much more important, increase the harvest, protect the vine and make the ewes healthy. Sometimes in the evening I crept down to watch the dancing on the common or join in the singing round the bonfire. There was something pagan about these peasant celebrations, with their abandoned dancing and cups spilling over with wine. We never know what will shape our lives. If I had not joined in these country festivals, would I later have understood what Homer was saying?

But if you think the life I led then was a dreamy, poetic life, you would be making a big mistake. I competed with the village boys in jumping, running and wrestling. We played hide-and-seek in the caves behind our house where once the Celts hid from the Romans. We swapped birds' eggs (I invariably got the worst of the bargain; I had not inherited my mother's gift). We climbed the chestnut trees that cast their deep shadows over the fields and caught birds in home-made traps. We took turns tormenting Denise, the local witch. She was a toothless old hag dressed in black, with a runny nose and bad breath. It was rumoured she could waken the dead from their tombs and throw spells on the moon to draw it down from the heavens. If any cattle became sick, she was always blamed. I sometimes dreamed that she chased me, muttering charms under her breath, into woods where flying phantoms clacked their teeth and hissed at me.

Every now and then I was invited into one of the squat little cottages in the village and there, sitting cross-legged on foul-smelling rushes, my friends and I would devour a piece of fatty bacon. My skin was as dark as tanned leather, I spoke like a peasant, and instead of a nobleman's doublet and hose I wore the ragged clothes of a village boy. My sister was ashamed of me in my coarse, dirty linen shift. 'Ugh, you smell,' she would say, taking her eyes off the mirror long enough to push me away. My mother ignored me.

The only time I was acknowledged to be part of the family was on feast-days, when all the household attended the parish church of Couture. Usually, we heard mass in our own chapel at La Possonnière, but on these special days I followed my mother and sister down paths where dew hung on the hedges like white pearls, over the wheat-fields to the village. The priest stood at the door to welcome us. Nodding distantly, my mother swept up the aisle, my sister and I in her train, to claim the family pew at the front of the church. I sat through those long services with head bent low, ashamed and uncomfortable at being cut off so suddenly from my ragged friends on the benches behind.

And yet there were parts of my life about which these friends from the village knew nothing. On rainy days, for example, I would explore our house, wandering from room to room (each one the size of an entire cottage), running my finger over the cool marble forms of Jupiter, Venus and Mercury sculpted on the pillars and chimney-pieces. In every room I came across inscriptions in a strange language. Even the larder was labelled in Latin, much to my mother's fury (like my sister, she was practically illiterate). My father, of course, read Latin fluently. No doubt he had intended his sons also to learn Latin, but this son at least spoke only peasant French. So I learned at an early age how the orders of kings disrupt the lives of private individuals. Not that I cared very much – what use was Latin to a soldier?

On my wanderings I found a discarded wooden rocking-horse. I brought it down to my room. In her better moods, usually when Claude was home, my mother would regale us with tales of her ancestors' military exploits. Occasionally, as an afterthought, she mentioned the Order of St Michel which my father had won in battle. It was a rare medal then, the utmost mark of honour for a nobleman. Now it has become debased and worthless, like so much else during these wars. But I am getting ahead of myself. Keep to the past. I desperately wanted to be a hero too. I rocked on my wooden horse for hours, laying waste whole stretches of Spanish countryside, till the Emperor himself knelt before me and begged for mercy. Curiously, he wore a huge cocked hat with a feather that trailed to the ground. I then rocked on to defeat the Turks.

Yes, it is coming together, it is taking shape at last. I am beginning to recapture something of the atmosphere of my early childhood. The mixture of peasantry and heroism in which I moved, both parts quite at odds with my later life.

I continued rocking till my sixth birthday, which my father arrived home in time to celebrate. It was a curious meeting. My mother had been busy for a month, supervising the cleaning of the entire house. Pomanders of crushed juniper and rosemary hung in all the rooms. My brothers came home from school and we were all given new doublets. Claude's was decorated with fur, and on his left hand he wore a fine gold ring. I saw little of him, as he was out every day hunting or overseeing the farmhands, who of course knew their tasks better than he did.

Charles, plumper and spottier than ever, sat around in the kitchen, coaxing the maids into letting him taste the special dishes that were being prepared.

'School is appalling. You want to avoid it if you can.' He plopped a slice of venison into his mouth. 'There's no heating.' He drew his chair nearer the stove. 'And nothing to eat.'

'You look fat enough to me,' I remarked, and dodged to escape a clip behind the ears.

'There are ways and means of staying alive,' he said darkly, licking his greasy fingers. I suppose he bullied the younger boys into giving up their food. 'Take my advice, Pierre, avoid school.' He pressed his hands to his stomach and belched loudly.

This was the only piece of advice he ever gave me. Whilst I was pondering it, my sister bounced in to show off her new dress ordered specially from Paris. She had curled and pinned up her hair.

'Hum! Not bad!' said Charles, leering at her low-cut bodice under which two small bumps were scarcely visible. He pinched the bottom of a passing maid.

'Your hair looks all funny,' I said, and crept up behind her to feel the shiny new material.

'Go away, you horrid boy,' she screamed, slapping my hand.

By the day of my father's arrival, I could stand it no longer. I seemed to have been pushed around, scolded and teased, for weeks. After mass I escaped into the fields for a joyful reunion with my friends. I was dreading my father's arrival – it would just add to the number of people in my life to be avoided.

We were playing leap-frog in the fields when I noticed a man in the distance coming over the brow of a hill. He sat straight-backed on his horse like a soldier. I shivered with fear and excitement. My father. I raced back over the fields, taking all the short cuts I knew, and arrived breathless in the yard just as my father came cantering in through the gate. There was no one else around. He had not been expected till later in the day.

He dismounted and stood uncertainly in the yard, holding his horse's reins. I ran over to him in my by now torn and dusty clothes. He turned to me.

'Hullo, young fellow. Is there anyone at home?'

'Yes, sir. They're all inside. I think they were expecting you later, sir,' I replied in my best peasant French.

'Well then, my lad, what would you think if I just slipped indoors and surprised them? Would they like that, eh?' There was a twinkle in his eyes.

'I think they would, sir. Shall I take your horse?'

'Thank you, my boy. Very kind.'

And my father, obviously impressed by the high standard of stable-boy my mother was employing, strode off towards the house. I led the horse, a magnificent Arab, over to the stables and woke one of the hands to unsaddle it.

In all the confusion of my father's arrival I managed to sneak back into the house unnoticed and took my place in the study beside Louise.

'Pooh,' she said, wrinkling her nose. 'Where have you been? You smell of the stables. And look at your clothes. All torn and dirty. You're a disgrace.'

With sinking heart, I prepared to meet my father.

The door opened. My mother ushered him in. We were all standing in a line, our hands neatly folded in front of us.

'Your children, Louis. Do you recognize them after four years?'

She escorted him along the line like a general inspecting his troops.

'Claude' (triumphantly). My father looked slightly shy as Claude held out his hand. His eldest son was as tall as himself. 'Very fine, my boy. You will make a splendid soldier, I can tell.' But I noticed his eyes linger for a second on the gold ring. A slight, wiry figure, my father was dressed in simple soldier's breeches.

'Charles' (a shade less triumphantly). My father took his hand affectionately. 'Are you enjoying your holidays, Charles?'

'Yes, sir.'

'Your mother tells me that you don't like school. Is that true?' He fixed Charles with a shrewd glance.

'Yes, sir.' Authority always reduced Charles to monosyllables.

'Well, well,' he patted his son's hand, 'we'll have a little chat and see what can be done to make matters better.'

'Louise.'

My sister performed an elegant curtsy. My father patted her cheek.

'Very pretty, my dear. We shall have to be looking out for a husband for you soon, I can see.'

My sister simpered and her blonde curls danced.

'And this is Pierre. Oh, Pierre.' My mother's tone changed to one of despair as she saw the state of my new clothes.

My heart sank further. Not knowing what to do, I executed a very slow, very deep bow. As I raised my head, I noticed a smile in my father's eyes. He placed both hands on my shoulders.

'So this is Pierre. And I took him for a stable-boy.'

'I'm not surprised,' sniffed my mother.

'So you wanted to observe me, eh, without being recognized? What did you find out about me, I wonder?'

'He's always prying where he has no business,' put in my mother.

'Not at all, he was very helpful.' And to my astonishment, my father winked at me. In that moment I began to have an entirely new outlook on families.

Yes, it's coming along. I'm starting to warm to the task. As I sit here, surrounded by ink-horn, ruler, wax and seal, I sense a pattern emerging, like the wings of a butterfly unfolding. My father's return marked the first turning-point in my life. There was now someone to take an interest in me.

Chapter 2

It's over a week since I wrote that last sentence. In the meantime, I have begun the move from Croixval to St Côme, the priory just outside Tours that I inherited on the death of my brother Charles. The poor Augustinian brothers saw quite a change of master. I have cut out lavish banquets. Instead of rich delicacies ordered from Paris to tempt my brother's palate, we eat crops grown by ourselves and meat from the local farms. I pensioned off the slut of a serving-girl who had been his mistress. It took them a while to adjust to the new regime. But now, as I travel in my carriage piled high with cushions, along roads lined with plane trees, I am sure of a warm welcome from the monks and most of all from their chaplain, Jacques Desguez, an educated man.

We bump into the cobbled yard of an inn to change horses. I descend painfully from my perch amongst the cushions. Travel is such a burden in old age. And with these wars one never knows when one will be set upon by a bunch of thugs. But I like to see my friends. The horses changed, we set off once more under the grey sky. Eventually we turn in through the gates of St Côme. Jacques is on the steps to greet me. He helps me out of the carriage, promising me a good meal of home-grown vegetables and local wine. After dinner we will play cards into the small hours. Jacques is the best card-player I know. Life is very pleasant, I decide, even in old age.

The next day, after matins, I return to my account, for of course I have brought my papers with me. The monks think I am writing poetry (best to let them go on thinking this – I don't want questions, not yet). The room in St Côme is almost an exact replica of my room at Croixval, with bed, table and a window opening on to a balcony overlooking the river. Instead of the oak chest there is a sideboard sent to me by the Queen of Scotland, Mary Stuart. It is one of my most treasured possessions. But no more delays. My youth is waiting for me, trembling like the wings of a butterfly.

My lack of education horrified my father. Whilst some of my contemporaries had mastered Latin and even Greek by the age of six, I could barely spell in my own tongue. My language was that of the peasants, a language of proverbs and swearwords, earthy and natural. I loved it then, and I still do, for its honesty and vigour. Quietly and without reproach to my mother (who after all had been moderately successful in raising her three eldest children), my father assumed responsibility for my education. He arranged for my Uncle Jean, a friar, to come over from his abbey nearby to give me daily tuition. He was an enormous barrel of a man with rosy cheeks and dark hair in his nostrils, though he had none at all on his head. His hands were as calloused as a ploughman's and when he celebrated mass, as he sometimes did in our family chapel, I could see the dirt encrusted beneath his fingernails. He was fond of his wine and smelled like a cesspit. 'All friars smell,' said my father. 'It's part of their religion.'

The first morning, my uncle arrived with two leather-bound volumes tucked under his arm. We went into my father's study, a great privilege for me. Two chairs had been placed on either side of the huge, carved fireplace. Suns, stars, lutes and cupids were sculpted into the stone. Across the top of the fireplace ran the motto 'Nothing in excess', a saying I have always found excessively restricting. I was somewhat disconcerted to see that the first thing my uncle did was to walk over to this magnificent work of art and pee into it. 'That's better,' he said, rearranging his robes. 'Now let me introduce you to Clément Marot.' Marot was at that time regarded as the greatest living French poet. It has always amused me that I can never think of his poetry without linking it in my mind with the stench of cooking piss.

In his rough country tongue my uncle read to me the poetry of our old French writers. I became acquainted with the delicate and subtle psychology of the authors of the *Roman de la Rose* who proclaim the goodness of nature and the beauty of love, and with the poetry of Jean Lemaire de Belges, who surpasses them all in music and voluptuous paganism.

I studied Latin and at last deciphered the inscription on our larder. The strange combinations of sounds intrigued me. Stray rhythms imprinted themselves on my mind and I chanted them under my breath as I played in the fields. So I first made friends with Virgil through the cracked, hoarse tones of my Uncle Jean. He pronounced Latin so badly, however, that I had to learn the language all over again later. At the time though, the poetry he read to me seemed the sweetest music, rivalling that of the lark.

The sweetest music. . . . As I sit here at the open window, looking out over the meadows diamonded with dew, I realize this is only part of the truth. Aha! Caught again, Pierre Ronsard! When will you learn to stop weaving fictions? I take a sip of home-made wine. All right, all right, let us be frank, then. The hours I spent with the village boys, trying to run and jump better than any of them, were more important to me than the poetry I read with my uncle. For by that time I had firmly made up my mind to be a soldier, and hugged the thought close to me during the poetry sessions like a warm and precious bundle.

There, it's out; now are you satisfied? You look astonished. No, whatever I might have said in my poems, I did not have a poetic childhood. The best times were the evenings, when the maids lit the tallow candles and stoked up the fire and my father came to sit with us. Whilst my mother and Louise busied themselves with sewing or embroidery and I sat warming my toes at the fire like the giant in Rabelais's stories, my father recounted his campaigns in Italy. He reminisced about the time the French army was besieged in Navarre – 'We had to eat rats to stay alive and drink rain-water out of our helmets.' Or the time they captured that notorious brigand, Ludovico Sforza, who hid amongst the Swiss mercenaries disguised as a monk. My imagination was set alight by these tales of heroism. I too was ready to sacrifice my life at a word from the King. I could hardly contain my excitement when my father said, 'When the time comes, little Pierre, we will send you away to be trained like Claude. You will go to the royal military academy and learn the skills of a swordsman.'

'And the pistol?'

I had never seen a pistol in action but I had been told it spat smoke like a dragon and could strike a man dead without touching him.

'It's better to rely on the sword than the pistol,' answered my father. 'A lot of people think that pistols and cannons will replace the skills of a swordsman, but I believe there will always be room in war for the nobleman and his horse. Things can go wrong with machines. Besides, gunpowder and firearms are robbing war of its glory. Anyone can learn to fire a cannon. If it goes on like this, our servants will be fighting our wars for us.'

We all laughed.

'No, Pierre, war is about honour and courage, cunning and discipline. The Turks know this. That's why their armies are so successful. They can survive for months on rice and powdered meat. In desperate situations they stay alive by drinking their horses' blood.'

The Turks. I shivered. They were – still are – an ever-present menace, hovering like vultures on the borders of Europe, ready to pounce at the first sign of weakness. France will always need her soldiers. I imagined a band of silent brothers, bound together by hopes of glory, waving their blood-spattered banners and uttering their soldiers' curses under a river of pure steel. At the sound of the trumpets, they would advance like oaks and destroy the enemy for France's glory. As I ran through the woods, frightening the demons with my imaginary sword, I could think of no finer thing to be than a soldier.

But this pleasant life came to a sudden end. Uncle Jean told my father that I would benefit from more advanced tuition than he could give me. My father decided that a spell at school amongst noblemen's sons would improve my manners – he had gently tried to prise me away from my friends in the village. To no avail. I took pride in spitting farther than any boy in Couture.

There were other things, too, about which he knew nothing. One of the boys and I had taken to sneaking off to the chapel beside our house. There we would pull down our breeches and gently caress each other's buttocks. We were both entirely innocent; there was just something so warm and comforting about the feel of soft flesh beneath one's palms. The smell of incense clung to the chapel walls and, for a long time afterwards, incense evoked memories for me of warm, childish skin. And mass became a struggle between spirituality and more earthy pleasures. Perhaps it was from this time that there sprang one of the most enduring conflicts of my life, one which I have not yet succeeded in conquering – even in old age, with masturbation the only option, one retains certain sharp memories. . . .

These strange, comforting trysts ended when I was sent at the age of nine to Navarre College in Paris. There began my education into the cruelty and petty-mindedness that exists in the world. At Navarre we rose silently at four in the morning to listen to prayers garbled in a Latin we could not understand. From six till ten we copied out pages from medieval authors (in Latin, of course) and recited mechanically the lessons we had learned by heart the day before. Between copying and learning there was no time for thinking, which I suppose is what our masters intended.

We then dined, if dining is not overstating the case, on watery vegetable soup, stale bread and overripe cheese. This delightful meal took place in silence whilst one of the masters read us some improving work, again in incomprehensible Latin (in any case, our attention was fully occupied with searching for a lump of carrot or a bean hidden amongst the brown water in our bowls). This is how the future leaders of France are educated. They say a nation gets the teachers it deserves: those at Navarre were limping souls unfit to be in charge of others. They worked there only for the money – indeed, conditions were so bad, with rats in the cellars and damp running down the walls, that any decent man would have steered well clear of the place. The classrooms rang with boys' shrieks and blood-stained willows strewed the floors as the masters vented their frustration, their poverty and their hunger on their pupils. I would not put such men in charge of a herd of animals, let alone human souls.

After dinner we had classes in grammar and rhetoric. We

spent an inordinate amount of time arranging words into clauses and then into sentences. We became expert at labelling ablatives and spotting conjunctions. We learned how to arrive at the perfect expression. Unfortunately we had no ideas to express; they had all been beaten out of us.

One boy, a little younger than I, called Charles, was held up to us all as an example of what could be achieved. Charles, immaculately turned out from head to toe, was adept at speaking elegantly on any trifle according to the best rules of Ciceronian rhetoric.

'But it's all nonsense,' I protested to him one day. 'You've just argued equally plausibly for opposite points of view. You twist words till there's no meaning left. You disguise ideas in rhetoric like the cook here who dresses up meat in sauces and spices to hide the fact it's stale.'

'Of course it's nonsense,' he said, nodding his powdered curls. 'But it's the system. You have to master it if you want to get on in life.'

The system certainly worked for him. He became France's most powerful cardinal – the Pope even granted him personal powers of inquisition. He was a good ally for Rome. He knew how to turn the shifting tides of court favour to his advantage. The system taught him how to tie his victims in knots with his tongue. That quicksilver instrument – I was caught by it myself when he commissioned poems and never paid me for them.

Fidgeting again? But this is important for what is to follow. You see, Charles was a consummate politician, and that has always been the difference between us, for politics is an abuse of words, whereas a poet (though I did not know it then) cannot afford to misuse language; it is his tool and on its sharpness depends the beauty of the object he fashions. A poet uses words in their deepest and truest sense.

So I never mastered the system (perhaps I have been too hard on myself, perhaps even then there was something of the poet in me, warning me that the gods punish those who abuse the language). I forgot all the Virgil my uncle had taught me – he was used only to explain points of grammar and was soon replaced in my head by garbled scraps from medieval commentators, paragraphs from churchmen like Aquinas and Scotus. And, of course, Aristotle. Everything went by Aristotle in that place. We were taught to reason in syllogisms – you know the sort of thing: all men are mortal (major premise), Socrates is a man (minor premise), therefore Socrates is mortal (conclusion). You can go a long way, reasoning like this. The best syllogism I have ever heard was told to me by Charles (he pinched it from Rabelais, but I didn't realize that at the time). It went like this: there is no need to wipe your arse unless there is dirt on it, there cannot be dirt unless you have shat, *ergo* you must shit before you wipe your arse.

After supper (usually something wholesome like tripe) we were trooped off to mass, where the old priest mumbled his way through the prayers in a race to get to the wine. We were taught to recite prayers over and over again during the services, like some magical incantation. If you repeat sounds too often, eventually they become meaningless. There were days when my head reeled from the dizzy inanity of our chants. How enormous the gap between the simple soldier faith of my father and this use of religion as ritual, to keep the world at arm's length.

This absurd ritual had one advantage, however – it helped me understand the calls for reform when they came. Indeed, during the very time I was in Paris, followers of Zwingli nailed placards demanding reform of the mass around the city and even on the King's door. François, incensed that his good-natured tolerance had been taken advantage of in this way, swiftly repressed the protesters. Shut in behind high stone walls, we heard only the far-off rumblings of these events.

On Saturdays they allowed us out for a walk. We marched in a line, flanked by masters, down to the Seine, where the yellow mud gave off an unpleasant odour (Paris always smells of mud and piss). On Sundays we bathed. Our unhealthy regime led to many disorders. I escaped lightly enough with lice, but two of the boarders died whilst I was there. We were never told the cause.

We slept on straw mattresses, twelve to a dormitory. One morning I was woken by groans coming from the next mattress. I looked over in alarm thinking that the boy, Michel, must be ill. I was astonished to see that he was holding his penis in his right hand and was gently stroking it. There was a strange, concentrated expression on his face. All at once he gave a fierce shudder and a sticky, white liquid spilled out over his stomach. Then his whole body relaxed and a little smile of contentment appeared on his face. He caught me watching him, stuck out his tongue and rolled over on his side with his back to me. So it was that I learned that the twice daily hardening of my organ which had amused and occasionally embarrassed me since the age of three did have some purpose after all. But however much I stroked my unpredictable member, at that time I was sadly unable to make it perform like Michel's. I learned other things too – some nights I would lie awake listening to muffled screams from the other end of the dormitory as an older boy roughly sodomized one of the younger ones.

Yes, college was both petty and brutal. I longed to be at home and ran away twice. The second time my father, being an intelligent man, took me away for good. I returned to the narrow valley of La Possonnière and the hairy nostrils of my Uncle Jean – the latter not for long. He died the following year, leaving his library to me.

How quickly events tumble from my lips. But I have to get on with it, there's so much to tell. . . .

The country was an explosion of senses after my time in the city. I scrambled out of bed at dawn to see the mist hanging like smoke over the meadows. I explored the ancient tufa caves and climbed trees to find birds' nests. I trained myself to recognize flowers and insects and birds. All nature came alive for me in colours, movement and song. I wandered through the vineyards on the sunny southern slopes of our valley, picking the half-ripe fruit and drinking water out of crystal streams. Flowers spoke their names to me as I passed, birds called out in welcome and trees nodded their heads. I had come home and nature was healing, as I had known she would, the scars that had been opened up in my soul by the horrors of school.

Most of all, I loved running through the green shadows of the Gâtine Forest which straddles the hillside above our château, the same forest where my father's family were keepers for so many generations and which even now is being felled to pay for a prince's bad debts, one more sacrifice to the wars.

These gentle, healing rambles were usually solitary, for, as my father had hoped, my absence had put a distance between my village friends and me. They saw now that I came from a different world; I had lived in the city which most of them would never visit in their lives. They watched their language in my presence and stopped sharing their jokes with me. Besides, they had grown up and were too busy to play (a peasant's son grows up more quickly than a nobleman's). They had to earn their keep, turning the hay, guarding the sheep and pruning the vines. Whilst I still dreamed of the glint of steel and the brave harmonies of war music. Gunpowder filled my nostrils as I roamed the hillsides.

And that's another thing. In my poetry I describe myself as a boy wandering through the countryside reciting Virgil to the trees and pausing now and then to scribble in my notebook. What nonsense! Actually, I had not written a line yet. It simply never occurred to me: I was going to be a soldier and that was that. How poetry loses track of reality!

The truth was that everything had taken on the flavour of battle. The farmers planting their vines on the hillsides were generals deploying legions in evenly spaced ranks for battle. The village boys who went around disciplining the plants and lopping off straggling branches, were the officers. The plough, the winnow and the mattock were the peasant's weapons in the war against unruly nature. If he slackened his efforts, the enemy would bring reinforcements of burrs, wild oats and weeds. The approach of winter demanded a full-scale planning operation – flocks had to be branded, corn gathered in, traps set, stakes and supports sharpened.

The battles I dreamed of fighting (how could I have been so naïve?) would be even more glorious than these wars on nature. On his visits home from court my father took me fishing and we discussed my future.

'You're still set on being a soldier?'

'Oh yes. I want to train like Claude and become tough and strong.'

'Well, first I must seek a position for you at court. A soldier needs a sponsor.'

A soldier's training is expensive, and though my father had tried to regulate his eldest son's spending on clothes, jewels, wine and mistresses, Claude's extravagance had made quite a dent in the family finances – in any case, my mother could always be persuaded into lending my brother money. So my father had to find me a job and a patron at court before my training could begin. I shrugged my shoulders and waited. Eldest sons are always privileged.

On entering the Church my other brother, Charles, had come into possession of several lucrative priories. In his black robes he looked fatter and more solemn than ever. He had engaged the first in a long line of mistresses to be his housekeeper. He spent most of the time at court, where he fitted in perfectly. He was unobtrusive in his opinions. He liked his food and wine. He sported delicate lace handkerchiefs, tucked into the pocket of his robes. He was made for the court. The best I can say about my brothers is that I did not choose them. My sister had left home several years ago. As my mother hoped, she made a good marriage to a nobleman rich enough to satisfy her craving for jewels and fine clothes. It is a mystery to me how different I am both in fortune and career from the rest of my family.

Sometimes my father brought with him on these visits a certain strange person called Bouchet. Bouchet's clothes never seemed to fit him, his breeches were always frayed and his ruff rumpled. His face was so thin that he looked as if he were constantly sucking in his cheeks. His eyes were red-rimmed through reading by candlelight. He was, my father told me, a poet. I was a little afraid of him.

When Bouchet visited us, our evenings were taken up with poetry. In my opinion this was much less interesting than listening to my father's tales of the wars. I sat glowering in a corner of the room to show my resentment at this unwelcome intrusion.

'As to whether it is possible for French writers to rival the Italians in poetry . . .' my father would begin.

'I very much doubt whether that is in fact possible,' Bouchet would reply, scratching his head (learned men were somehow always associated with dirt when I was a child). 'Our language is still so impoverished, so crude and unpolished compared with Italian, and as for the classical poets . . .'

'Impossible!' agreed my father. 'We moderns can never

hope to compete with them. No, you are right, all we can do is follow the example of Italian writers and hope that we don't fall too far short of their standards.'

I listened, astonished that they so calmly accepted the inferiority of French literature when they would have been ashamed to admit military defeat by the Italians. I had been rereading a volume of Marot I had found in my uncle's library and one evening I asked warily, 'What about Clément Marot? Aren't you forgetting him? I've heard he is popular at court. Surely he is as good as any Italian writer?' I put as much scorn as I could muster into my voice.

Bouchet exploded into laughter. 'I see you have inherited your father's patriotism, at any rate.'

I went red.

'There's a very great difference between the witty, satirical verses of Marot and the learned style of, say, Petrarch,' explained my father, gently. 'Of course we all like Marot, but even he himself wouldn't claim to equal the Italians.'

'You should read some Petrarch,' put in Bouchet, taking notice of me for the first time. 'He is our first modern lyrical poet. He has perfected the language of poetry in Italy.'

'Pierre doesn't read Italian.'

This was as close as my gentle father ever came to reproaching me for the abrupt way in which my schooling had ended. I loathed Bouchet.

But perhaps . . . yes, perhaps during evenings such as these I caught a glimpse of a different kind of battle to be fought, the battle to restore our country's confidence in her language and poetry. Who knows? I certainly realized for the first time that a poem does not spring whole and perfectly formed from the poet's mind, as Pallas Athene sprang from Jupiter's ear, but that it must be changed and moulded into shape like a living being. Bouchet was always changing his poems. His poetry was the kind that was popular then, full of complicated rhymes and plays on words. Those were the times when poets were tricksters, performing juggling feats with words to impress the court. He would read us a poem one evening and the next day he would have altered it, omitting lines, changing words here and there. Sometimes he even added lines from other poems – he was not averse to swapping his poems around, I noticed.

'The poet must be a magician,' he told me when I asked him why he altered his poems so much. 'His task is to perform miracles with the language.'

And so the first inklings of the creative process began to filter into my sleepy mind. Years of schooling at Navarre could not have done so much (though later I was to regret bitterly my lack of formal schooling). It was Bouchet also who first told me about the legend of France's Trojan origins – but more of that later.

Sometimes, if we were sufficiently persuasive and if my mother was out of the room (she regarded all poetry as unhealthy and particularly objected to Bouchet's fleas), my father would recite one of his own compositions, adopting a casual tone and a deceptively offhand manner.

'I much prefer your poems to Bouchet's,' I told him one day. 'They are easier to understand, for a start.'

He laughed and ruffled my hair. 'That's because you've had no training.'

Could one be trained in poetry? Like a soldier? It was a curious idea. Why then had my father not chosen to be a poet like Bouchet instead of a soldier?

'Look at Bouchet's clothes,' he said, smiling. 'If I didn't give him money, he would starve. There's no money in poetry – Homer went begging from door to door and even Clément Marot needs patrons. Besides, it's not fitting that a nobleman should be a professional writer. Poetry is beneath the dignity of a nobleman except as a pastime.'

There's a contradiction here – serious poetry can be written only by full-time professionals, they said, but nobles shouldn't be professionals, therefore no nobleman can ever be a good poet. *Ergo gluc*, as Rabelais's dotty professor says after a particularly nonsensical piece of academic jargon. No wonder French poetry was in a mess.

I tried another tack: 'At least Bouchet is free to come and go as he pleases.' I was thinking of my father's enforced absences at court.

'Starvation is an enslaver in its own way.' He was serious now. 'To earn enough money to eat, Bouchet will write whatever the King and the court require. All poets do. Whereas a nobleman gives his services unforced, because he has chosen of his own free will to do so. He is loyal to the King as long as the King deserves his loyalty. In this way, he retains his independence – unlike the poet.'

How those words ring down the years! My poor father. He believed in a strictly organized society where subjects gave unquestioning obedience to the monarch in return for his protection (he even wrote a poem about it). To overturn this system by protest or rebellion would have seemed to him perverse. Thank God he did not live to see the day when kings, encouraged by that sly Italian Niccolò Machiavelli, would claim freedom from all such moral and social restraints and trample on their subjects' rights. What would he have thought of our present King Henri, grandson of the great François, who struts around the court in ear-rings and puts taxes up three times a year to pay for the clothes and jewels of his band of homosexual followers? Would he have thought such a ruler deserves his subjects' loyalty?

By coincidence, as I am at this point in my narrative a letter is delivered – the King's call falls like a thunderclap, summoning me to court. I say coincidence, but of course there is no such thing. Fortune is an artist too. Beneath a surface appearance of chaos she weaves her patterns.

Once more I heave my pack of aching bones in amongst the cushions and say goodbye to Jacques for the present.

Chapter 3

We pull in for the night at an inn. Soon I am sitting up in bed wrapped in furs, my toes resting on the hot brick thoughtfully provided by the innkeeper in consideration of my great age. The coarse sheets smell of wood-smoke. At my elbow there is a glass of white wine to help me as I try to recall my feelings on arriving at court for the first time all those years ago. Come, Bacchus, set memory's old cogs wheeling.

My father had been pulling strings on my behalf and in 1536, the year the first French sonnet was composed (though I did not know that at the time) and exactly a month before my twelfth birthday, he summoned me to Avignon to serve as page to the frail youth François, heir to the throne of France. It was the first time I had travelled so far south. I was overwhelmed by the brilliant white light and the heady perfumes of the orange and lemon trees.

What a splendid place the court was in the eyes of a country boy! Satins, velvets and silk brushed past me. Dresses flamed silver and gold. The graceful dancing of the court ladies was like the ever-changing pattern of a flight of birds. The air was filled with their Arabian perfumes. I took a bath every day and rubbed my skin with olive-oil till it gleamed.

I was laughed at by the other pages on account of my country accent and Vendômois slang. I spent hours practising in front of a mirror, tugging my mouth into positions where the proper vowel sounds would come out. Later I was punished for my snobbery: when writing poetry about my birthplace I had to learn my native dialect all over again. Vice is very contagious at court; you either copy it or hate it. I began by trying to copy. I did not know then, you see, that for me the court would always be a whore who flirted with me but saved her favours for someone else. Each time I have tried to pin her down, she has slipped out of my grasp as lightly as a will-o'-the-wisp and bobbed and danced above my head. Yes, you say, but an old man sees everything with jaded eyes. Well, I can't decide for you. There are some things you must make up your own mind about.

I was impatient for my training as a soldier to begin. However, 'In a monarchy every noble has to become experienced in the ways of the court,' said my father. So I learned how to be a courtier. It took a long time, I can tell you, there was such a frightful amount of etiquette. I learned how to walk gracefully (never run), salute with my plumed hat trailing to the ground, shield my mouth when coughing, and how to kiss the hand of a lady. I, who had been used to rampaging through the countryside like a ragamuffin, now strutted as primly as any courtier and remembered to dodge the dogs so that my cloak wouldn't get splashed by mud as I hurried through the streets on some errand.

I was like Theseus, abandoned amongst the intricacies of court life without Ariadne's thread to guide me. Mealtimes were the worst. The first day I was so hungry that after going through the rigmarole of washing my hands in a bowl of perfumed water, drying them on a fresh linen cloth and standing ten minutes for grace, I dived with both hands for the lump of meat on my plate. I was conscious of giggling and whispers behind the candelabra. I noticed one or two frowns. I looked round. 'Three fingers, silly,' whispered the page sitting next to me. From then on I ate my meat holding it in three fingers like everyone else. I took up my goblet in my left hand like everyone else and drank it at one draught like everyone else. At the end of the meal, like everyone else, I picked my teeth. It was puzzling. My life, which I had thought would be altogether nobler and grander at court, was becoming hemmed in with petty restrictions. It was practically like being back at school. I felt myself shrinking – and no wonder, life is difficult enough without all the artificial burdens imposed by the court. There are ways round it, of course:

nowadays I just go through the motions, with my eyes shut.

In those days, however, Avignon seemed to me as splendid as the court of Urbino described in Castiglione's book (a dangerous work that one – it substitutes appearance for truth). Nobles arrived daily from all parts of the country to join the King's army, for hostilities had broken out again between François and the Emperor Charles. The court was becoming more brilliant by the minute. It was a long time before I saw down into the rottenness beneath – though an early incident should have warned me. Is it worth recounting? The passage will have to be cut, of course, if these memoirs ever come out – only an historian is allowed this much freedom. Never mind, I shall write it down anyhow; let it be the printer's responsibility.

When I arrived at court, one person had particularly impressed me. That was my master, the Dauphin of France. I joined him in his daily exercises – his skill in hunting, jousting and vaulting was amazing. The future King of France seemed very great indeed. Six days after I entered his service, the Dauphin drank a glass of cold water after a heated game of tennis, caught a fever and died. I never admired kings so much again.

With all the preparations for war, everyone was very jumpy and rumours flew round the court that the Dauphin had been poisoned by the Spanish. An autopsy found nothing suspicious, but naturally that did not put a stop to the gossip. We pages were forced to be present. Holding a handkerchief soaked in vinegar to my face, I watched as the knife slit open the lump of dead flesh laid out upon the table, its poor limp member nestling in its blond bush. For the first time I looked on a human body as an object, a thing for pumping blood.

To put an end to the rumours which were dividing the court, Montecuculli, the page who had given the Dauphin the fatal glass of water, was arrested. As an attendant who had been present when Montecuculli handed the water to the Prince, I was required to be one of the chief witnesses. The night before the trial my father, who had been appointed one of the judges, came to my room. He sat on the side of my bed looking troubled.

'You know why the King has ordered this trial, Pierre? He needs to put a stop to these rumours of infiltration by the Spanish. They are weakening the court at a time when the country can ill afford it. The Emperor is waiting with his army at the borders, ready to pounce at the first sign of divisions amongst us.'

I sat up in bed. 'But it was a fever, Father. The Dauphin died of a fever.'

'Hush, Pierre.' He looked uneasily over his shoulder. 'Kings don't admit to accidents. Someone has to be blamed and then the matter will be closed.'

I pulled at the edge of my blanket. 'So Montecuculli is being sacrificed to keep France safe.'

He looked away. 'Just tell them what you saw.'

Don't judge my father too severely; the court takes away something from us all.

The next day, Montecuculli was brought shivering into court. They had to get a box for him to stand on, since he was too short to see over the prisoner's bar. I hardly recognized my father in his judge's robes. I was called into the witness-box. A huge man, with a nose hooked like a bird's, leaned forward.

'You were present when the accused handed the glass of water to the Prince?'

'Yes, sir.'

'Did the accused pour the water out himself?'

'Yes, sir.'

'Where did he get the water from?'

'A jug, sir.'

'Did you see him put anything into the water?'

'No, sir.'

'Would you swear to that?'

The beak was thrust up against my face.

'Yes, sir.'

'He didn't drop some powder into the water perhaps?'

No! No, no, no.

The little page was found guilty of poisoning the Dauphin. He was sentenced to be dismembered by horses, and beheaded. In our lawcourts, there are some sentences more wicked than the crime. The court turned out in huge numbers to watch. An execution livens up the day no end. We pages were forced to witness the spectacle also. Montecuculli screamed so much that in the end they had to drug him in order to get him tied to the horses. As the horses gathered speed, blood and pieces of bone spattered around the square and even on to the ladies' dresses. Montecuculli became a little bit of red meat lying in the mud. It was a terrible warning. I pressed my hand to my mouth. I had suddenly remembered: it was I who had been detailed to hand the water to the Dauphin, but at the last moment my attention had been distracted by a shout. It could have been . . . my insides turned liquid. I rushed round the corner and was violently sick.

I became page to the King's third son, the eloquent and debonair Charles, Duke of Orleans, His brother Henri, the young thug, was now heir. Extremely dim-witted, his only talent was for warmongering and he spent vast sums of money on his suits of armour. Because he had been only second in line to the throne, his education, for which he had showed no aptitude anyway, had been neglected. It saddened his father that the future ruler of France had no interest in literature or the arts. Little did I think then that one day Henri's indifference to learning would have a direct impact on my own life.

James V of Scotland, nicknamed the Red Fox on account of his long red hair, came to Paris to claim a wife and ran through the streets disguised as a workman. The whole city crowded to Notre-Dame to watch the marriage ceremony performed by seven cardinals. The streets were hung with tapestries; the horse-racing, fencing and jousting went on for days. Wine gushed laughing out of fountains. And in the midst of it all was the Princess Madeleine, the Red Fox's new wife, heavy-eyed and flushed with fever. Breathless, I watched fireworks explode in the sky like some heavenly battle on Olympus. They were golden days; I was a butterfly chasing after all the pleasures the court had to offer.

It was with mixed feelings, therefore, that I received my master Charles's orders to join the retinue escorting Princess Madeleine to her new home in Scotland. To leave the golden elegance of court for that barbaric country! Why me? Perhaps because the Prince Charles had glimpsed some spark of promise in me. If there is one thing I have learned during my long years at court, it is that the orders of kings are inscrutable (and frequently illogical). Forlornly I put on my new Spanish cloak and leather riding-boots and joined the Princess's governess, her doctor, midwife, cook and jester for the journey to the coast.

The sea was a foaming monster, lashing the rocks with its vicious tongue. I was seized by an unaccustomed desire to pray. The journey to Scotland took five days. One of the musicians Princess Madeleine had brought along with her taught me to play the lute. Like Orpheus charming the wild beasts, I lulled away my terror of the waves with the simple rhythms of popular songs.

Walled in by waves, Scotland is indeed a savage country. Grey sky even in the middle of summer. Eternal wind and mist. The natives live in thatched houses and eat porridge and fish. Perhaps their dull diet accounts for their grimness – I swear I never saw a Scotsman smile all the time I was there. After Paris, Edinburgh was tiny. Icy winds howled down its dark, narrow streets and the inhabitants shuffled by wrapped in deer-skins.

The barbaric climate carried off our Princess, our fragile French flower, soon after her arrival. The court exchanged their fine silks for black mourning. We stayed on in Scotland till the following summer (though all the seasons are alike in that country), moving between the strange little castle at Holyrood and the Gothic abbey of St Andrews by the sea. I spent the winter wrapped in my cloak, playing the lute by the fire in one of the dark, panelled rooms. In the evenings a nobleman who had come over with us, Seigneur Paul, read poetry and made us homesick for France.

On fine days we went fishing for perch and pike and hunting for deer. Venison is the best thing about Scotland, and riding over the tough heather, stopping for beer at the local taverns, these are perhaps the only things I missed when I returned to France.

I scarcely had time to congratulate my brother Charles on his promotion and be introduced to Claude's new wife, a pale-faced girl, already pregnant, when I was off again. The Red Fox, eager to keep up the links with France, had selected another of our noble ladies to be his second wife, Marie de Lorraine, sister of my schoolfriend Charles. It was December when we left. This time we went by way of the rolling Flemish plains. Flanders was a very prosperous place, full of round-bellied burghers dressed in furs. But the sea crossing proved very nearly fatal. For three days storms drove us perilously near rocks which could have shattered men's bodies like eggshells. I was more frightened than the cowardly Panurge in Rabelais's stories. I learned by heart all the patron saints of the sea and a few more besides.

My second stay in that constipated country was pleasanter than the first, for the Red Fox's new wife was determined to make the Scottish court as civilized as the French. She brought over writers and artists from France. She held tournaments and fêtes. She planted vineyards, for the dour Scots had not yet tasted the sweet fruits of Bacchus.

We returned to France by way of London and saw the English sheep, the white swans on the Thames and the handsome lords at Hampton Court.

Now, at last, I was too old to be a page. Charles released me from his service and, as my father had hoped, paid for me to be educated at the Royal Stables, the military academy for young noblemen. The serious business of training to be a soldier got under way. Instructed by my tutor, Carnavalet, I learned to ride bareback, fence and handle arms. Athleticism came naturally to me and I enjoyed showing off. Sometimes the Dauphin Henri came to visit us and we would ride or play football together. He was an excellent fencer. He amazed onlookers with his skill at breaking in a rebellious colt that no one else could handle. When he jumped a hedge, it seemed as though he and his horse were one, a centaur. But he was a strange, sad youth – perhaps thug is not the right description for him. He dreamed of being a medieval knight. We went hunting together at Fontainebleau and, riding at the Prince's side I felt that at last my life was taking on a serious purpose.

Yes, but . . . at the same time the persona I was creating was being subtly complemented by another self. It was a long time since I had done any studying. An Italian friend of mine, Claudio Duchi, who was also training at the Stables, persuaded me to open up my Latin books again. He was elegant, graceful and charming, like all Italians. His sister had been the Dauphin Henri's mistress. His aura of sophistication and worldliness impressed me. I have reason to be grateful to him, for he taught me the correct way to read Latin verse, how the metres worked, where the stresses fell. For the first time I was hearing the true rhythms of Virgil and tasting the sweet honey of poetry. Somewhere, but still far off, the wings of poetry faintly stirred in my soul.

Let's not exaggerate; however much pleasure my reading gave me, it came very secondary to my main goal of training myself for army life. How nearly my vocation slipped through my fingers.

The day creaks into action. I dress in my warmest furs (it is always so cold in that great barn of a place, the Louvre). I pick up the diamond ring given me by Queen Elizabeth of England in return for a volume of poems I dedicated to her. It slips on painfully over my gnarled finger – arthritis has twisted my joints into unnatural shapes – but it's necessary to remind my enemies that once I was famous and courted by rulers.

I am staying at the Boncourt College where my friend, Jean Galland, is principal. I gave up my house in Paris – well, it was hardly worth keeping it on for the few times I visit the city nowadays. From my window I can see the students sauntering in pairs in the garden or talking in animated huddles as they wait for their next lecture. Threadbare hose and holes in their shoes, I'll be bound. It seems like a century ago since I was one of them. A knock at the door. It's Amadis, come to accompany me to the palace. I pick up my walking-stick.

As we walk through the narrow streets with the smell of mud filling our nostrils, I say, 'Tell me, my friend, since you are now so much at the centre of court affairs, why does our King wish to see me?'

Amadis gives me a wry glance. 'It won't please you.'

'He's not asking me to give up one of my priories, is he?'

'No,' he laughs, 'though, God knows, he needs the money.'

'To spend on his dogs, or the band of pimps he calls his bodyguard? Tell me, what is the going rate for offering your backside to the King?'

'Hush, you're too harsh on him, Pierre. And very unwise.

You aren't in the country now.' He looks uneasily over his shoulder. 'Even the walls have ears – but you have lived long enough at court to know that.'

The wrath of a monarch means death. Who said that? The Englishman Thomas More, if I'm not mistaken.

'No, you must give him credit,' Amadis continues, 'he's doing his best, but the monarchy is bankrupt, he is overwhelmed by debts . . .'

'Then why does he continue wasting large sums of money on masked balls and festivals?'

'To impress the foreign ambassadors, of course. The country has at least to look as if she's still a world leader.'

We pass a group of women bargaining over a leg of ham. I point to them. 'See those women? That's like our princes. They dispute territory like a bunch of housewives haggling in the market-place.'

Amadis pulls a face at my cynicism. 'He's not a bad king, just weak and unable to refuse his followers anything. In any case, he needs them as a defence against extremists. And as you know, he takes an interest in things of the intellect, especially philosophy.'

'Ha ha! That's all we need, Plato's philospher-king, the ultimate illusion. What this country wants is a good politician.'

Amadis ignores this outburst. 'In fact that's why he has sent for you. He wishes you to make one of the speeches at the next meeting of his academy.'

'But I loathe making speeches.'

Amadis sighs. 'Look, I know that. I tried to suggest other names. Believe me I did. He wants you and no one else.'

I am suspicious. 'Who will debate against me?'

There is a silence, then, 'Philippe Desportes.'

So that's it. The King has called the old poet out of retirement to watch him perform before the court like a dancing bear. I feel the anger rising in me. I am being set up like pins to be knocked down, as undoubtedly I shall be, by the King's favourite poet. I am old and slow of speech. My rival is a young man. I am a relic of a past age and the King wants to prove this in order to rob me of my few remaining supporters.

We pass the hanging bodies and the open sewer in the place Maubert. I retch a few times and not only from the stench. Amadis gives me a handkerchief.

'Think about it carefully, Pierre. Can you afford to refuse?'

Of course I can't. Even in old age there is no peace. The old man must still perform his tricks.

We turn into the courtyard of the Louvre. Horses and nobles mingle in the mud. Women hurry past in tight-waisted dresses and black velvet caps. Today their Indian perfumes smell sickly and cloying, as if they were being used to disguise the rotting flesh beneath. Everywhere there is a mad bustle. Monks and bishops stride briskly across the square, servants dash past carrying messages. I am nearly knocked down several times, but Amadis supports me with his arm. No one stands still in the Louvre. If you do so, it looks as if you are out of a job.

We go past the Swiss guards, through the guardroom and up the staircase to the waiting-room. By the time I get to the top, I am out of breath. I pause outside the room. From it issues a noise that would rival the chatter of fishwives at the Petit-Pont. The courtiers hang around dressed in their best velvet and silk doublets. Do I imagine it, or is there a hush as I enter the room? There's a general crablike shuffle to the other side of the room. I don't smell bad (at least I don't think I do), but I am out of favour and they know it.

We wait around for over two hours. Finally we are ushered into the royal presence. Down on my knees. A huge emerald ring is held out for me to kiss.

'We are pleased to see you. You may rise.'

I find myself face to face with the King. I note the rouged cheeks and gold hair-powder. Nowadays it is fashionable to be absurd.

'Our secretary, Amadis, has informed you of our wishes?'

'Yes, Your Majesty.'

'You are willing?'

'Willing and honoured, Your Majesty.' (I am a fox amongst foxes.)

'The debate will be held in two weeks' time.'

My heart sinks. Two more weeks in this stinking cesspit.

'Our desire is that you should speak on the virtues of the

active life. Philippe Desportes will argue in favour of the contemplative life.'

Oh, very clever – naturally the King prefers the latter. He's an artist, this king, an artist in the pursuit of pleasure. I look into his eyes for a second. Empty, like the eyes of all the kings I have known. He eats alone at a huge table, waited on by the band of youths who, it is rumoured, provide other services as well. Alone and yet pursued – he can't even piss in private, for his chamber-pot must be held out for inspection.

I bow out in suitably humble fashion, leaving him, a tiny solitary figure, in that huge, magnificent and empty room.

I return to Boncourt College and work fruitlessly on my speech for a couple of hours. Time, that is what the court steals from me. I have never been mercenary, only of my minutes, because I knew they were owed to poetry. And now? Ah, now, I have only this mental masturbation to occupy me. Stroking memory, a task well suited to an old man. Yes, but wait, insects scrabble in my stomach when I remember what comes next. So what, Pierre Ronsard? Surely you didn't expect that telling your life story would be an easy task, did you? How like you, the eternal optimist, always hoping to escape scot-free. Pour yourself another glass of wine and get on with the story.

Chapter 4

'How would you feel about a trip to Germany?' asked my father.

The guzzling Germans.

To initiate me into the art of diplomacy, my father had got me a post as secretary to his old friend Lazare de Baif; for, if I were to be an officer of the King, I must learn to be a diplomat as well as soldier and courtier. Lazare was on a delicate mission to win the German Lutherans over to François our King and away from the Emperor Charles V.

I said goodbye to my friends at the Stables and rode round to Lazare's house in the Fossés St Victor feeling somewhat nervous. For Lazare had the reputation of being a formidable scholar. He had published a translation of Sophocles' *Electra* and was on friendly terms with some of the most learned men of the day (he had corresponded with Erasmus). I had heard it rumoured that he wrote his letters in Greek rather than the usual Latin. I felt a little uneasy and my uneasiness increased when I stopped outside his house and saw that the entire façade was covered with Greek inscriptions, of which I understood not a word.

Lazare himself opened the door. He was dressed in a long velvet coat with fur edging. I was struck by the warm expression in his eyes.

'So you are Louis's son. Tell me, do you like poetry too?' he asked as we shook hands.

I mumbled something about reading Virgil at the Stables with a friend. I had hoped not to have to reveal my ignorance too early on; after all, I was supposed to be acting as his secretary.

'The Stables – ah, yes. Well, it's a fashionable place to be educated – no Greek there of course . . . still, Latin will stand you in good stead in Germany. You may take notes in the vernacular if you wish,' he added, seeing my face drop. 'The main thing is to record accurate minutes.'

I followed him as he led the way to the library. A thin, pale-faced boy of about eight was sitting at a table reading a large tome with an air of intense concentration. He jumped as Lazare put his arm on his shoulder.

'Perhaps my Antoine should do a spell of training in the Stables – get rid of these hunched shoulders, eh?'

The boy scowled and made some reply in Latin, too quick for me to catch. Lazare, noticing my confusion, patted his son on the arm and said gently, 'I think our friend here would like you to repeat that.'

'I was quoting Juvenal, Father. *Mens sana in corpore sano.*'

'Very good, Antoine.'

I swore under my breath. What a swot! Thank God he was being left behind.

'Antoine is to stay with Jacques Toussaint, the famous Greek professor,' Lazare said, proudly. 'It's a great honour. Toussaint hand picks his pupils.'

'A talking library,' one of my friends had called Toussaint. No doubt he and Antoine would get along fine.

On the day we set out, Antoine stood in the doorway reciting Greek verse as a farewell. With his lank brown hair and high forehead he was an unprepossessing sight. But wait now, who would have thought that one day he would become my closest friend? Hush, come closer and let me whisper – such things should not be said out loud for fear of misunderstandings. As I write, I have the feeling that all this time I was simply someone else's plaything. Humiliating, isn't it? But then perhaps it's only because I know what's coming next.

Lazare was very proud of his clever son and spoke about him often during the journey to Germany. 'I have been both father and mother to him,' he said, tapping his chest.

Antoine was born during Lazare's spell as French ambassador in Venice. His mother was a Venetian courtesan. When his period of duty as ambassador ended, Lazare had taken his son away from the atmosphere of pimping and prostitution which was his mother's world and brought him in a basket to France. Oh, I see you are shocked. Why? That such a respectable man had an affair with a high-class prostitute? Surely not, it happens all the time. Or that he took so little trouble to hide it? (In which case, you are something of a hypocrite.) I ask you, how many men acknowledge their illegitimate children? How many take as much trouble over their children born in wedlock as Lazare did over his son? He gave Antoine the best Greek and Latin teachers he could find (though whether in fact . . . but he couldn't have predicted the profession his son would choose; he thought Antoine would become a scholar like himself).

We had a riotous time in Germany. I was dazzled by the brilliant conversation of the scholars and politicians who called at Lazare's house. Coming from the blunt world of the Stables, I found myself completely out of my depth amidst the clever repartee. Understanding very little of what was being said, I took down copious notes in my capacity as secretary. My diligence amused Lazare, though I think he sometimes wished I was more efficient.

Lazare took me to hear gloomy old John Calvin speak. He was a man of obvious integrity, passionate in defence of his interpretation of the Scriptures though, as my father often said, fanatics rarely advance the cause of piety. Nevertheless, despite my father's warnings, I found something attractive about the sheer uncluttered nakedness of the religious system he preached, the harsh light he turned on abuses in the Catholic Church.

Even more impressive than John Calvin was the Germans' capacity for drink. The Germans drink their wine neat instead of mixing it with water as we do. Unlike Socrates, I was unable to drink glass after glass of wine and remain sober. Midnight very often saw me with my head on the table, dead drunk. Lazare looked on in wry amusement. He himself drank very little.

'Drink and diplomacy don't mix,' he said, but he thought a few excesses no bad thing in youth (also, that if I carried on long enough, my head would grow stronger).

Protocol required us to attend or give at least one banquet a day. These were held in overheated rooms and the staple fare was always sausages, ham and salt beef. I put on weight through overeating and lack of exercise. At night, I dreamed drunkard's dreams of men without heads, dwarfs with eyes in their stomachs and horned beasts.

One day, in the company of another secretary, I visited a brothel. The atmosphere was thick with music, laughter and perfume. Half-naked girls lay sprawled in armchairs, watching disdainfully as their customers were shown into the room by the madam. A girl with an oval face framed by dark ringlets caught my eye. 'That one,' I said, pointing to her. But the madam, taking advantage of my obvious inexperience and lack of German, chose to misinterpret my signal. She beckoned to someone in the corner and the next minute I saw a stout forty-year-old matron bearing down on me. She was dressed incongruously in some pink wispy material and there was a thick moustache on her upper lip. As she took my arm to lead me away, I cast a desperate glance backwards at my friend the secretary who was doubled up, laughing. The woman led me into a room where a bed with grubby sheets stood waiting for me like a threat. Taking a deep breath, I blew out the candle by the bed, got undressed and lay down beside the heap of quivering flesh. Keeping the girl with the oval face firmly fixed in my mind, I finished the whole business as quickly as I could. I staggered home, my head swimming with beer, and fell asleep. In this glorious way I lost my virginity.

I woke up with a fierce hangover the next morning and a determination to return to the brothel and get the better of the madam by insisting on the girl with the ringlets. I am glad to say I succeeded. I grew quite expert after that first fumbling encounter. There were women of all nationalities in those German brothels, each country having its own speciality. I sampled them all. It was a skill to be mastered, as much a part of a soldier's training as handling the sword or throwing the javelin. I turned sex into a battleground with fixed rules and operations. My approach to it was that of a soldier; later I regretted it had not been as a poet that I met my first experiences. (We have all of us so many different selves. How can we be sure we shall be the right one at the right time?)

Towards the end of our three months in Germany I became conscious of a severe pain in my left ear. At first I ignored it, though I eased off the alcohol. One day, as I was taking notes for Lazare, he noticed me wince and clutch my ear.

'You must see a doctor,' he insisted.

Speaking in Latin, for I knew no German and he no French, the doctor explained that I had some sort of infection in my ear. His examination caused me great pain – as is often the way with our doctors, he increased rather than cured my suffering. He gave me an opiate to dull the pain, but as we made our way back to France it was obvious to me that I was going deaf.

There, it's out now, but perhaps you knew already? Ironic, isn't it? France's leading poet, deaf as a doorpost.

Our mission in Germany had failed. The Lutherans remained loyal to the Emperor. Lazare went up to Paris to face a difficult interview with the King whilst I went home to La Possonnière to recuperate. By now the pain had spread to my right ear. My mother sniffed in disgust when she saw me. My father summoned several doctors to examine me, all of them incompetent. Why is it that medicine, the science most important for our preservation, is yet the one that is the most uncertain and confused? One doctor even had the nerve to suggest that my deafness had been caused by venereal disease, a diagnosis my enemies were later to seize upon with delight, I may say. It is possible that I picked up something in Germany – not from the pink-moustached wonder, I hope. No, as far as I can remember, I have never been seriously affected by this complaint (a few rashes here and there, possibly). It is strange, though, how many people have accused me of it. I wonder if there's something wrong with my memory.

They say hell is soundless. A skeleton on a black horse, with dogs barking at its hoofs, chased me through a dark forest. Winged phantoms ground their teeth after me, furies lashed me with their whips. I woke screaming, to feel the wind thunder through the poplars behind our house. It was winter. I got up from my bed and, wrapped in furs, went for lonely walks through the fields of my childhood. The widowed forest with her bare head, the veiled and saddened sky, were a perfect reflection of my feelings.

I could never be a soldier, the role I had created for myself had collapsed. My life had become useless, empty, without a scrap of purpose. The future stretched before me, monotonous and blank. I would live out my dull existence without heroics and without glory. My mother made no secret of her satisfaction that I had turned out exactly as she had predicted, the runt of the litter, the sickly last-born. 'I told you you were wasting your time on him,' she said to my father. My father hid his disappointment, but I knew I had let him down.

During my solitary rambles I chose my burial-place, a little green island at the confluence of two streams. Entombed under grass and water, shaded by trees instead of marble, I would be visited every year, like Pan, by peasants who would sprinkle my tomb with new wine and handfuls of rose petals. No, that's wrong, I had hardly heard of Pan in those days. Fiction again.

I avoided the company of others. Lazare called. I refused to see him. He left a message. 'Tell him that only letters last.' I shrugged my shoulders. I had no time for a scholar's riddles. I went days without washing or changing my clothes. I attended mass in our chapel, mechanically reeling off the responses, but a God who could shatter my life seemed very remote. I believed in his wrath but not in his mercy.

The months drained away. I lived like a stone or an empty, hollow vessel. The April sun slanting through the fingers of the trees left me unmoved. Joy was a dim memory of the past. No, no, I can't go on; to describe what I felt at that time brings back memories unbearable in their pain. And yet it is the mark of an artist to face, to welcome even, the unbearable. Have I lost that gift too? My hold on life has never been so frail as it was then. I thought of suicide but, unspeakable as life was, I feared even more the great black void beyond. It was my first taste of melancholia, Saturn's gift, familiar to all artists.

Gradually the pain in my ears subsided to a dull ache and a persistent ringing which has never left me. I was not going to be totally deaf. Over the years, by dint of much application, I have learned to follow quite rapid conversations by lip-reading. I have been helped by the fact that in most situations people say what you mostly expect them to say. But the birds no longer sing to me and I no longer hear the patterned rhythms of the streams. Nature has been, from that time on, a silent picture for me.

In desperation, I turned back to those poets who had amused me during my army days. I reread Horace; his poetry was like a cry down the centuries. He spoke of death and change, of the shortness of life, things I could feel and understand, important themes not touched on by our French poets, who masked their emotions behind a complicated jingle of rhymes. Fifteen hundred years ago a Roman had experienced the same pain as I was going through. In my mind, the Sabine hills became the fertile meadows of the Loire, the Fons Bandusiae became my own Bellerie fountain. I tried my hand in a desultory fashion at imitating some of Horace's odes.

One night I looked out of my window and saw moonlight falling on the snow. I wanted to reach out and touch the brilliant radiance of the night's eye. From that night on, leaving behind my childhood's easy familiarity with woods and fields, I began to recognize the mystery and authority of nature, mother of my Muse. I began to know that sense of wonder, prerequisite for poetic vision.

But my Latin was still shaky. I could not hope to rival Horace in his own language, the language he had spoken daily. I did not take these experiments very seriously; they were merely a distraction from the pain in my ears and the deadness in my soul. But slowly, slowly, the Muses were drawing nearer, beating their steady wings, unheard by me as yet.

My father, the only person who might have helped me, had become an old man. He had begun to suffer from kidney-stones, which made him uncharacteristically irritable. My presence was a constant reminder that his hopes of seeing me continue his career were at an end. I felt I was darkening his last days. I also felt resentful, I remember, that he had encouraged me so much in my dreams of glory – how unfair we humans are to one another! I have often been glad that my only offspring will be my poems; who at Rome would not rather have given birth to the *Aeneid* than to the handsomest youth in the city? There is no guarantee that one's children won't turn out to be imbeciles.

'We must think of some other profession for you,' said my father one day. 'As the youngest son, there'll be precious little for you to inherit, I'm afraid.'

It was decided that I was not sufficiently educated to be a

lawyer, nor sufficiently a charlatan to become a doctor. I chose the only other profession open to me: I became a cleric like my brother Charles and dedicated myself to a celibacy which was against my nature and a God whom I found increasingly hard to worship.

I notice a few eyebrows raised. I see I shall have to defend myself (this was before the Catholic Church reformed, of course). In the light of later events it would be easy to be critical of my decision to enter the Church. But think back to those years – I don't believe my motives were very different from those of the majority of my contemporaries, namely a wish to please my father and the need for a steady income. No, I was no worse than they, but I was certainly ill-educated (and much too uncertain in my own faith to care adequately for anyone else's).

'I've always thought there was something monkish about you,' sneered my mother.

We made the journey to Le Mans in slow stages, since travelling aggravated my father's condition. We arrived in time for the funeral service of the great general, Guillaume Du Bellay, with whom my father had fought in Italy (we were distantly related to his family on my mother's side). The lesson was read by a fat, round figure in monk's robes, a pair of spectacles perched comically on his nose. I heard later that this was Dr François Rabelais, whose giant stories had entertained me so much in childhood.

As they lowered the coffin into the grave, I felt as though the soldier in me was being buried too. (What I did not know then was that there was someone else amongst the crowd of mourners whose dreams of being a soldier had ended with the general's death.)

The next day, I knelt by the altar in a cassock (hateful garment!), with a folded surplice over my left arm and a lighted candle in my right hand, whilst Guillaume's brother, the Cardinal Du Bellay, clipped four chestnut locks from my head. They fell into a golden bowl held by a choirboy. The Cardinal took the folded surplice and slipped it over my head. I was now a tonsured clerk of the Church. My heart sank.

During the incredibly long and tedious service I noticed a thin figure dressed in black leaning against a pillar. I was struck by the long, sallow face and the lost, hungry eyes. After the service, I inquired who this person was.

'Du Bellay's nephew. Odd sort of a fellow. Always on his own. Doesn't do anything in particular. Writes a bit, I think. He's a little deaf, which I suppose accounts for . . . oh, sorry.'

It was like looking into a mirror. The first feelings I associated with the general's nephew were ones of bitterness and pain.

I was introduced to the Cardinal's secretary, Jacques Peletier. He had studied medicine and law. At twenty-seven he was already known as a bit of a wandering scholar. He asked me why I had decided to enter the Church. I shrugged my shoulders to imply family pressures. I certainly did not wish to pretend, even to the Cardinal's secretary, that I had a vocation.

'So . . . you will need some other occupation, otherwise your duties, which are light, will bore you. What were you thinking of? The court?'

'Theoretically I'm still in the service of Charles Orleans.' My tone betrayed my indifference. With my affliction life at court would be intolerable.

Peletier put his arm around my shoulder (we were walking in the cathedral garden). 'You know, you ought to take up writing. Your father's a friend of Bouchet, isn't he?'

I confessed, a little uneasily, that I had tried my hand at some Latin imitations of Horace.

'Splendid, splendid. You must show them to me some time. I'm working on a translation of his *Ars Poetica* at this very moment.'

'Yes, but you're a serious scholar. I'm only playing. My verses limp along, getting entangled in their own rhymes.' Even then I knew that it is a bad poet who is hindered by rhyme.

'You should be serious about your writing. This country needs poets,' he insisted.

'What, one more court monkey, composing jingles to please the ladies and flatter the rich?'

'And Petrarch?' he said, quizzically.

I was reminded of those conversations long ago at La

Possonnière between my father and Bouchet. I repeated their argument, partly to see what he would say.

'Of course, French writers can't hope to rival the Italians.'

He stopped in the middle of the path, feigning horror.

'Why ever not? Besides,' he went on, 'I'm beginning to think that we could be capable of leaving the Italians behind and rivalling the classical poets themselves.'

'You're mad,' I said.

'No, listen – Horace's theories of poetry are nobler than anything we've yet heard of in this country. For Horace, poetry isn't a trade but an art, an art too full of magic to be the work of men. The poet is chosen and at the same time a consummate craftsman. He purifies himself in order to be a worthy vessel for the Muses, but he also devotes a lifetime to perfecting his technique. Horace's poet doesn't rush his poems into print like our courtiers. He keeps them in a drawer, taking them out from time to time to polish them till they are worthy of publication. His whole life is a disinterested effort towards beauty. Such a poet would not dream of prostituting himself to the highest bidder. Bad poets crawl along the ground like slugs. Horace's poet flies upwards towards heaven. Incidentally, such a concept is not totally out of keeping with the role of churchman, if you are determined to be bothered about that.'

And so I heard for the first time, explained to me in the walled garden of a cathedral, the classical definition of a poet, where poetry is no longer a game, as it was for our poets, but the highest form of human activity. It seemed a noble profession, nearly as noble as that of soldier. But who would accept a poet who thought so highly of himself? The court would laugh.

'These ideas are in the air, my friend, they're very much in the air. Oh, not at court, but amongst serious-minded people. Your friend Lazare is a great supporter of the new ways of writing. He and a group in Paris spend a lot of time discussing how our country's literature can be made great again. I'm surprised he hasn't spoken about this to you.'

I shook my newly tonsured scalp. 'I've had a bad education. I'm lost among such men. All this may be true, but even if we allow your preposterous statement that we, mere moderns, can rival the great classical writers, such a task can't be for me. My Latin is rusty and I know no Greek at all. I'm too old to begin my school-days over again.'

'Nonsense, it's never too late. Have you heard of Jean Dorat?'

Needless to say, I had not.

'Lazare is thinking of getting him to tutor his son in Latin and Greek. I'm sure he would help. Shall I write to him?'

Now I was certain that Peletier was more than a little mad. I extricated myself as well as I could by promising to give the matter some thought.

Nevertheless, the conversation had sown its seeds. I returned from Le Mans with the outward vocation of a cleric, but in my soul Peletier's vision of a poet had started to take hold. And so my poetry began in sickness; as a revolt against the abyss I had glimpsed opening up beneath me, an instinctive gesture showing that I was not about to give in to the powers of darkness that had threatened to swallow me up. (I did not know then that all poetry is an affirmation, a movement outwards to embrace life.) Peletier had opened the way to the mountain-tops. Imperceptibly, my life was changing shape, like clouds on a summer's day. I have said before that fortune is an artist.

We are shown into a little room without windows. Here, the King holds his academy by candlelight and expounds eloquently on philosophy whilst his country is torn to pieces by civil war. I begin my speech on the virtues of the active life, pronouncing it in my flat deaf man's tones to which the court has become accustomed over the years (only a few new arrivals snigger). I intend my speech to be a rebuke of the King's indulgence in philosophy and scientific research at the expense of his subjects' welfare.

'What use is astrology to a state at war?' I ask. 'Determining the exact position of the stars won't help me live any better. The peasants know only how to plough and till the land, yet they live more simply and virtuously than many at court.'

I might have added: does Aristotle help them when they get

gout? Does a farmhand, for being ignorant of Greek, get a smaller erection?

'A bad housekeeper', I continue, warming to the task, 'spends in a few days, on feeding his astrologers and fortune-tellers, what has taken his ancestors a hundred years to earn.'

The King raises a royal eyebrow. I see Amadis frowning in the corner. Well, what does it matter? A poet speaks in images and metaphor; he should not be forced to explain in prose the ideas that are hidden like jewels amongst his verse. It is something of an anomaly that I am here at all. But if the King insists on plain-speaking prose, then he shall have it.

Desportes, tall and curly-haired, jumps up eagerly to argue. 'Moral virtue springs from the intellect and therefore a life of study is best. You yourself, sire,' he says, the flatterer, the toady, turning to the King, 'have set a shining example to your subjects of a life devoted to philosophy and contemplation.'

Odd, I think to myself, that Desportes, who has never expressed a serious thought in his life, should be defending the study of philosophy, whilst I . . . but that's the court for you; it makes monkeys of us all and men are praised for qualities not their own.

As Desportes's speech comes to an end, an expectant hush descends on the small room. The King rises and beckons us both forward. We approach, heads bowed, and go down on bended knee in front of him. A royal hand reaches out and raises up my rival. 'My beloved Desportes,' says the King. Desportes kisses the emerald ring. The King places an arm round his shoulder and they sweep out of the room without so much as a backward glance. I am left foolishly on my knees.

As the room begins to clear, Amadis comes over and helps me up. He walks me to my carriage, sternly rebuking me for testing the King's indulgence. 'You go too far, Pierre.'

'You'll see,' I say, merrily, wagging my finger at him from the carriage, 'when this new edition comes out, I shall regain my place at court!'

But I touch wood as I say this.

On the way home I call in at La Possonnière, now owned by my nephew Louis. In addition to managing the family estate, Louis is military governor of Vendôme. He is a devout Catholic and tells me he has joined that bunch of Catholic extremists, the League. They have pledged themselves to keep France for the Catholics and expel all Lutherans. I find it hard to sympathize with a religion established by violence: though he is the soldier and I the cleric, I come away from the family home with a bitter taste in my mouth. From my carriage I watch the rain dropping tiny pearls into the hearts of roses. Admit it, why not? I am jealous. My nephew has succeeded, as I never could, in carrying on the military traditions of our family. All the same, his religion is too extreme for me.

As always after visiting La Possonnière I stop the carriage at the churchyard in Couture. I walk through the damp grass till I come to a headstone slightly more ornate than the rest. My father. Gentle and loving, yet with enough ambition, ruthlessness, call it what you like, to adapt his soul to the tortuous path of life at court and carve himself a comfortable position there. 'Don't always be in a rush to tell everyone what you are thinking,' he told me once. He would have known how to handle this present King. I bend down to clear some of the weeds around his grave. And yes, I was waiting for this: guilt and sorrow that his last days were saddened by my deafness.

Softly, the Muses were drawing near. It was impossible, though, to think of acting on Peletier's words whilst my father was still alive. It would have completed his disappointment in me if he had guessed I was considering the career of a poet. He was too old to change his views that poetry was merely a pleasant diversion, unworthy to be the profession of a nobleman. So I trailed round after the court, playing football with the future King Henri, who seemed more of a lout than ever.

Secretly I got hold of a copy of Horace's *Ars Poetica* and read it through to myself in my halting Latin. I composed some more imitations of Horace's odes. But the rhythms that were beginning to dance and sing in my head, limped and stumbled under my pen. And I had no idea how to bridge the gap between the sounds in my head and their transposition on the page.

One day I did a stupid thing. Feeling desperately in need of advice, I swore my brother Claude to secrecy and showed him some of the poems I had been working on. Whilst I paced anxiously up and down the room, he sat in a chair by the open window, dressed in soft leather boots and a silk shirt, reading through my poems. At last he paused and took out a lace handkerchief to wipe his face.

'Well?' I snapped.

'Can't you find a more serious subject? Wine and sex are all you seem able to write about. Why don't you try describing battles and heroes?'

He had seen in my poems only as much as he could understand and had completely missed all the passages on Horace's philosophy. It was my first lesson in the importance of choosing responsible literary critics.

My father was increasingly crippled by the stone. He coughed blood regularly and his urine was thick and dark. The doctor advised bleeding and confinement to bed. More sensibly, my father drank quantities of water and took as much exercise as he could bear. He continued to carry out his duties at court. 'Nature understands our illnesses better than we do,' he told me when I begged him to rest. 'Our own body tells us what's good for us. We should listen to it rather than to the doctors.'

In this way, my father prolonged his life until June. I accompanied the body back to La Possonnière and stayed to sort out the will and act of succession. The estate passed into the predatory hands of my brother Claude, who descended on us the day before the funeral with his pale-faced wife, Anne, and his four children. All the fruits of my father's careful economies were about to be squandered.

My father's death finished a stage of my life. His and my dreams of heroism on the battlefield had led to a dead end. You see what I meant when I said how little we control our own lives. Horace was right, we are just the playthings of fortune, that cruel and beautiful woman who delights in teasing her lovers. Yes and . . . how strange – in that same year, Clément Marot died in Turin. It really was the end of an era. Not knowing that she had already prepared the way, I decided to call fortune's bluff, to see what role she had in store for me next. The day after the will was settled I wrote to Lazare in Paris. Two weeks later I was on my way to that city to study with his son under Jean Dorat.

I finish pulling out the weeds on my father's grave. I get up stiffly and start to walk back to the carriage. I am looking forward to the peace of Croixval after the noise and bustle of the city. It has always been like this (I settle back amongst the cushions): a constant swing between solitude and the crowds. Being tossed back and forth like a cork. Embracing the court (that whore who dazzles with her perfumes and silks), fleeing to the country to preserve my purity, fearing failure and oblivion there, running back into the whore's arms to receive her kisses, which are death to poetry. And in the end, extravagant mistress that she is, she has destroyed my happiness, my youth, my trust in others – she has taken them all and flung them to the winds. Now I approach her only in a mask and reduce my gestures to those of a puppet. It is always a relief to return to the country and tear off the mask.

PART TWO

SCHOLAR'S APPRENTICE

Chapter 5

I entered Paris with hope faintly stirring inside me. The plague had recently swept the city, leaving it crouching sullenly under an autumn sky, racked by coughs and fevers. But as I rode through the city, the narrow streets seemed paved with jasmine. All kinds of delicious scents floated out of the apothecaries' shops. Musk mingled with spices from the grocers'. Tennis-courts were springing up all over Paris that year. The court was going through a fitness craze. Juvenal would have been pleased – this reminded me of Lazare's son, *mens sana* and all that. What could I have in common with a boy of twelve who spoke Greek and Latin fluently? Would Jean Dorat be as formidable and arrogant as the scholars I had met in Germany? Or gloomy like Calvin? By the time I arrived at Lazare's house I had worked myself into a fine sweat.

As I was dismounting, a large, ruddy-faced man with a mop of flaming red hair and a beard to match opened the door and rushed down the steps two at a time to shake me by the hand. 'Welcome, welcome,' he said, pumping my hand up and down. 'Welcome to the home of Minerva and the Muses, home of gracious conversation and civilized living. I'm Jean Dorat, by the way. So', he stood back to get a better look at me, 'you have come to us to make a scholar of you. Jacques Peletier spoke highly of you. Well, well, but first you'll be wanting some food and drink inside you after your journey, eh?' And he winked at me.

He pronounced all this without pausing for breath. I noted his provincial accent with surprise. I had somehow expected this famous professor, this oracle who unravelled knotty passages of Greek and charmed the ears of his students, to speak in the aristocratic tones of Lazare and my father.

Lazare then came forward, gently expressing his sorrow at my father's death. 'Your home is here now, Pierre, with us, as long as you wish to stay.' He beckoned Antoine who had been hovering in the doorway. 'It will do my son good to have a companion in his studies. He has been too much on his own.' Antoine nodded solemnly. After all the grief and pain of the last few months such a welcome, so unexpectedly warm, made tears come into my eyes. I looked round at all the kindly faces. At last I had found a home, I thought.

Later that evening, after I had washed and changed and rested, there was a meal in my honour. The food was simple but wholesome, without any of the heavy spices I associated with meals in Paris. But the conversation was brilliant. Lazare kept open house for scholars and literati – any writer fallen on hard times could always be sure of a meal and a bed at the house in the Fossés St Victor. As Peletier had said, the discussions centred upon the revival of learning in our time. They spoke of the trilingual college founded by the King where for the first time Greek and Hebrew were taught in France and the Bible could be read in the original rather than in Jerome's translation. Like a long-buried treasure, the classical languages were being hauled up to the light and the dust blown off them.

'New ground is being broken every day. Scholarship is proceeding at a pace not seen for centuries.'

'God is moving in history, literature is being reborn, light is coming into the world after the darkness of the past ages.'

'Nevertheless, the Sorbonne has accused Erasmus of heresy.'

'There will always be vested interests who see progress as resulting in loss of power for themselves. It's not a reason to call a halt to the progress. The Sorbonne theologians are like the Druid priests – they want to keep all the mysteries of religion to themselves.'

'But it's true that by comparing Jerome's translation with the original text of the New Testament Erasmus has found errors in the Vulgate. Since the fourth century the

Catholic Church has based its doctrines on what Jerome said, and now we're told he mistranslated the original Greek.'

'I agree. To publish such things disturbs the faith of ordinary believers.'

'I would never willingly shake anyone's faith, but we can't hide the fact that Jerome made mistakes. The Church will survive, it always has.'

'But to criticize the book on which the tenets of the Catholic faith reside, this is to give fuel to Luther and his followers.'

'That old story – Erasmus laying the egg that Luther hatched. I believe that Erasmus never intended the Church to split. Things have gone further than he wished.'

'In the name of truth and progress. . . ?'

'You can't stop men learning and speaking out about what they find, however uncomfortable it may be for everyone else.'

'Even if it destroys our certainties about the world and peace with it?'

'Anything that imprisons men's minds in darkness is evil. You know that saying of Pico's: God has placed man at the centre of the world so that he may fashion himself into whatever shape he chooses. There are no limits on man, except those he fixes himself.'

'And Ecclesiastes? He that increases knowledge increases sorrow.'

'I believe', put in Lazare quietly, 'there will come future generations who will be capable of resolving those truths which now seem incompatible to us. We shall uncover and a later age will synthesize.'

'Yes,' agreed Dorat, 'Luther and Erasmus are part of a spiritual force rising up in our time to break down the narrow categories of the past and usher in the future. I would even include Agrippa of Nettesheim in this.'

'What! That magician?'

'A white magician. Ficino said that white magic is not incompatible with the Christian religion. Our century is weary of dialectics and seeks answers in intuition.'

'I agree. Philosophy can no longer be a dialectical exercise. That only leads to a dead end. The modern philosopher must prepare himself to receive intuitive knowledge of the divine by purifying his way of life. He must be a magus.'

A hundred different strands of knowledge have opened up in our century and as a poet I have had to be receptive to them all. I may not have recorded the conversation exactly, for it is too long ago for that. Yes, it's occasionally necessary to improvise. The names of the speakers? They do not matter. As Peletier said, these opinions were very much in the air, they could have been expressed by any number of people. But it was the first time I had heard them. Listening to those men that first evening, I found ideas thrashing around in my head like flies.

I was amazed at the freedom they permitted themselves in talking about religion. My father's faith, which he had tried to pass on to me, had been that of a soldier, loyal to his country's Church and to the religion of his ancestors. I had scarcely heard the name of Luther pass his lips. For him, Luther had been a scandal, a drunken monk who expounded the Scriptures between the soup and the fish course, with one hand round his goblet and the other on his wife's knee. He had admired Erasmus but had been afraid of what his writings might lead to. And now here, just a few yards away from the Sorbonne, these men openly discussed ideas that were sufficient to have any one of them sentenced to death for heresy by that bastion of conservatism. It was my first taste of intellectual freedom and my head was spinning.

Dorat banged on the table with a spoon. 'Come now, we're exhausting our new friend here with all this talk. How about a song?' He struck up a drinking song. Everyone joined in and it was followed by several more, not always the most decent. Decidedly my view of scholarly life needed revising.

Lazare smiled across the table at me. 'We work hard here, but we play hard too.'

About midnight, the party broke up.

'See you in the schoolroom at seven,' grinned Dorat.

'Now, Pierre.' Dorat tapped the desk with a ruler. 'Latin is all very well, but to be any kind of a scholar Greek is essential. The Roman culture is a second-hand one. Everything in it originated from the Greeks. That's why we put so much emphasis on learning Greek here.'

For the first few weeks my mind was in a state of turmoil. I felt intensely humiliated at having to labour over elementary Greek grammar whilst beside me a boy of twelve was reading Homer fluently. Fencing and horse-riding had come easily to me. It was galling to have to wrestle with lists of verbs.

Antoine offered to help me with my homework.

'No, thank you,' I replied gruffly, damned if I would let a mere boy explain grammar to me. I preferred to sit up till two in the morning. He offered to test me on Greek verbs. I told him to go and play outside.

One day I was feeling smug. I had translated a passage correctly at last whilst Antoine had made a small slip. He probably did it on purpose – he was a sensitive child under all that Greek.

Dorat shot me a glance from beneath his bushy eyebrows. 'This isn't a competition I'm running here. You know, Pierre, all over Europe there are scholars writing to each other asking for help on some point or other. Learning has to be shared or there would be very slow progress indeed. Scholars help one another. They don't compete for prizes like soldiers.'

I blushed scarlet, swallowed my pride, and from then on never refused Antoine's offers of help. I struck a bargain: in exchange for help with Greek I read him some of our old French poets – Jean Lemaire de Belges, the *Roman de la Rose* – all the books I had brought with me from my uncle's library.

All the same, it was humiliating to have to make so much effort over what came easily to others. Many times I cursed my inferior schooling. The masters at Navarre College had stuffed Latin down our throats, made us learn verses by heart without giving us the slightest insight into how those verses had come into being. Under Dorat we were expected not only to read and admire, but to question and even criticize classical authors, something that would have been considered blasphemous at Navarre. For the first time I began to see the imperfections of the ancient authors, to judge Virgil's *Georgics* better than his *Aeneid*, to learn that even Homer nods.

'Poetry is a gift from the gods,' he said, 'and therefore the poet is free to write on any subject he chooses – wine, myth, erotic love – but in order to do this, he must first understand what men have been in past ages and other countries.'

He taught us by comparing Greek with Latin to show how from an impoverished language and literature the Romans, by imitation, created poetry to rival the Greeks'. The comparison with the state of French literature was obvious. If Dorat had taught me nothing else, this alone would have been enough to earn my gratitude, for he pointed the way to go. But I owe him more than that: listening as he read to us the sweet strains of ancient poetry, my sleeping soul began to stir and waken. Slowly, slowly, I began to shake off earthly dross as poetry, like a magnet, drew my soul upwards.

Last night I dreamed of Philippe Desportes. Or rather, not at night but at daybreak when, they say, all dreams are true and foretell the future. Dressed in furs and holding a rolled tobacco leaf carefully between two fingers, he leans against my bedroom door.

'My dear Ronsard, all that effort,' he smirks, 'just to be a poet. Was it really worth it?'

Was it? I don't know.

'You really needn't have gone to so much trouble, you know.' With the back of his hand he stifles a laugh. 'Your problem is you went the wrong way about it. The court doesn't care a fig for all your learning. See how successful I have become and with so little work. You shouldn't have made things so difficult for yourself.'

I wake up shivering. No, I can't bear consciousness yet. I reach for the opiate by my bed.

One evening, about a month after I had arrived in Paris, as I was working in my room swotting up verbs for the next day, Dorat knocked on my door.

'Come along,' he said, 'put away your books. We're going out.'

He led me down narrow back-streets, sheltering under night's brown wing, till we reached the river. We walked along its banks for some time. He stopped outside a tall house where all the windows were brilliantly lit up. From inside came the sound of women's laughter. Dorat winked at me and knocked on the door. It was opened by a plump woman in a low-cut dress.

'Ah, it's you, Jean,' she cried, enveloping him in a huge embrace. 'And you've brought a friend.'

We went inside. The place was thick with the scent of Arabian perfumes and the smell of fornication. A young girl in a cotton shift brought us wine.

'*Vivamus, mea Lesbia, atque amamus,*' said Dorat, nuzzling into the neck of a passing whore.

'Get along with you. You and your Latin,' she replied, gently pushing him away.

On a low stool a dark-skinned girl sat strumming a lyre. Her black hair streamed wildly round her shoulders like that of some follower of Sappho. Her almond-shaped eyes were languorous and tempting. I went up to her. She smiled and shook her head. I retreated in embarrassment, much to Dorat's amusement.

'Come, Jeanne,' he said to the woman who had opened the door. 'Find a ripe young chicken for my friend here.'

I blushed as she brought forward a young girl with breasts like tiny rosebuds and skin a colour between white and red, like a rose under glass. I took her arm and led her into a quiet alcove away from the grinning Dorat. I motioned her to sit down.

'What is your name, child?'

'Marguerite, sir.'

'Marguerite.' I rolled it around my tongue. Margarita, pearl. I looked at her. She was small and thin and looked underfed. She could have been no more than twelve years old. 'How long have you been here, Marguerite?'

'I was born here, sir.' She lowered her black lashes. 'My mother worked here. She went away when I was six . . .'

'And left you behind?'

'A shopkeeper offered to marry her. It was an opportunity. She couldn't take me with her. I would have been a . . . a reminder. I have been fortunate. Madam, instead of throwing me out on the street, let me stay. I earned my keep by cleaning.'

'And now you've been promoted?'

She blushed. I kissed her naked shoulder.

'I am a student, Marguerite. I have very little money, but it doesn't please me any more to sleep with different women. I am looking for something more . . . settled. Do you think you could come to like me?'

She looked at me shyly through black lashes.

'I think I could, sir,' she replied.

I kissed her on the lips, gently. After a while she led me to a room and we made love at first shyly, then more fiercely. It was with Marguerite that I discovered I was capable of passion. Her kisses sucked the very soul out of me. As I came inside her for the third time I cried aloud for joy. She reawakened the sensuality that had slept since my return from Germany. It was only as I dressed to leave that I noticed the blood-stained sheets and realized that I had taken her virginity.

I visited my Marguerite often in the brothel by the banks of the Seine. It was a relationship fuelled purely by our delight in each other's bodies. I flattered myself that though her trade was to sleep with men she kept a soft spot for me in her heart because I had been her first lover. I was probably wrong. Though she could not even spell her own name, passion gave me the illusion that we had things in common.

One day, not long after that first visit, I showed Dorat some poems I had written for Marguerite. They were imitated from Catullus and very bawdy.

As he read them through, his craggy face broke into a smile.

'I like them well enough, but they'll never do for the court, you know. This kind of thing is out of date. You should read some Petrarch.'

So in the evenings by the fire Antoine and I began to learn Italian. (At least we were equally ignorant in this.) For Antoine, the language had an added significance, since it was, literally, his mother tongue, the language of the Venetian courtesan.

Let me see: I think it's going to be necessary to describe my reactions to Petrarch. Yes, it is important for what comes later (what a utilitarian attitude you have). I suppose it is my fault if you are restless, writing about poetry when I am supposed to be recounting my life. Well, it can't be helped. Poetry is knotted into my life – it marks off all the important parts. So, taking up my teacher's pen and pointing it at you, let me begin. Petrarch is the first modern poet to put melody above content. His verses are pure music. Bouchet was right when he called him the greatest lyric poet. His lines quiver between laughter and tears; he has sounded out the slightest movements of the human heart, explored all the emotions and created a new note in poetry. Here was a poet who could help me. I recognized at once that he was much superior to Marot or indeed any of our French poets. Marot is all playfulness. Petrarch's verses float between light and shade; his awareness of the fleetingness of earthly life casts a shadow over his love for Laura.

Yes, but his ideas on love! I thought these highly amusing – to place a woman on a pedestal and worship her as a goddess! Women were accommodating like Marguerite or stuck-up bitches like my sister. There was nothing divine about them. Nevertheless, Petrarch wrote great poetry, and so I adopted a style of writing that was foreign to my nature, which at that time was more at home in the brothel than amongst goddesses. I composed several poems for Marguerite; their persistent sensuality dissatisfied me. It was not Petrarchan. Yet how could I write in any other way about a girl whose skin was as familiar to me as my own?

'There's no doubt about it,' laughed Dorat, 'you'll have to fall in love.'

My ideal was a black-haired woman with mother-of-pearl skin and a mouth like a rose opening in the May sun. I found her at Blois in the spring of 1545, sitting by a window playing a lute and singing softly to herself. Perhaps it was the sadness of seeing a beautiful woman sing a song, the words of which I could not catch, or the sight of a lute which always caused me pain, since I could no longer play one myself. Perhaps it was her noble name I fell in love with. Cassandra, the beautiful Trojan prophetess with leather sandals and unbound hair who scorned the love of Apollo himself.

That night, watching her dance by torchlight under the blue and gold dome, her eyes shining like the fires of heaven, she seemed pure beauty; her steps weaving in and out of the dancers like the meanders of a river, the exact equivalent of a Petrarchan sonnet. 'The gods themselves must have fashioned those eyes,' I whispered to myself. Her laughter opened the way to the stars for me. As I gazed on her I felt heaven brush past my cheek; and youth paid homage to love.

Now comes the hard part. I have to disentangle the truth from the fictional role I created for myself over the next few years as Petrarchan lover of Cassandra. Did I love her? For her beauty, yes – it was said at court that her beauty would have made the heavens themselves jealous. My friend, Nicolas Denisot, drew her portrait. But I have never (except in my poetry) espoused that foolish notion of Plato's that we can judge someone's soul by looking at her face.

And there was another side to Cassandra, oh yes. She came from that wealthy family of Florentine bankers, the Salviatis, distant relations of the Médicis. She had the easy confidence that wealth and a good family brings. Some people called it arrogance. She certainly kept me in my place. I was allowed to visit her in the presence of her chaperone. I was allowed to address my poems to her. I was allowed to be present as she sang the latest sonnet I had composed for her, her fingers plucking at the strings of the pear-shaped lute. Occasionally, as a reward, I was granted a peck on the cheek. (Yes, Cassandra was definitely virtuous: as far as that goes, she was the perfect subject for a Petrarchan sonnet cycle. She had found the pedestal and stood on it long before I came across her.)

She kept me on as a kind of performing monkey – every lady at court worth her salt had verses composed for her. The trouble was, she could never be entirely sure I was writing solely about her. Once she flung down her lute and stamped her foot in annoyance. 'There is nothing of me in these verses except my name. Look, you have even made my hair blonde!'

'It's you alone, Cassandra, your beauty which inspires me,' I replied.

She pulled a face. 'I deserve better than this.'

This was not the last time a beautiful woman was to say those words to me. And of course she was quite right, I was as often thinking of Homer and Petrarch, of all the women I had known and loved, even for only a night. Beauty in all its forms, that was what I was trying to capture. Cassandra was merely the catalyst for my imagination, the woman who had made Petrarchan love possible for me (for the other, I was still visiting Marguerite).

Yes, it's my belief I loved her for my poetry's sake, though whether that is sufficient to count as love. . . . She embodied all that was young and beautiful and joyful in the world. My hair was already turning grey; her youth intoxicated me. I became like Pan, changing my mistress into a reed to fashion a flute on which to pay homage to her charms.

Yes, and out of my passion for her beauty, lyric poetry was born in France. For in that year the Muses finally sought me out. Bending close to me till I felt their soft breath brushing my cheeks, they summoned me out of the crowd to serve them. I wrote and wrote, sitting up late into the night. And suddenly the heavens unfastened for me, I saw the planets whirling in their dance and Apollo beckoning me up into the clear night. I became intoxicated and wheeled drunkenly amongst the stars. The whole earth behind me seemed suddenly scented with heaven. I had discovered a new kind of faith. Every morning I picked up my pen like an old friend.

But if you think then that I didn't love her, you'll be grasping only half the truth. How can I explain? You see, fact and fantasy became so mingled in my mind that I found myself acting like a Petrarchan lover, sighing and blushing as she went past, stammering when she spoke to me, worshipping to the point of tears her black hair, her gowns, her skin white as alabaster. Love with Cassandra was a courtly game and there are scars. . . . She was Alcina, the beautiful and wicked enchantress who would turn me into a myrtle tree when she tired of me so that I would tell no one of her fickleness. At balls, she moved amongst the dancers like a silver wave, outshining them all. To speak of 'truth' and 'reality' in such circumstances is impossible, for they belong to the language of prose, and in my thoughts imagination had completely taken over.

And then, of course, reality intruded. I was in the habit of riding over to her château at Talcy, which was not far from La Possonnière. I came more as a family friend than as Cassandra's lover. Any thought of being accepted as a serious suitor was out of the question. Even if as a cleric I had not been pledged to celibacy, my deafness and poverty would have made it impossible for me to marry into the wealthy Salviati family. Her father, a shrewd business man, enjoyed relaxing of an evening and listening to my verses being sung by his favourite daughter. 'Nothing wrong with a bit of poetry now and then,' he would say, settling himself comfortably in his chair and undoing the top of his breeches. 'Not all men of my profession would take such a tolerant view, mind. I've known some who consider that poetry leads to unnatural vices, debauchery, effeminacy, that sort of thing. But we Salviatis have never objected to a bit of culture, in moderation of course.' At the same time, he was carefully looking out for a nobleman for Cassandra to marry. Tired of being reminded that he belonged to the money-making middle classes, he was determined to haul himself up into the nobility, even at the expense of his daughter's happiness.

One day I arrived to find a red-eyed Cassandra. She dashed out of the room when she saw me, leaving me alone with her father. The old boy coughed and shifted uncomfortably in his chair. 'Women!' he said, apologetically. 'Wish I'd had all sons – less bother. She's upset just at the moment because I've told her that she is to be married to our neighbour, the Lord of Pray. A mighty fine match it is, too. Can't see what she's worried about. Of course it's the end of her freedom. No more flirting with poets, eh?'

He slapped his ample breeches.

'She likes this man, then?' I asked.

'She'll come round to him eventually. It's a good match.' He mopped his brow. I remained silent. He glanced shiftily at me and then looked away. 'That's the way these things always happen. Her mother and I believe it's for the best. It suited us. As you know, there's more than oneself to think of in a marriage. One doesn't marry for love, but for the family and posterity. That's what I told her.' He shot me another sideways glance. 'She'll come round in the end.' He coughed and blew his nose loudly on a lace handkerchief. 'I hope your visits won't stop just yet. She needs cheering up. Come, let's have a glass of beer.' He filled two tankards. 'Your health.'

The white foam dribbled down his chin.

Like many fathers, he was sacrificing his daughter for the glory of his family. Marriage is women's one great adventure; it has always seemed to me cruel that they have so little say in the matter.

During the months leading up to her marriage I felt curiously protective towards Cassandra, as if towards a sister. We went for picnics in the country and ate strawberries and cream. Once when she got bitten by a snake, I carried her back to La Possonnière and laid her on my bed. Aha! I know what you're thinking. Sorry to disappoint you: my relations with Cassandra were always chaste and never more so than at that time when she was betrothed to someone else. . . . As her father had predicted, she eventually 'came round' to the idea of marriage and resigned herself to her change of status, even in the end looking forward to the position she would occupy at court as the wife of a nobleman.

Seventeen months after I had first set eyes on her at Blois Cassandra was married to the Lord of Pray. I rarely saw her after that, except in the distance, walking in the Tuileries with a friend or dancing by the crystal fountains. But I no longer needed to have her by my side; she had given my creative impulse its shape and theme, my poetry could fly by itself now. It needed no earthly presence to help it along.

Over the next few years I continued working on my poems for Cassandra, suppressing some, rewriting others as my knowledge of Greek increased. I worked in lots of references to pagan mythology. Like colour in a painting, these old fables catch the reader's eye and hold his attention. In them are veiled more mysteries than we mortals can hope to understand. I rounded off the collection with a lament for Cassandra's marriage. I am afraid that, for artistic reasons, her husband came off badly. I should like to set the record straight: he was a decent sort, if a trifle dense. The marriage seemed no worse and no better than many others.

Chapter 6

What's this? A parcel from my old friend at Boncourt, Jean Galland? I open it greedily. He has sent me cuttings from his garden, as I requested, and the latest edition of Desportes's poems, which I certainly did not ask for. I suppose he thinks I should keep up with the latest publications, but I am old, my mind cannot absorb new ways of writing. My own poetry, which I have lived with so long, pleases me best. I am too old for new mistresses. Of course jealousy comes into it as well (I see you nodding your head). It is not without a feeling of trepidation that I pick up the book. His third collected edition in three years – this man is killing himself for glory. Envy pecks at my stomach as I slit open the uncut pages and sniff the ink fresh from the press.

But it's all right. Love poetry, well written of course, dainty, flowing verses (I could learn a thing or two from his technique, though it burns my tongue to say so). But nothing great, nothing startlingly new. I heave a sigh of relief and sit back in my chair. What is it his poems lack? I try to work it out. Boldness . . . intensity, perhaps (they say he runs away at the first sign of emotion – and he's never been known to quarrel). As a result, there's a certain . . . vibrance lacking in his verses. Yes, that's it – he seduces readers by his daintiness but they very quickly end up with indigestion, as if they had been forced to eat too many sweet things. Good: hold out the basin, I've just been reading Desportes. (Of course the court doesn't see it that way, and more's the pity.)

Now, now, try to be a bit more dispassionate. All right, he is not a bad man, but he is weak, and weakness is bad for poetry. He is too concerned about what the public thinks: for instance, he never dares change his style for fear of what they might say. (I'm glad about this, it will stand me in good stead in centuries to come when they measure us beside each other.) You can tell he is more interested in making money than in preserving the integrity of his poetry; he doesn't polish his verses half enough. I think he regards poetry as a way of making a comfortable living for himself. Ah! It wasn't like that in my day. No, in my day when you chose poetry as a profession, you knew you were embarked on a lifetime of poverty – and perhaps, after all, it's better like that, we had nothing to distract us.

Yes, a volume of chaste love poems in the light Italian vein to please the court. They'll be as popular with the ladies as Marot's poems were at the beginning of the century. Hum! How strange that my career should be bounded at either end, like a book, by rivalry with these two poets. Marot and Desportes: so similar in many ways, so bad for serious poetry. The first I defeated and supplanted in popularity, the second I fear will outlive me. The wheel has come full circle. We have passed the best of our age; poetry is falling asleep again.

For a brief moment poetry flashed into existence in our century, beating out its rhythms in the hearts of kings and peasants, the years of my glory. Now the world has fallen back into triviality and become drained and shallow. The court has turned back to its jingles, the Muses wander ragged and homeless and the sweet, sad music of the spheres has faded from our planet.

What's this? A tear fallen on the page? From such an old man? Surely you didn't expect poetry to earn you gratitude? Come come, shake yourself out of this melancholy. It's time to tell of your fight with Marot, or rather his supporters, for by then the poet was dead.

Love poetry was not the only thing occupying me during my 'Cassandra years', as I call them. Around the time of her marriage, I began composing a new kind of ode and Pindar entered the French language for the first time. In modelling myself on Pindar I knew I was taking a risk. His kind of lofty, difficult poetry had never been attempted in France before, and I was still a beginner. When my poems were published, years later, I was criticized for trying something new which very few people could understand. Typical! The masses always cling to the past and think nothing new should be attempted. In adapting Pindar to our language, I had set myself a difficult technical problem, but the general public is interested in themes not technique – they even made up a verb 'to pindarize', meaning to speak very obscurely. The technique was for my fellow craftsmen.

Of course, I blame Dorat – it was he who encouraged me to model myself on Pindar in the first place. It was his fault if I found myself out of my depth. 'What is difficult to understand is beautiful,' he would say. 'Beside Horace's murmuring brook, Pindar is a rushing torrent, an eagle beside his raven.'

He was wrong, you see. Whenever I followed Horace, I kept within the bounds of my abilities and my temperament. Whenever I strayed too far from Horace, I overshot the mark. It was a valuable lesson, had I but realized it, in choosing to imitate only those authors with whom one feels a natural affinity. I was never so much myself when imitating Horace's native sweetness and so little when following Pindar. And staying true to oneself is everything in poetry. Writing from the outside in, I had tried to force my muse to too austere heights. As I say, I blame Dorat.

My studies under Dorat continued, not without a certain sense of dissatisfaction. It gradually dawned on me that we were pursuing different aims. He was concerned with the revival of learning. To this end, no subject was too obscure or pedantic – indeed the obscurer the better (he often seemed to me to equate obscurity with scholarship).

His lack of literary discernment was brought home to me one day when he placed that pedant Lycophoron on the same level as Homer. I have often thought that teachers are not the best judges of literature. The syllabuses in our schools and colleges would be better designed by poets. There are only five or six Latin poets worth studying – Horace certainly, Virgil, Ovid, Catullus, Propertius and, yes, Tibullus. All the rest write history disguised as poetry.

Dorat had rubbed against some of the finest minds in Europe, yet he remained strangely provincial in outlook, ready to admire any writer so long as his books were a thousand years old. He wrote Latin poetry as an exercise (of course he couldn't hope to rival the ancients). I thought it a betrayal to write in a language not one's own. I was right in a way – his poems are a faded bouquet of other men's flowers.

Dorat read books from cover to cover whilst I, wanting to read only those things which could be of use to me in my poetry, would pick up a book at random and flick through the pages, dipping into a chapter here and there, letting my imagination wander freely, not knowing what chance word or image might spark off a poem.

'You have a mercenary attitude to books,' he would say, banging his knife on the table. 'The true scholar delights in knowledge for its own sake.'

'No one can delight in Lycophoron,' I would reply. 'And that text you're currently editing, it's sheer bad poetry.'

'The least amongst the ancients was better than the greatest of the moderns. Even bad writing deserves to survive so that future generations can learn from it.'

'No, it does not.'

We had reached an impasse. I shall not be so arrogant as to say I had outgrown him. That I shall leave for you to decide.

Around this time also I quarrelled with Antoine (I can't deny that our friendship has drawn blood on occasions). He had begun writing poetry himself and often showed it to me. One afternoon, having a headache and feeling sleepy and irritable, I took him to task for weighing his poems down with scholarship. He stared at me.

'But surely a writer should put all that he knows into his poems, plundering the ruins of the ancients and gathering all he can, as Aeneas bore Anchises away on his back from the ruins of Troy. . . .'

I felt it my duty to cut off this flow of erudition in midstream.

'A poem must have other things as well, it must be musical for a start,' I snapped. 'Music prolongs and colours the emotions. Look at Petrarch. All poetry aspires in the end to the perfection of music.'

Antoine had no ear for melody. 'One single error of scholarship makes a poem bad,' he insisted.

'No. Perfection lies in the choice of a word, the richness of a rhyme. A good poem seduces and rapes the reader's judgement so that academic errors go unnoticed.'

He shook his head. We never resolved this basic difference. Antoine was a victim of his learning. He swallowed Dorat's teaching in huge gulps and spewed it out undigested into his poetry. I teased him that the reader would need a dictionary at his elbow to decipher all the learned references in his poems (mind you, people have said the same of my poetry, but there is a difference). Up till this time, you see, Antoine had studied rather than lived – all right for a scholar, but a great disadvantage for a poet. The poet has to write about what he discovers within himself, there are no rules. Antoine's poems are aesthetic exercises, based on theories about poetry. He was never relaxed about his poetry. He was always trying too hard.

I felt lonely in those days, surrounded as I was by scholars and teachers who piled commentaries on commentaries, grafted opinion on to opinion, in order to multiply doubt. You could not have a simple conversation without someone butting in to say 'That argument is illogical' or 'I find that viewpoint rationally indefensible'. Those learned academics who visited Lazare's house had the analysis of literature down to a fine art, yet they never appeared to allow themselves to be affected by what they read. It was as if they lived in one way with their minds, in another with their emotions. They had everything defined and labelled and stored neatly away in jars where they could not be touched. Whereas I had begun to be intoxicated by words, to drink in the pure wine of language. A line from Pindar would send my spirits soaring in an excited wish to imitate; yet there were days when my pen trembled in my hand and I could not write, overwhelmed as I was by my student notes and the vast erudition of Dorat and his friends. My courage was failing me, all this learning was stifling my inspiration. I longed to free my Muse. Most of all, I wished someone would come who thought the same way as myself.

And then, suddenly, Lazare was dead. We laid him out under a white wool coverlet. Spices burned in the brazier. Death did not rob his face of its sweet expression – if it is true that death is the final test of what we are, then Lazare's death was consistent with his life. We put on mourning. Learned men came from all over the city to pay their last respects at the foot of his bed. He is one of the few people I have seen sincerely grieved over by those he left behind. I don't expect the same privilege for myself – perhaps a handful of the monks here will feel something, a few of the young poets I have tried to help. Perhaps not even that.

Am I giving too much away? It's rude to chatter on so about oneself. But maybe an old man may crave a little. . . ? No, no, too obsequious (it annoys the reader). Who am I writing for anyway? The King? No! I have said too much, he would not be pleased. Friends, then? Perhaps; but not my friends so much as friends of my poetry. Yes, that's whom I am writing for – those who feel friendly towards my poems. But then these old man's excrements are neither here nor there. My poetry can speak for itself. Doubt flutters in my stomach. I'm confused. Oh, get on, get on with it. You can't stop now.

Lazare's death left Dorat without a job. He took the post of principal of Coqueret College. Just before we all moved out of the Fossés St Victor to take up residence in the college I had a visit from Jacques Peletier. We stood in the hall, talking amongst the packing-cases and boxes. The translation of Horace he had told me about had just been published, he was becoming quite famous. So my heart leapt when he asked me to compose a prefatory ode for a volume of poems he was bringing out.

'I've persuaded Joachim Du Bellay to contribute something, too.'

I remembered the curious sensation of seeing myself reflected in that thin and interesting figure leaning against the pillar in the cathedral.

'Where is he now?'

'He's struggling at law school, trying to make up for lost time. His education has been shamefully neglected. He showed me some of his writing when we met, but he is familiar only with medieval writers and with Marot. I advised him to compose sonnets and odes. These are the forms we need in France at the moment. I told him he should come to Paris and see what modern writers are up to.'

Again I felt a strange sense of identity with this man whose life had seemed to follow a course so similar to my own. I knew sooner or later fortune, that weaver of men's lives, would cause us to meet.

In September my first poem was published in Peletier's book, alongside a dizain by Joachim Du Bellay. I was ecstatic. At last I had joined the creators. I had become a craftsman, a maker of things. I had rediscovered a role in life. My ode was a light piece detailing all the ideal qualities I wished for in a mistress: youth, firm breasts and plump thighs. A warm-hearted, fun-loving woman who would know how to creep up behind me and hug me without being asked. A lively girl with a roving eye (I like a bit of jealousy, it sharpens the tooth). I carried the published poem around with me for several weeks, eager to read it to anyone who would listen. In November we moved to Coqueret College. A month later, encouraged by Dorat's growing reputation as a teacher, Joachim joined us.

Chapter 7

He turned up on the doorstep in a frayed black cloak, clutching a bundle of clothes and books. His long, thin face was half hidden by an enormous black hat. For the nephew of such a distinguished general he looked decidedly shabby. We shook hands.

Later that evening, after a meal in college, we walked through the streets with the chill December wind slapping at our faces to our local tavern, the Three Fish. Men sat around on upturned barrels, talking and gesturing or just staring morosely into their beer. The beams were low, the atmosphere thick with smoke. André Thevet, the explorer, had returned to our shores bringing supplies of tobacco from Brazil (years later he was to import the pox and lie sweating and dribbling in his bed). The weed was being smoked in every tavern in the city. Joachim, up from the country where tobacco was unknown, began to cough and splutter. We ordered a couple of bottles of wine and brought them to a table.

'Pierre here has been learning Greek with us,' began Dorat, stroking his beard. 'I've finally convinced him of the superiority of the Greeks to the Romans.' He grinned. 'Do you have any Greek?'

'None at all, I'm afraid,' replied Joachim. He had discarded his hat but remained huddled in his cloak despite the stuffy atmosphere.

'We must start you off tomorrow,' said Dorat, tapping his knee. 'In three months you will be reading Homer fluently. I guarantee it.'

Joachim moved his knee.

'Thanks. I hope I shall have time. I want to set aside a few hours every day for writing poetry. I may have to make do with reading Homer in translation.'

To say such a thing in Dorat's presence amounted to heresy. I bit my nails in anticipation of a confrontation.

'You're making a big mistake, you know,' began Dorat with his usual lack of tact (or usual frankness, depending on your point of view). 'Everything that men have said, has been said best in Greek.'

'Yes, the only truly inspired poets were the Greeks,' put in Antoine. 'They felt all our sorrows. They must speak through our writing.'

'But not instead of us,' said Joachim, twisting his long, bony fingers. 'We have to find our own voice, a voice to suit the age in which we live. If French poetry is to be of any value, we must come out from beneath the shadow of these men's minds and stand face to face with them, ás equals.'

'Yes,' I added eagerly, 'and we shall need a new language, our own words for our own thoughts.'

We looked at each other. I felt a shiver of recognition run down my spine. This was it, the moment I had waited for. I was no longer alone. I was going to have to share my glory, if glory there would be, with this man who sat wrapped in a black cloak. Together we would lead a revolution in the arts – no, not so much a revolution as a rediscovery of the ancient music and a search for new forms and a new poetic language through our contact with the great authors of the past.

We walked back to college together, deep in conversation about the future. The air was sharp as a diamond. Suddenly Joachim stopped and looked up at the spermy whiteness of the Milky Way above our heads.

'They say the stars are God's signature, only we mortals are too blind to decipher it.'

The reflection in the mirror had been false. He was quite different. I was in the presence of a deeply religious man.

How can I describe him? (And have I the right to do so, to fix his character for posterity? Well, never mind.) He was the child of elderly parents who died early on in his life, leaving him in the neglectful hands of his elder brother. Like me he was partially deaf, owing to an infection and his brother's failure to summon medical help till too late. His deafness and solitary childhood in the country had given him an acute sense of the insecurity of human life. This emotional perception had been reinforced by his study of philosophy which he had done on his own, begging books off his uncle, the Cardinal, since he was too poor to buy them himself. Whilst I had been loved by several people, my father, Lazare, Marguerite perhaps, he claimed he knew nothing of love. It was a fragile thing, he said, better to recognize that there is nothing permanent in life. He was an exile on earth: I have sometimes come across him standing in silence looking at a stream or a flower and sensed a soul in prayer. Too sentimental? Yes, I'm afraid so. But these are the facts – blame them. There was always around him the sweet sad music of melancholy and exile. I felt that fear of exposing my triviality which every man experiences in the presence of a deeper thinker than himself.

And yet it was he who had the gift for friendship. He was the one people took to instantly (whilst I was thought aloof and cold). I can be open only with people I have known for a long time. Small talk does not come easily to me. I can never think of things to say to someone who is only feigning interest in me and my poetry. I cannot get used to holding myself back, nodding my head politely and uttering a few empty phrases. I would rather remain silent in such circumstances. People always made friends with Joachim first.

We sat up late into the night discussing our plans to revive French poetry. We both possessed a sense of urgency. Whilst Dorat and his scholarly friends were content to speak of the rebirth of our literature as taking place some time in the future, we wanted to see it in our lifetime and we wanted to be part of it, the greater part.

'It matters enormously that great poetry should be written in French,' said Dorat. 'It matters not at all by whom.'

For myself, I could not go so far. History was being made and I wanted to help shape it.

'Poetry is like a will-o'-the-wisp, flashing over meadows and streams, brightening now one country, now another,' said Joachim. 'We must catch her and hold her tight for France.'

We kept awake by drinking coffee, that strange Arabian brew, which made my heart beat uncomfortably.

'There will have to be new ways of writing,' I said. 'We must extend the range of subjects for poetry, stretch our art to its limits. The Italian sonnet must be developed in France. We must master all the metres and forms known to the ancients.'

'Not only will there be new ways of writing, but also a new language. French is still in its infancy, and there has never been a great work of literature written in an inferior language.'

'New words must be grafted on, from Greek, Italian, even from our own French dialects, till our language is as rich and varied as a garden full of flowers.'

Did we really speak like this? No, we were much more . . . groping, much more in the dark. Still, that's the essence of what we were struggling to express in our discussions.

Undeterred by the enormousness of a task that would send me nowadays scurrying for a bottle of wine, we set to work to create the language we needed. Yes, and from these conversations sprang the modern French language, the language used by poets today, yes, even by Desportes. They are all tributaries of that great river which burst forth from Coqueret College.

I feel a sudden chill come over me. The pen drops from my fingers. I sense a presence in the room. The clouds part. Picture Joachim as a white skeleton with a noseless, swollen face and a stomach dripping with worms. I cower behind my desk.

'Still courting kings, Pierre?' His voice is high as a cricket's (how strange, I always thought ghosts spoke in low, booming voices). 'The world's an illusion, I would have thought you'd have realized that by now. Why don't you stay at home and fear God instead of rushing back and forth to court?'

I feel myself slipping from my chair. I clutch the edge of the desk. This is not my gentle, kind Joachim but some monstrous product of my imagination.

'And incidentally, this new edition you're working on, I see you have cut out several passages praising me and taken all the glory for yourself now. Have you forgotten how we worked together at Coqueret, side by side as equals? I see you have even made me your pupil. Very nice. I wouldn't have done it to you, you know, if you had gone first.'

'No, no, you don't understand,' I stammer, half under the desk. 'It's not like the old days. Everything's so much harder now.' I reach out a hand to him, but he vanishes.

'You must have nodded off, sir,' the monk says, putting a hand on my shoulder.

I rub my eyes. No, it was not my Joachim. Some demon must have taken his shape. My Joachim knew all my faults, my little betrayals and treacheries. He would have forgiven.

The routine at Coqueret was severe. We rose at four for prayers. From five to ten o'clock we attended lectures, resting our tablets on our threadbare breeches, stamping our feet to prevent frostbite. We ate dinner, salted meat and watery vegetables, and had lectures again from one till five. Supper was at six and then we were free for the evening. That was when Joachim and I retired to our rooms to write, inspired more often than not by the particular author on whom Dorat had expounded that day. This was the period of our apprenticeship when we tried out many different styles and subjects. We filled basketfuls of discarded poems.

Each evening around ten o'clock one or other of us would give in and suggest a trip down to the Three Fish. There we would order two tankards of beer and sit around reading our poems to each other (and to anyone else who cared to listen). Joachim was readier than I to accept criticism.

'There are two things one should always be honest about,' he said, 'poetry and wine.'

Whilst I revised my poems to Cassandra, Joachim was composing his own collection of Petrarchan love sonnets. They were dedicated to a certain Olive, a lady I must admit never existed. Distrusting love, he preferred to invent a fictional woman who could be relied on not to alter during the process of composition. In this way he fled from the insecurities of life into the surer realms of the ideal.

'There are two sorts of writers,' he said to me during one of those evenings in the Three Fish. 'There are those who write of other people's inner lives because they have no inner life of their own. These kind feel that nothing exists unless they write about it. And then there are those who create a fictional world as a refuge from reality. They compensate for their fear and loneliness by creating a world they can control. I am of this second type. I think you belong to the first.'

He was right of course.

Occasionally, we went on outings. Our favourite haunt was the little village of Arcueil whose legendary founder was Hercules. Just as night was throwing off its black veil, we interns would be woken by the students who lodged outside the college. Abel the porter would unlock the huge iron gates and off we would go, laden down with hams, sausages, artichokes and melons. And bottles of sweet white wine. We would sing as we strolled along, bawdy drinking-songs made up by Dorat. And there in the fields, where the light fell like dry water, we would play tennis, fish and hunt for hares whilst Antoine chased after the brightly coloured butterflies that weaved and dived, drunk on the sunlight. When our city-dulled senses had been sufficiently revived, we would descend on the local tavern to drink tankard after tankard of warm beer and sing to the accompaniment of a lute. Our enemies later accused us of debauchery on account of these excursions. Pure malice. Menander says it's wise to play the fool occasionally.

Sometimes we took a boat down the river and visited the country estate of Jean Brinon, a friend of Dorat's and councillor in the Paris parliament. On these occasions Brinon and his beautiful mistress would throw open his house and gardens to us and we were lavishly entertained, drank wine out of golden cups and recited scraps of poetry to each other. Or we went to the home of Jean Morel in the rue St André, where his charming wife Antoinette and their three lovely daughters played host.

A year after he had taken up his post as principal of Coqueret, Dorat, much to his surprise, found himself married. It happened like this. He had for some time come out of the brothels to frequent the house of a young Parisian of good family, named Marguerite de Laval. This girl was rather taken with our Dorat. She became pregnant, whether by design or accident we could never quite make out. Dorat refused to marry her, claiming he had been tricked. 'I am a scholar,' he thundered. 'You don't hear of Erasmus dragging a wife around with him, do you? It's all a trap set by that wretched woman.' After the birth of his daughter Madeleine, however, the 'wretched woman' took Dorat to court, claiming breach of promise. The judge ordered Dorat to marry her unless he wished to find himself faced with an expensive lawsuit.

Dorat had no money to defend himself. So one morning, very early, he was spotted walking sheepishly out of a nearby church with his new bride on his arm. I will say this for her: she was a good judge of character. Contrary to all expectations, the marriage was a great success. In fact soon Dorat could be heard proclaiming the felicities of the married state. 'Much more in keeping with my station in life,' he would say, patting his belly, which grew rounder by the day on his wife's good cooking. 'No more wasting my energy on acrobatics in the brothel. Marriage gives one a settled routine, frees one from the vagaries and whims of lust, not to mention the clap. Pity you can't marry, my boy.'

He took a proud interest in his daughter Madeleine. He was determined to bring her up speaking Greek and Latin. ('If that Englishman More could do it with his daughters, so can I.')

We discussed the marriage, Joachim, Antoine and I.

'There's the difference, you see, between the scholar and the artist,' said Joachim. 'A writer's task is to guard his independence, to keep watch in the interests of society as a whole. He has to be an individualist, because everything to do with the masses – convention, ignorance, brute force – is unconducive to art. Poetry is a garden, it has to be tended and protected from *them*.'

'So in your opinion the poet must always be alone?'

'I can't see how it can be any other way,' he replied. 'The artist's life is a bondage to pain and loneliness, with intervals of illusory warmth when he imagines, or pretends to himself, that he has come close to another human being.'

'I see it another way,' I said. 'The poet has to retain his capacity for spontaneity, the freedom to fall in love with anyone capable of rousing his soul from the dullness of routine, which spells death for the artist. For a scholar, it doesn't matter so much – in fact routine helps his work.'

'And happiness?' asked Antoine (appropriately enough, since he was the only one of us to find, after a fashion, a sort of happiness in love). 'Where does it come into all of this?'

Joachim looked sad. 'For an artist? None. At least not what you mean by happiness and not what society means either. The artist is driven on by doubt and insecurity. His art feeds off his insecurities. He knows there may not be one other person in the world who understands what he is doing. And still he has to go on creating.'

Listening to Joachim, I often had the dizzy feeling of standing at the edge of a precipice. One push of hostility from the outer world and we would both tumble over the edge. Apart from the period of my illness, my world had always been sunlit, filled with wine and song. Joachim taught me to look into the darkness. He taught me to question authority and social convention in a way that would have horrified my father. But I could not go so far along the path of rebellion as Joachim. There was something in me that would always bend at the last minute. Was I then the lesser artist?

'You don't like me speaking like this, do you?' he said, noticing my expression.

I shrugged. 'You make me feel as though . . . we lived in different worlds. You turn things upside-down . . .'

'But that's the poet's task,' he interrupted. 'He deals in shifting levels of reality.'

'I believe in the sweetness of life' (I was thinking of Marguerite). 'Joy is there to be grasped with both hands. Hell is only an invention by men.'

I did not know then, you see, that pleasure is always mixed with pain.

Chapter 8

One evening, around the time of Dorat's marriage, Antoine came to my room in a state of unusual agitation.

'Have you seen this?'

He slapped a loosely bound pamphlet on my desk. I looked down at the cover. It was entitled *The French Art of Poetry*. I turned over a page.

'No name?'

'None. Rumour has it that it's by some bastard at court. Read it. Fetch Joachim and read it together.'

To our consternation, we discovered that this unknown author had expressed many of our own ideas on the rebirth of French literature, ideas that we had prided ourselves were the very height of modernism. Not only that, but he had muddled in ideas that were positively medieval – according to him, court poetry was the ultimate in sophistication. As if that were not enough, he held up Clément Marot as a model for the aspiring writer, claiming that Marot had already contributed greatly to the revival of poetry in our country. We would have been annoyed in any circumstances that someone had expressed publicly ideas we wanted to be the first to announce. That he had done so so badly was unforgivable. What, Marot! That rhymster! Why, he knew no Greek at all, had never tasted the Attic honey, how could he be the model for our new poetry?

'This must be answered,' said Joachim.

We set to work on *The Defence of the French Language*. This was to be our reply to those who claimed that nothing great in the arts could come out of France. All languages are equal, we said. French can be as great as Greek and Latin and we explained how. Instead of Marot's psalms, we proposed secular and pagan models, Virgil and Homer. Poetry must no longer be a game played by self-seeking courtiers, we argued (thereby condemning all our French predecessors to oblivion). Poetry is a serious art form. If it is to become a moral force in the life of the nation, poets must free themselves from all triviality and profit-making. (I apologize for insisting on details – this was, after all, our literary manifesto.) Poets from now on must be prepared to sweat and suffer in the studious solitude of their rooms. None of this dashing off of poems on the back of a napkin. Only by prolonged intellectual and moral training can the mind catch a glimpse of the divine; only in this way can the poet become the 'winged and sacred being' described by Socrates.

Needless to say, all this amounted to a frontal attack on Marot and his followers at court. We accused them of cheapening the Muses, turning them into whores for the sake of gain. We insisted on that old idea of Horace's told to me all those years ago by Jacques Peletier, that the poet must lop and prune his verses as a gardener cuts away the dead branches of a tree and never publish them without first getting the opinions of friends. If only we could have lived up to the ideals of this polemical and hastily written pamphlet! Perhaps Joachim did – I know I have not always been pure in my contact with the Muses. There were times when I polluted the strings of my lyre for profit.

We all worked together – Antoine, Joachim, Dorat and myself – but it was decided to publish the pamphlet under Joachim's name, since he came from the most distinguished family of all of us. For added protection we dedicated it to his Uncle Jean, the Cardinal. We were already becoming wise to the ways of the publishing world; but even this foresight could not save us.

The *Defence* came out in April. It annoyed many distinguished people at court. The anonymous author who had preceded us into the field, openly attacked it. We replied. The battle between the supporters of Marot, the old guard, and ourselves was started. Our poetry was born shouting. We were called young and arrogant. It was said we would never rival the great Marot. Our pamphlet was attacked as illogical and unreasoned. Naturally our attackers did not see that we had been writing passionately as poets, not as theoreticians of literature. Joachim wrote a bitter counter-attack on those old crows who were preventing the young swans from singing in France.

Oh, Joachim, how I wish you were here with me now, to help me fight off my enemies at court again. It's harder this time, much harder. Now I am the older generation – and trying to prevent the rise of youth is as unnatural as attempting to turn back the waters of the sea. I am tired, so tired. The names of the months sound like threats in my ears. My days are the heavy, dull days of old age. I have become an old, old man for whom the nimble Muses no longer deign to linger. How comforting it is to escape into the past.

Joachim published his poems to Olive. Right from the start he was the precursor, the one who experimented with new forms, whilst I, whether from timidity or a desire to polish my work beyond criticism, would correct, revise and wait. The lines flowed easily from his pen, more easily than my own if truth be told – and he was even more impatient than I of 'futile scholarship', as he termed it. Perhaps he was already aware of how little time would be granted him (his judgement was always incredibly accurate). One thing though: because he published first, it was easy for people to say that he was the first Frenchman to write lyrical poetry. I should like it to be known that I was writing lyrical poems years before him. A small point, but an important one (to me).

I published only two poems that year – praising France and the King. I had decided it was time to earn some money from my poetry. I had plans, you see, to compose a grand epic poem in honour of the Valois dynasty – a poem that would allow me to live in comfort, subsidized by the King's vanity. So, remembering that it is the aim of the lyrical poet to praise to the utmost those he has undertaken to write about, I congratulated Henri, the idiot, the thug, on the treaty he had signed with the English (we had got Boulogne back at last). It was a pity, though, that François had died. This son of his was keener on jousting and fencing than on France's cultural rebirth.

Eventually, I published my four books of odes. The reviewers said: 'Sustained lyrical poetry has entered the French language for the first time.' The Calvinists said: 'This man is a pagan. He peoples the countryside with spirits and invokes the gods of ancient Greece.' The Calvinists are wedded to literalism. They pervert literature to fit in, not with life or truth, but with their own dogma. They fail to notice the universal soul of man trembling in these fables they affect to despise. Over the years, my struggles with them grew more embittered.

Marot's supporters said: 'Marot didn't write like this'; and 'He throws dust in the eyes of his French predecessors and dismisses the court's poetry, but he does not hesitate to pinch lines from the ancients' (not realizing that there are no frontiers in the world of art). Vermin! One of them, Saint-Gelais, attempted to discredit me with the new King. As Joachim said, Henri didn't think or read, but we needed to get him on our side if our careers were not to be abruptly ended by the vicious rumours circulating at court.

'If only he was as eager to fight for his language as he is for his country,' sighed Joachim.

This Saint-Gelais, this mocker of men, read out some of my odes in the King's presence, deliberately emphasizing all the wrong bits and mimicking my flat deaf man's tones. The King laughed heartily, I was told.

'What are all these absurd classical references?' he asked. 'What do they mean?'

'Nothing at all, sire,' replied Saint-Gelais with a smile like a knife. 'They are utter nonsense.'

This satisfied the King, who didn't like to think that there were things beyond his understanding.

'Sing me some of your own compositions then, my dear Saint-Gelais.'

So Saint-Gelais got out his harp and, choosing some of his easier poems, entertained the King and the court.

For a few days after this, my reputation and all our fates hung in the balance. Messengers arrived at Coqueret at all times of the day, bringing conflicting reports.

'The King is angry with the new poets and will not have Marot criticized.'

'The King wishes you to withdraw from court.'

'The King is thinking of having your books seized and burned.'

In the end, the King's sister Marguerite intervened on our behalf. She was a gentle, cultured lady to whom Joachim had given the title of Minerva on account of her quiet intelligence. She shone like a burning planet in the brown night of ignorance at court. She understood and sympathized with our aims. She begged the chancellor to support us. It worked. The King graciously agreed that there might be a possibility of writing in a new way without prejudice to the old. (It was his sister who framed the reply, of course. Henri was incapable of diplomacy.) We had won.

Sensing the tide had turned in our favour, Saint-Gelais dedicated a poem to me and came humbly to ask my pardon. I was touched and forgave him. He was not entirely mediocre as a poet; his poems have a certain melody about them, but he was born too soon, the times were not right for serious poetry. And now he belongs to the past.

No, no, it's too easy to take refuge in others' expectations. The fact is, I wrote quite a good poem of reconciliation for him. No one can be angry for ever, I said, nothing is permanent under the heavens (a nice philosophical touch, I think you will agree). I gave a few classical examples of people whose rage had given way to forgiveness, sketched in the bad effects of anger. I pride myself it was a dignified forgiveness. All the same, I could not resist later dedicating my 'Hymne des astres' to him. You don't follow me? Say it quickly and you'll see what I mean. What? Surely you didn't expect me to be a good man because I am a good poet? I have my vanity like anybody else. There are no heroes in this story.

My role of apprentice was coming to an end. My ideas were beginning to be listened to and approved by a small group of people whose judgement I trusted. I had found a friend in Joachim. The knowledge that we were working towards similar ends was to sustain me even in his absences. I published my poems to Cassandra. They were moderately well received (some people even went so far as to call me the

French Petrarch – yes, you may not believe it, but it's the truth).

Once again, though, I encountered criticisms for being obscure and pedantic. Readers objected to myth and philosophy being introduced into love poetry (again the battle against trivial minds who want to debase poetry into entertainment). The famous professor of Greek at Boncourt College, Marc-Antoine Muret, offered to write a commentary on my Cassandra poems, explaining the classical references. I was flattered and honoured. Which other French poet had been complimented in this way? I was being treated like an ancient. And it was important for me that others worked out the meaning of my poems. I don't always want to know what's going on – if I did, I'd be finished. The act of creation must remain a mystery, most of all for the poet himself.

Despite all this flattering attention, I realized with greater urgency the need to free myself from Dorat's influence if my verses were not to become merely fit for a school textbook. I had served my apprenticeship as a student of literature. It was time to feed the artist in me.

PART THREE

THE PEASANT

Chapter 9

My dear Jean Galland,
    I have received the cuttings (thank you) and the volume of Desportes. That man heaps up adjectives like an Italian, but no doubt it will go down well at court. Gout, arthritis, rheumatism, the diseases of old age follow on each other like a string of curses. I'm afraid I'll go this year with the autumn leaves . . . sweet-natured Jean, you have all your life before you.
    I am pinning my hopes on the success of this fifth edition. You, my dear Jean, my second soul, can help. I am determined this time to wring some money out of those publishing sharks. Look around for me in Paris, if you will, to see whether there are likely to be any offers. A little money for logs to keep me warm in the winter would be very welcome.
    I know, my gentle Jean, that you have sometimes reproached me for boasting too much, as you see it, about my work. But if I am conscious of the value of my poetry, it is because I recognize that my verses come from God, a reward, over-generous, no doubt. And how incomplete the gift because how incomplete the man.
    Which reminds me, you will never guess what I am working on at the moment – an account of. . . .

I pause, my pen hovering above the page. No, I cannot tell anyone yet. These old man's babblings give away too much. The time will come – perhaps. I tear up the letter. Enough for one day. I am going to bed.

Tentatively, I began to develop that part of myself which had been suppressed in the scholarly atmosphere of Dorat's lecture-rooms. I still believed that poetry was a serious art form, but having made my point I was prepared to climb down a few rungs and write in a lighter vein. My poems to Cassandra had been published with musical settings. Friends told me that they were being sung in villages all over France. I discovered that a poet needs a public. It meant more to me that my songs were played in some village square by strolling fiddlers than in the châteaux of kings, with commentaries by scholars. Isn't an artist's sweetest music that which can be understood by the people, by the ploughman in the field, the kitchen-maid hurrying through the streets of Paris? Composing a poem that nobody understands is, as Ovid says, like dancing in the dark.

Art, I have always thought, should be a constant surge forward (to copy oneself is disastrous). Every great artist must know how to change direction, go back on his tracks and start off again, strengthened by new discoveries. He must constantly be on the look-out for new ways of expressing himself. There is more than one way to describe reality, more than a hundred. My task was to uncover as many ways as possible, so far as my talent and my century would allow.

So I sought a simpler kind of poetry, one that would not have to dress up in learning like a peacock to attract attention. I was helped by a find of Henri Estienne's. On a journey through Italy he had come across a lost manuscript of Anacreon. The discovery of this sensuous poetry written in old age by a man still conscious of the sweetness of life encouraged us all to write more openly of our feelings. Joachim published a clever, biting satire which mocked all the clichés of Petrarch's poetry. It took our foolish imitators completely by surprise and marked a change of direction for French poetry. I left my books and began using instead memories of the countryside where I had grown up. The fountain at Bellerie which bursts forth from caves hollowed out of tufa. Women coming through the meadows at harvest time balancing wooden trays on their heads, bringing supper for their men at work in the fields. Rifling through the images and experiences of my childhood I found my life was taking on a sort of unity. I recalled the language of my childhood, the speech of the peasants and the chamber-maids, and I realized that good poetry does not necessarily lie in using rare words, but in finding new ways of using everyday ones. I had been in awe of the old writers for too long; it was time they were knocked off their pedestals. I wanted a language more my own, not borrowed from Latin or Greek, a style not influenced by the latest poet I had read.

I wanted to celebrate the delights of wine and love in poetry which would throb with life, that greatest mystery of all. I wanted to leave Pindar's churning torrents for the cool, clear streams of Marullus and Theocritus. I dreamed of a poetry as vital and various as nature herself, a celebration of the world as I found it.

Professor Muret, who had by now become my friend, gave a series of lectures on Catullus. Muret was more of an artist than Dorat. In his spare time he wrote erotic Latin poems, imitations of Catullus. Reading Catullus or Ovid or Anacreon to us, he bore us away with his voice to sweeter places where the meadows were always in flower, the grapes were always ripe and there was no sickness or war or death. His lectures encouraged the vogue for Catullus amongst us poets. Our critics accused us of licentiousness – they had obviously not heard Catullus' saying that it is not necessary for verses to be chaste, providing the poet is. If I had been drunk or in love as many times as I have described those events in my poetry, I should have had no time to write. Wine can be useful for releasing certain emotions, helping to recall certain painful moments and images that would otherwise have remained buried. But when I sit down at my desk, what I need most of all is a clear head.

Under Catullus' influence, love too was changing. Petrarch was a frigid old cleric, we decided, tormented by fear of damnation on account of his love. The perpetual agonizing struggle between heart and head was not for me. What a fool Petrarch had been to cling for thirty years to his unrequited love! (In French we have a proverb: the lover who waits, grows old in a day.) I looked around me – all nature beat with the sexual instinct, the bull and the cow, the oak and the clinging ivy. Nature cannot lead a soul into damnation, I thought, she is the voice of God. Petrarch was wrong – fidelity to a sterile love is unnatural (and there is no forgiveness for those who betray nature). Sensuality is a basic creative drive, inconstancy in love a guarantee of the poet's inspiration.

I was still visiting Jeanne's brothel on the banks of the Seine, but I had begun to imagine a love that would satisfy completely, that would be more than just a spasm of the flesh. Besides, we had quarrelled.

'You're going grey, dear,' said Marguerite one day as she tried to pull out the offending hairs.

'So what?' I replied, jerking my head away. 'It's natural, isn't it?'

'Madame Jeanne has some ointment we could put on to colour the grey bits. Shall I ask her for it?'

'No! I shan't disguise my age to please you.'

The courage of youth! Latterly, I have been known to use a touch of vegetable dye to confound my enemies at court. But in those days I believed there was something false about these city women who swallowed ashes to give themselves a pale complexion, who pulled out their teeth to alter their voices and burned their skin to give themselves a new face. Marguerite was at home in this world of artifice and pretence. As she had told me herself, she had been born into it, she would never change. Meanwhile I longed for a more natural kind of love, the love of a peasant girl perhaps, someone who would know how to love simply. Everyone at court loves because of wealth, fame, ambition. Does anyone love simply, I wondered, out of an abundance of youth and life and joy?

A dull, familiar ache nudges me out of my memories. I am back at St Côme. Looking out at the garden, a little to the left, I see a single pine tree – Attis, priest of Cybele, castrated himself in ecstasy and was transformed by her into a pine. Whilst all around me, in the stones, the leaves, the branches, is the steady throb of nature's sexuality, I alone sit here, impotent, castrated like Attis, cut off in old age from the world of fecundity and natural abundance, from the world of passion. Peasant women from the village no longer visit my bed, or leave bunches of wild flowers and nosegays of thyme on my doorstep. Sometimes I think it is true the gods gave us sexuality to make us their playthings. Speaking of love without making love is like seeing the sun without loving its light. Mortal women have deserted me. Only in dreams does satisfaction come. Dreams are the consolation of old age, dreams and self-deception.

What! No woman to heat this chilly blood? And yet an old

man has more need of comfort than a young one. 'Hey, slow down, slow down, once is enough' (if I could even manage that). 'I suppose kisses wouldn't do?' No, I thought not. I, who peopled the trees with song, who made the nymphs leap for joy, am become in old age a perfect image of sterility. My fingers have slipped from the lyre. Sexual and poetic powers have waned together.

Stop moping at once. Get back to the facts, continue your mental masturbation (for that's what it seems like). I was having my first taste of power at court. Despite the inconvenience of my deafness, people no longer avoided me. The King's sister had interceded for me; who knew but that one day I might have the ear of the King himself? I was worth getting to know.

Our followers too were gaining ground. Étienne Jodelle, a withdrawn, rather melancholy youth with dishevelled hair and a long beard, who had first been a supporter of Marot and then on the fringes of our group, suddenly surprised us all by composing the first tragedy in the French language. The theme was the downfall of Cleopatra and it was performed at court with the King himself in attendance. Étienne had fulfilled one of our greatest ambitions: to create a French theatre modelled on the Greek. The day after the performance we took him off to Arcueil to celebrate.

We descended on our usual tavern where a long table awaited us, laid with a white cloth and glasses. The fire had been lit and the plump hostess beamed as we trooped in, kissing her on the cheek. We ate venison done in a heavily spiced sauce and washed it down with several glasses of the local wine.

'A toast. A toast to Étienne, the new Sophocles,' cried Professor Muret, banging on the table. He had been instrumental in encouraging Étienne to write tragedy whilst he was studying under him at Boncourt.

'To the new Sophocles.'

We raised our glasses and stamped our feet under the table.

'We must present him with a ram,' said Antoine. 'The Greeks gave Sophocles a ram as a prize for being their greatest tragic writer.'

(This was generous of Antoine, since he had been the one expected to become France's dramatist. His earliest compositions had been plays, translations and adaptations of Greek tragedies. But none of them had been performed, even at college, and now he had been overtaken by Étienne.)

Antoine's idea caught on. Half drunk, we all ran out into the fields.

'There's one,' said Guillaume Cappel, a student of medicine and part-time translator of Machiavelli.

'But is it a ram?' asked someone else.

'Never mind,' I said, 'it will do.'

Staggering around the field, we eventually managed to corner the sheep, and amidst much laughter we pushed the stupid creature through the tavern door. Antoine adorned it with a garland of ivy which kept slipping down over its face, making it look even sillier. By dint of much pulling and shoving we got it over to where Étienne was sitting, cool and detached amongst all our drunken merriment. Whilst Guillaume held it down, Antoine recited a few verses appropriate to the occasion. When we let it go, it scuttled out of the tavern scattering sheep-shit all over the floor, about which our hostess had much to say.

We settled down to some serious drinking till evening drew its dark veil over the sky and it was time to return to the city. We had great plans then for the theatre. Professor Muret had written for the stage and together with his colleague, the Scotsman George Buchanan, he was encouraging his students at Boncourt to write plays. Several of our best tragedies and comedies have come out of that college. (I once tried my hand at drama – a translation of Aristophanes' *Plautus*, which Dorat set Antoine and myself as a project. We never finished it. Neither of us was equipped to write for the stage.) Despite our plans, I do not think that future generations will judge our century as being rich in drama. The present Queen Mother Catherine, the Médicis widow with the bad breath, has banned all tragedy from the court – just another of the annoying superstitions in which she is encouraged by that swarm of astrologers and magicians she keeps at the palace. Our greatest playwright can no longer get his plays performed.

With their eternal literal-mindedness the Calvinists later accused us of celebrating some ancient Hellenic ritual with the ram and declared we were no better than heathens. So what?

Homer himself was fond of wine and a good meal. If to be a pagan were to be like Homer, I should have no objection. Better a good pagan than a bigoted Christian. But leave them; they make my blood boil with their absurdities.

One person was missing from our festivities at Arcueil: Joachim. He was preparing to leave for Rome as secretary to his uncle the Cardinal. He was journeying, he said, like Astolfo to the moon, to find his wits. Whereas I thrived on fame, he shunned it. His deafness had grown worse, making life at court difficult for him. His elder brother, the neglectful guardian, had died leaving the family finances in chaos and a son of eleven who needed a guardian. Joachim was obliged to bring a long and frustrating lawsuit on his nephew's behalf over succession rights. He spent several months at the family home in Anjou trying to sort things out. He returned tired and melancholy.

More than all this, he had even begun to doubt his capacity to create. He had published a volume of odes but the form did not suit his style. Loss of confidence in his poetic powers made him turn to translation as a way of enriching our literature. He published a fine translation of the fourth book of the *Aeneid*, but this did not satisfy him. 'Poetry hardly ever works in translation,' he said, bitterly.

When his uncle offered him the post of secretary, he saw it as a chance to renew his inspiration at the very source. Rome, the centre of the ancient world, city of endless renewals and change, sloughing off its skins like a serpent, but never perfectly, so that the old skin is never entirely shaken off and the different layers remain on top of one another, overlapping. We were all a little envious, imagining gardens of statues, vaulted rooms piled high with rare manuscripts, beautiful Roman women, Venetian glass and solid silver goblets at table. Joachim had plans to study philosophy, mathematics and theology. The morning he set out he stubbed his toe on the doorstep.

'The Romans would say that was a bad omen,' he joked.

In the same month that Joachim left for Rome the great François Rabelais died. He sat astride the chasm between the dark Middle Ages and our own golden age like one of the giants in his books. In that same month, too, an anonymous collection of erotic verse appeared at Paris. Yes, perhaps it was a little cowardly of me, but remember I had my reputation to consider. (In any case, several of my friends guessed the name of the author and I was gently rebuked for allowing such poems to be published.) Permit me to review this anonymous collection: 'It is the revenge of a temperament too long restricted by Petrarch's pinching verse. The author lets his sensual joy in life break out, unrestrained. The language he uses is rustic and earthy, exulting in sexuality (you know the sort of thing – stiff golden rods and red slits, pikes and lances and velvety cunts). He playfully parodies ancient themes, reducing them to ridicule.' How am I doing as a critic? 'The author seems to have undergone some sort of crisis – at any rate, he exaggerates the importance of sexuality.' (The author, receiving the review by courier, reads it, laughs, and tears it up. What does the critic know about poetry? He's probably impotent into the bargain. He has a good laugh with his friends.)

Like Joachim, I needed to renew my inspiration. Staying on at court meant the temptation to write more and more poetry to please the King. Henri had deigned to listen to a judiciously chosen passage from my epic, read to him by Bishop Carle. 'It is to be our national poem,' I said, 'a poem to glorify your dynasty, sire.' I had remembered Bouchet's story that the French were descended from the Trojans. It pleased the King to think his ancestors were warriors. I had included a description of a particularly bloody battle which I knew he would enjoy. I was made 'Poet to the King', only, curiously enough, the post did not appear to carry any money with it. Ah, the court, the court, its tortures are worse than Ixion's on the wheel; once it has started turning, there is no going back. Human bonds dissolve, people put their good actions on display and expect to be repaid with admiration, men communicate in lies and flattery. A touch too cynical? No.

I fell ill with a fever and spent weeks in a room with only a drunken nurse and a plant to keep me company. The fever restored a kind of balance. I began to realize that writers who live entirely at court are doomed, for courtiers turn everything they touch to trivia and an artist needs to live his life at its deepest level. He must continually surprise: I could no longer, as they expected, imitate Petrarch and Pindar. My freedom was shouting out to be claimed. I spent most of the next few years in the country playing the part of a peasant.

Chapter 10

In those days I had a very poetic view of the countryside, coloured by my reading of Theocritus and Ovid: Pan leapt to the sound of my flute, nymphs and dryads capered to my songs and tall oaks bent their heads to listen. All nature seemed touched by the divine. To capture its essence would be to put the divine into poetry, as a magician harnesses the spiritual powers of the universe to work his spells. In my childhood I had looked on nature with soldier's eyes; now I saw her with the eyes of a poet. The streams ran with nectar and wine, vines sobbed and every morning the dawn sprinkled the roses with her tears.

But I am getting carried away again – nowadays, I am glad to say, my views are much earthier. I see the calloused hands of the ploughman, the purple veins on a woman's legs after she has stood all day in the fields. I believe now that a poet's emotions must not come between his writing and the landscape he is depicting, for that would be to come between God and his handiwork, to trivialize God's creation by the intrusion of a human personality. Nature is sacred. I have learned to stand back and simply look, and I see things I never noticed then, filled as my head was with the pastoral poetry of Greece and Rome.

And I see that, like poets, the peasants are makers, makers in wood and stone and bread. Despite the wars and the plagues which cut them down like flies, they go on doggedly coaxing crops out of the hard earth. The land belongs to them, not to the nobles who live at court and return once a year to collect the rent. Their courage has earned them the right to it.

That is why I became involved, a few years back, in a long

and costly lawsuit against that unscrupulous Fortin who built a dye factory here at St Côme and was polluting the river. He had taken our land and claimed he was using it to enrich the neighbourhood (the bastard didn't lower the price of his dyes for us, however). For the sake of profit he was destroying the countryside. My poetry had prepared a place for me in these country people's hearts and they asked me to be their defender. Knowing the number of vile and dirty tricks lawyers practise, I wouldn't have undertaken the case had it not been for their insistence. The laws are always changing nowadays and judges hardly ever agree on a case. What is more, judgements are being reversed all the time. But I am rambling. (You may like to know, however, that the lawsuit ended with Fortin being ordered to pay the inhabitants of St Côme an annual rent for the privilege of having their water polluted. Neither side was satisfied.)

I made a friend, the young poet Rémy Belleau, who shared my love of nature. He came to visit me one day in the country. I shall always remember it. It was pouring with rain. There was a knock and I opened the door to find Rémy huddling in the porch for shelter. There were holes in his shirt and he had only one shoe on – the other had got left behind in the mud. As he dried himself and put on some of my clothes, I got out the smoked ham and the spiced wine. 'I've come to discuss poetry with you,' he said. 'There's no one to talk to in Paris.'

He was a poet of nature, a craftsman in words, creating a fantasy world inhabited by stones and jewels and tiny animals. His subjects were the tiny things of nature: the butterfly, the snail, the oyster and the glow-worm. He traced out his miniatures as delicately as if he were working in ivory. His palette shone with every colour of the rainbow. I loved him for his shy, gentle soul, for his total lack of ambition. Right from the start he took his own path: he was not one of the swarm of slavish imitators that sprang up in France as soon as we published our first books.

The country had a good effect on my poetry. I published a volume of light poems on rustic themes, dedicated to friends rather than princes. I tried to imitate Rémy's delicate brushstrokes in the poems I addressed to him on tiny subjects – the frog, the hornet, an ant. In return, he composed a graceful poem about a butterfly. That's all we poets could give each other as gifts, our poems. I dedicated another volume to my patron, Jean Brinon, who had showered me with presents – a glass, a statue of Bacchus, a snub-nosed hunting-dog with sparkling black eyes and droopy ears. Much good did the dedication do me (excuse me a minute for being mercenary). Brinon died whilst the second edition was being printed and I had to add an epitaph. No money: I judged that badly. As for the first volume, it had been dedicated to that impostor, Pierre Paschal, who promised to write a history in which we would all feature. He never did. I've scrubbed his name off now, of course.

All was not rusticity, you see. I polished up my odes for a new edition, adding several courtly pieces, of which the general point was money. France needed an epic poem, so why shouldn't she pay for it (in advance)? I composed short odes to the King's wife, his mistress and all the royal children (three little princes and three little princesses). I thought I deserved something after all that. But there was no reply. Shelving my epic for the time being, I returned to country matters.

One day in Aphrodite's month I was riding through the countryside with Rémy. We were on our way to go hunting with my friend, Charles de Pisseleu, Abbot of Bourg. The wind-blown blossom left splashes of pink on the brown soil. Over the patchwork of fields in front of us the sun was trying its best to push its way through the clouds. We stopped by a stream to rest our horses and drink the wine we had brought with us. Rémy tethered the horses and strolled beside the water's edge, looking for stones. I lay back on the grass watching him. Presently, he came and sat down beside me. 'Look,' he said. He held out a stone of a deep red colour. It was smooth and polished by the water. He turned it over in his hand, lovingly. 'It's the colour of rubies. They say rubies protect you from bad dreams and melancholy.'

'That's the stone for me,' I laughed. 'But what about love. Is there no charm against that?'

'The diamond.'

'Much too expensive.'

'Then you must remain defenceless against love's arrows,' he said, smiling. 'But come, I know you don't believe in these old charms and I'm hungry.'

I broke off some bread and cut portions of cheese. We passed the flagon of wine between us. A cloud moved and the sun came out to slap us on the cheek. I asked Rémy how his translation of Anacreon was progressing.

Suddenly he nudged me. I looked in the direction he was pointing. Standing on the bank looking down at us were three curly-haired young girls with bundles under their arms. We had surprised them at their favourite bathing-place. Rémy stood up and held out the flagon of wine as an invitation to join us. They looked at each other and giggled a bit. Then the youngest and boldest deposited her bundle on the ground and skipped down the bank to take the flagon. She drank, fixing us with large brown eyes over the top of the rim. Her hair was the colour of ripening corn, her skin like a milk-white rose. As she handed the flagon back to Rémy and turned to go, I put out my hand to detain her.

'What is your name?' I asked and saw a flash of fear in her eyes at the sound of my strange voice. I made a sign that I was a little deaf.

She stared for a moment, then replied, 'Marie. What's yours?'

'Pierre – and this is Rémy. We are two poets on holiday for the day. Why don't you get your sisters to join us?'

For a second she looked doubtful.

'We're perfectly harmless,' laughed Rémy. 'We might even put you in a poem.'

Then she smiled, turned and called up to the other two, Antoinette and Anne, taller likenesses of their sister. They were still standing at the top of the bank, staring down at us with their huge does' eyes. Marie beckoned them to come down and we all sat by the slate-grey stream sharing the wine till there was no more to go round.

In this way my friendship with Marie began. No, more than friendship – love, perhaps. I was grey-haired and thirty, at the mid-point of my life. She was fifteen, an innkeeper's daughter. Her parents owned the Tall Pine in the village of Bourgueil. I asked permission to call on her there. She was open, simple and direct. She was just the model I needed for my rustic love-songs. I made arrangements to stay in Anjou.

At first her mother was cool towards me, suspecting, I think, that I might 'lead Marie on'. But when she saw that what I most wanted was to write about her daughter, she left us alone, judging me odd but harmless. Despite my shabby clothes and irritating deafness, she was flattered by these visits from a nobleman, believing they would raise Marie's status in the village and make it easier for the girl to make a good match (such are the mercenary concerns of mothers).

There are holes in my memory. All that remain are chance images. The mornings writing in my room, the afternoons with Marie in the woods and fields, her skirts fluttering through the corn like a mixture of wind and leaves. The heavens themselves fell in love and bent to look at her. Love wove the threads of our life – as we walked in the vineyards or sat on the river banks, singing, weeping, dancing, smiling. And all around us the steady throb of nature's sexuality which found its echo in our hearts. In the evenings she would serve me my tankard of ale in the Tall Pine, where the beams were smoky and the oak floors uneven. Her body smelt of thyme and jasmine, her legs were frail as a deer's. Marie! Sister! I did not think I would outlive you.

Bringing her presents – a pincushion, a purse, a green belt. Hunting for wild boar with my friend, Charles de Pisseleu, knowing that at the end of the day Marie would be waiting for me. Love is a sickness for which there are no herbs – no, not even Rémy's diamond could have protected me from her charms. It was the countryside that had brought us together. It was there I found all the flowers and fruits of happiness. She inspired in me poetry as clear and simple as drops of rain against a window.

It was Marie who led me into the world of women. Not their outer, social world, but the secret world of their bed-chambers known only to their husbands and sometimes not even to them. She told me her girlish dreams. The kind of husband she hoped for, someone not too stern, someone who would not be for ever spying on her or rob her of the little corner of freedom she had made for herself. Like a sister she gave me privileged glimpses into the secret fears of a young woman's world. It seemed indeed that the odds are stacked against their happiness in our society.

'I shan't have child after child, just to please him,' she said. 'I must keep a part of my life for myself. I would almost prefer he took mistresses.'

She told me of other things – the oils she used to soften her skin, the rose-water her girlish vanity prescribed to ward off the dreaded wrinkles. The veil into the secret world of women was lifted for a moment, as I think it could only have been, by a young girl unschooled (thank God) in the sophisticated ways of the court. I was privileged. Most men are never allowed behind the veil.

Sitting by the stream where we had first met, I would read some of the poems I had written for her, and she would laugh in delight when she recognized the nightingale I had given her, or the scarlet covering she had woven for my bed (I still have it in my room at Croixval – but you know that). 'That old thing! Fancy putting that in a poem! It took me ages to finish.' But in general, poetry was as remote from her experience as soldiering would have been.

I went back to Paris to see the volume of poems I had written at Bourgueil through the press. Rémy added a commentary and new poems on a snail and a cherry. The faithful people of Toulouse sent me a statue of Minerva in solid silver. I presented it to the King to make amends for my long absence from court. For this piece of diplomacy I was rewarded with the curacy of Evaillé au Maine. But no money for my epic and not a kind word from the King.

My new patron, the Cardinal Châtillon, had been working steadily behind the scenes for me (he's not like those courtiers who promise the world and then pass by on the other side of the street when asked to do one a favour). It was he who wangled the curacy. I built a temple of white marble for him in my poetry, which later a Protestant defiled, a Protestant very close to me . . . but I mustn't give away all my secrets at once.

I spent a lot of time tramping the streets of Paris trying to rake up money for my epic. I hung around doorways, stationed myself discreetly in public places, hoping always to catch the eye of some rich noble (it's remarkable how skilled these courtiers are at looking away, down, sideways, as they rush past you pretending they have not a moment to spare). One day I caught sight of my old schoolfriend Charles, now Cardinal of Lorraine, walking in the Louvre. I was afraid to approach him (he had taken to walking with his chin in the air and it was rumoured he expected to be Pope one day). A week later, however, we were unexpectedly placed opposite each other at dinner. He smiled across at me.

'I haven't forgotten we were pupils together, Pierre. Friendship that goes back to school-days is always the best.'

Oh, fool! I was taken in again by his flattering words and asked if I could have an interview with him. My request was graciously received, but I wore the carpet thin outside his room before finally, after many days, the door was opened to me. A splash of red. Yes! At last.

'I'm not looking for public office or a bishopric. All I need is a little money to enable my Francus to set sail.' The words came tumbling out in foolish order. Damn, all my rehearsals down the drain! I swallowed and began again.

'An epic, a national poem for France, will take me eight, ten years to write. During that time I shall be absent from court, so I shan't hear if any posts fall vacant. You know how these things work, sir,' I pleaded. 'Just a little money, to guarantee my independence whilst this epic is written, so that I don't have to interrupt it constantly to look for commissioned work.'

He heard me out, his elbows resting on his desk, the tips of his fingers touching. He coughed impatiently as my words petered out into thin air (well, after all, he's the wizard at rhetoric, not I). Looking me straight in the eye, he said he would see what he could do.

'In the meantime you will write some poems for my family and me, yes?'

It was an order, not a question. I nodded.

And that was that. Finished in five minutes. Wily old Ulysses.

I saw some other old friends in Paris. Dorat, who had just been appointed tutor to the royal children (a great honour but very tedious work for a professor of Greek). Antoine, whose own volume of love poetry had come out (as I had suspected, it was more impressive for its learning than its poetry – the reader needed to be a good swimmer if he were not to drown in the murky depths of his scholarship). He was bitterly disappointed by the public's indifference to his book. We quarrelled again. He accused me of artistic insincerity, of altering the facts to fit my poems.

'You're becoming a Calvinist about poetry,' I retorted. 'Leave history to the historians. Poetry doesn't need to tell the truth. It's concerned with other things.'

We did not speak to each other for a long time. We were too incompatible in our approach to poetry. I felt he lacked the spontaneity of the true artist. He imitated and adapted more than he invented.

'Your poems are a patchwork of quotations from different authors,' I sneered, unforgivably.

Poor Antoine! I have watched him grow more and more bitter over the years. His is the hardest pill of all to swallow – he knows just what makes poetic excellence, but he is unable to achieve it. He has all sorts of projects, and leaves half of them unfinished. The glorious reputation of his father, Lazare, gnaws away like a worm at his stomach when he sees how few rewards his own efforts have brought. He grumbles and thunders against the meanness of kings, the ignorance of the public, and hides from himself the bitterest knowledge of all, that his ambitions have outstripped his talents.

And yet he has done some important experiments in the field of versification, juggling with rhymes and metres. He has been daring in exploring the relationship between music and language, and in his spelling reforms. Poetry needs its technicians.

But throughout my time in Paris, discussing poetry, wandering through the halls of the rich, Marie's face haunted me like an unfinished poem. I left the mules, the merchants and the stink of Paris and returned to the country.

Chapter 11

Before going to Bourgueil, I first had to call in at La Possonnière. Claude had died, leaving his pale-faced widow Anne with five children and ruinous debts. I had been appointed guardian of his two sons, a dubious honour, since it meant dipping into my own pocket for their education. I had a pleasant surprise, however, when I reached La Possonnière. Now that her spendthrift husband was no longer in charge, Anne had unexpectedly blossomed into an efficient manager. The estate was starting to run as smoothly as in my mother's time (and certainly a great deal more quietly). Anne welcomed me and gave me a good meal of roast deer and home-made cherry brandy. I was touched when she said, shyly, 'You are welcome to come and live here any time, Pierre.' All the more so, as my last meeting with Claude had not been a success.

He had come as usual to borrow money, and as usual I had lent him some. Then he took the opportunity to attack my poetry.

'Why do you stuff your verses with Latin and Greek? Nobody wants to read that old rubbish. They want to be entertained. No wonder Marot's still popular. Your poems are too much like hard work to read.'

I threw him out and that was the last I saw of him. I have few regrets it ended like that.

It was a different Marie I found at Bourgueil. She was growing up, losing some of her simplicity. She never tired of hearing me repeat what a great success her poems were in Paris, how the noble ladies read them aloud to each other after supper.

'I wish I could go to court and see all the lords and ladies. It would be lovely.'

'No, it wouldn't,' I said, 'they would spoil your naturalness. Do you really want to have to pluck your eyebrows every day and lace yourself in tightly? And wear a horrid little black cap instead of letting your hair fall naturally around your shoulders?'

'Oh, you! You never understand!' She turned away in disgust.

To please her I sometimes wrote poems to her as if she were a noblewoman living at court.

I have loved two Maries. This one let me less often into her private world. She was young and lively, suddenly aware of her power to attract. Village youths hung around the tavern waiting to catch a glimpse of her. She wanted to make the most of her freedom before marriage claimed her. When I went hunting with the dashing Charles de Pisseleu, whose sister had been François I's mistress, she begged me to take her with me. I brought him back to the tavern one day. Her two sisters sat wide-eyed, their hands folded in their laps. Marie sprang forward to make an elaborate curtsy at his feet.

'You have made a conquest,' I said sadly to Charles. He was much amused.

The day she heard he had been hurt in a fall there were tears in her eyes.

I put a hand on her shoulder. 'Noblemen are fickle, Marie. As soon as they've made one conquest, they're on to another.'

She frowned and pushed me away. Oh, Marie, my pale violet, did I corrupt your sweet innocence by my verses?

My old-fashioned clothes and my deafness were beginning to irritate her. One day she pulled at my ragged beard. 'Why don't you shave this old thing off? No one wears beards any more. It makes you look ancient.'

'It hides my weak chin. I would look a thousand times worse without it, I can tell you.'

She pouted and tossed her silky hair. 'I deserve better,' she muttered.

I couldn't deny it. Our love born amidst the flowers and fruits of nature was becoming sterile. She wanted me to fit in, be ordinary – 'normal' she called it. Her head had been filled by her social-climbing mother with notions of what should and should not be done by fashionable people. Her mother had taught her to be calculating. Peasant simplicity had turned into peasant cunning.

Still I lingered on, composing a second volume of poems for her, hoping vainly to re-establish our friendship. But the veil had been drawn down for ever. However hard I tried to play the peasant role, I would never succeed well enough for Marie. She made me see that I didn't fit into her world. Our love had wilted like a flower dashed by the spring rain.

For when I look back, this was as much a period of role playing as any other. At the same time as I was extolling the pleasures of country life and love, I was writing hymns. Into these I put all the subjects missing from my light-hearted poems for Marie: religion, mythology, philosophy and history. I described the movements of the planets, the origins of the seasons, the influence of the stars. I tried to cram the whole world into those hymns (some of them are a little long-winded – I've cut out a lot of lines in this latest edition).

Like a magician, I wanted to uncover the secret workings of nature and lay bare the intricate relations between the different parts of God's creation. A poet, however, has no need of magic charms; everything comes from himself and the language. He performs miracles with words, seeking to capture the voices of the gods.

'These hymns are to close the mouths of those who say I can only write about humble country things,' I told Rémy. They were also a way of gaining patrons: I still needed sponsors for my Francus if he were ever to set sail at all. 'I shall dedicate the whole lot to the Cardinal Châtillon and make a present of each individual hymn to a prominent person at court. That should do the trick.'

'Humph! Don't expect anyone at court to listen to you,' replied Rémy. 'They are all too busy renovating their castles and palaces. And the abbeys and benefices that should go to us poets, go instead to the architects.'

(He had a point there: I myself had often compared architects to greedy harpies, devouring the nation's wealth.) But I refused to be put off.

'I shall even dedicate one of my hymns to the King himself,' I said.

Rémy pulled a face. 'That's a sticky one.'

'Not at all,' I replied, blithely. 'I shall praise his horsemanship. The King is silent and thoughtful? Give him the benefit of the doubt. Perhaps he's thinking about his kingdom, which town needs fortifying, where the frontiers need strengthening, how to surprise the Spanish. The King is white-haired? It's a sign of hard work and immense wisdom.' I held up my right hand with fingers crossed.

Rémy looked sadly at me. 'What's happened to the poet of the countryside?' he asked.

I uncrossed my fingers. 'I feel restless,' I replied, a little guiltily. 'I want a change.'

Yes, it seems one can lose one's self as easily in the country as at court. I would never be a true peasant, because I would never be able completely to throw off those long years of study under Dorat, when I learned that poetry is not just a pleasant distraction but a way of heightening men's awareness of the world. Books would always be my best friends, silent friends that never hurt. I have found more real joy sitting at my desk than running to greet a friend, however old. For when I write, I feel solid and true to myself. And there is no substitute for that peace.

And so in old age as I try to be honest with myself (and perhaps it is only in childhood and old age that we can be honest; in between we are occupied with different things, often incompatible with truth), I realize that I was covering myself with layer upon layer of pretence – scholar, courtier, peasant – till I could no longer see where my true self lay. I have borrowed many different lives and lived perfectly in none of them. Perhaps that is the fate of the poet, to be for ever shivering behind a mask.

Friends wrote daily from Paris urging me not to bury myself in the country for ever. I was needed in the capital, they said, why was I delaying so long? Eventually the second volume of poems to Marie was completed and my hymns were ready for publication. I wrenched myself away from Bourgueil and set off for the city. Marie was sad to see me go, but I knew that, while her fame flew up to heaven on the wings of my verses, I would be replaced in her affections by some livelier and younger man. I should have learned the lesson long ago. Poets can never expect to profit personally from their poetry.

Paris was cold, vast and unfeeling after life in the country. The city was racked by catarrh and fevers. The skies were heavy with rain. The stinging wind rushed to meet me round every corner and winter's lazy moon made the nights unbearably long.

My second book of hymns was published, dedicated to the King's sister, Marguerite. People congratulated me, few of them sincerely. Their conversation fell like a knife on my nerves. Dorat had been made Professor of Greek at the Royal College founded by François I. He talked in editions and footnotes. I felt we had little in common any more. The only person who might have provided some link between my time in the country and Paris, Rémy Belleau, had gone off to Italy, fighting in the King's army. He had left behind for me a tiny, uncut diamond. 'A charm against love and demons,' the note said. It had come too late.

I spent a lonely winter readjusting to the cut and thrust of life in the capital where no one says what he means and each one looks out for himself. By the spring, I had come to terms with this life again. But I had left the deeper, the best part of myself behind in the country. And that vital simplicity of a country girl, which had touched me more deeply than anything yet, was gone for ever out of my life.

I saw her from time to time over the next few years. If I was in the area, I would call in at the Tall Pine and exchange polite trivia as Marie sat sewing or spinning by the fire. Sometimes we walked out by the river. The last time I saw her was at a wedding. Antoine and I (we had by then patched up our quarrel) had been staying at La Possonnière. The wedding was to take place on the island at St Côme – my brother Charles was still in charge of the priory then. Antoine and I set out to cover the thirty miles between La Possonnière and St Côme on foot. We called in on the way at my cousin's house. He gave us such a good meal and we sat drinking so long that it was quite late by the time we started out again, and we had to spend the night under some willow trees. We woke up to find the dew covering our faces.

After the wedding there was a dance, to which people from the neighbouring villages had been invited. Amongst the dancers I spied Marie. She had green ribbons in her hair and was dancing gaily with several young men in turn. I own I felt a pang of jealousy. She started and blushed when she saw me out of the corner of her eye. She turned back and said something to her partner, then suddenly darted over to the table where Antoine and I were drinking beer.

'Hullo,' she said, half shyly, twisting a strand of blonde hair around her finger. 'How are you?'

'Well. And you? You seem to be enjoying yourself at any rate.' I gestured towards the group of young men she had been dancing with.

She blushed. 'Oh, them. They're not important. They're only cowherds. I'm . . .'

'Marie!' Her mother came up behind her and said something in a low voice, or at any rate a voice too low for me to catch more than 'Martin', and 'spoil things'. Nodding distantly to me, she took Marie's arm and led her firmly away. Six months later I heard that Marie had married a rich farmer of the district.

Marie! When I heard that you were dead I wanted to fill your eyes with rose petals, sprinkle perfume and honey on your body, place lilies at your head. Nothing less would be worthy of you, girl of butterflies and roses.

PART FOUR

DEFENDER OF THE FAITH

Chapter 12

This part will need some explaining. How did a writer of love poetry become involved in politics? And why did a lover of pagan myths and a more or less indifferent church-goer become defender of the Catholic faith? Oddly enough, I think I can best explain it by talking a little about my friends.

They were returning to the capital. Rémy took up his studies again. Jacques Peletier moved up from Lyons; not to write poetry but to study mathematics and medicine. Genius never falls in the expected places. At forty Peletier had come to terms with the thudding recognition that he lacked a real talent for poetry. The first to sound the notes of a new kind of poetry, he had quickly been eclipsed by the younger poets he had tried to encourage. These others possessed the gift he had thought all along belonged to himself.

'It's unfair,' I said. 'If you hadn't introduced us to the ode and the sonnet, you would have been alone in your field now, way ahead of anyone else.'

He shook his head sadly. 'There are no rules in poetry. Art is as incalculable and unfair as nature herself.'

And he was right. The poet describes what he finds within himself. There are no laws determining where poetry will flourish best, though I have often been asked to give some and have occasionally done so. Poetry is a bitter gift – it refuses to flower according to men's notions of justice. Some of the silliest and most selfish people have been great artists; some of the wisest have seen their gift peter out.

Finding himself on the wrong track, Peletier resumed his medical studies and got his doctor's degree.

'You've become a taster of men's urine,' I teased.

I still have in my room here a bouquet of herbs he sent me to ward off Saturnian melancholy.

From medicine Peletier turned to mathematics, discovering that numbers, like poetry, hold a key to the divine.

'Proportion – this is the link between man and the world he lives in,' he told me eagerly. 'Like the poet, the practitioner of Pythagoras' art uncovers the hidden laws of the universe.'

Peletier is turning into one of the great polymaths of our time. His whole life has been a flight into the light of knowledge. Completely self-taught, he has made himself equally at home in mathematics, law, medicine and astronomy. He has attempted to bring some logic into our muddled spelling.

'All knowledge is ultimately linked,' he explained to me, 'and Saturn holds sway over all – poets, prophets, seers and mathematicians.'

Why have I chosen to describe at length one man's failure and change of direction? What has this to do with the story? you ask. Well, it's because, yes, because I think Peletier's brave, disinterested exploration of all branches of learning (and other men like him) had something to do with the stance I later took up in defending the faith. You'll see what I mean. Don't rush me, these motives are hard to untangle and my friends are as involved as I am.

If Peletier came to Paris feeling the loss of his poetry, Joachim returned from Rome having rediscovered his powers – and greater than ever. It happened like this. Whilst we in France had been resenting his good fortune, Joachim had arrived by the yellow waters of the Tiber to find a noisy, dirty city filled with crumbling ruins, of people as well as buildings. Instead of the serenity and majesty we had imagined at Rome, the air was filled with the clamour of traders, the whispers of financiers and, yes, a kind of spiritual anxiety. A blanket of foreboding hung over the city. It was feared that Rome would be sacked again, unemployment was rising, shops and businesses closed down and the streets were crowded with soldiers. Priests practised exorcism daily on young girls thought to be possessed by demons. Everyone was nervous about their jobs. There had been two papal elections in quick succession, each involving huge shifts in the balance of power. If the present Pope so much as spat into a fountain, the pompous troop of cardinals crowding at his heels would turn pale and sidle up discreetly to examine the colour of his spittle. A pope who coughed blood was not a good horse to back.

Rome, the glorious cradle of the classical world, had proved to be a stinking sewer. Joachim turned the merciless light of his poetry on to the darkest corners where corruption lurked. Nothing escaped his disillusioned eye – the bribery during papal elections, the idle courtiers curling their hair, plucking their eyebrows and dowsing themselves in perfumes to cover the smell of rotting flesh, the courtesans who freely walked the streets dressed in brightly coloured gowns that successfully hid the crabs crawling at their groins. He painted Rome in all its colours – the blood on a toreador's cloak, the red of the cardinal's robes, the sickly pallor of the courtesans, their faces caked with powder.

In verses pure and strong he alternately laughed and wept over the disasters of Rome. He saw at first hand, and realized before any of us, that the Catholic Church was heading for disaster. 'Rome is a rat race,' he said. 'Anyone can become Pope in three days and the clergy spend huge sums of their parishioners' money for self-advancement.' Nepotism was rife. He told us about the handsome young Ganymede who looked after the Pope's monkey and, it was rumoured, performed other services as well. This Ganymede had recently got a cardinal's hat. 'Why didn't the Pope make the monkey a cardinal as well?' asked some wit. It was impossible to get an audience, for the churchmen were too busy playing like children with canons and trumpets and banners. 'The Vatican needs a good clean-out,' wrote Joachim. 'It has accumulated as much shit as the Augean stables, where thirty thousand oxen lived for thirty years.' Naturally, such outspokenness got him into trouble with the censor and with the Cardinal, his uncle. He wrote in his verses what he did not dare say out loud, jotting down his observations to make a kind of journal of his life in Rome. In this way, poetry acted as therapy for him, a much-needed distraction from his irksome duties.

'Tell us about your life there,' we said, not believing that it could have been as bad as he made out.

'If you think that traipsing with my uncle from embassy to embassy trying to catch up with the latest political gossip, signing petitions, drafting reports and warding off creditors is interesting, then you're welcome to it,' he replied. 'Personally I think there are more important things in life than running from banker to banker arranging new loans for my uncle, knowing that he'll never have the money to repay them. And then there's all the entertaining to be done. . . .'

And so Joachim had learned to navigate his way through the perilous Roman sea of intrigue, bankruptcy and fraud. He learned how to flatter and serve, how to obtain money by dubious dealing, and how to break promises. He learned never to speak without weighing his words carefully. And all the while he knew that time was running out for him and that every minute spent with bankers was a minute lost to his poetry. How many marvellous poems may have failed to be written because he was placating his uncle's angry creditors!

He used his poetry as an escape, as a galley-slave chants songs under his breath to lull away the cramps and the agony of toiling for hours at the oars. And out of his sadness came laughter, a sardonic kind of laughter that saw through the street theatre of Rome and vented its venom in verse.

What! Impatient again? Why am I lingering so long over another man's poems? A debt, my friend, a debt long overdue. You see, whilst Joachim was in Rome, he wrote me many poems of encouragement and friendship, poems comparing me with Virgil and Homer, poems urging me to complete my epic. When I was melancholy, he cheered me up with a comic hymn on the blessings of being deaf. And I? Not one word in reply. Why? Oh, fear, I suppose, that I would be eclipsed at court when Joachim returned with his new collections. Yes, that's it, fear and jealousy. I was eaten up with it – till he came back and published his poems and I saw, with tears in my eyes, that he had deliberately chosen another path so that there would be no comparisons between us. He stated it very clearly right at the beginning: he was not writing my type of poetry.

Others had written to him in Rome. I suppose he thought me indifferent, too preoccupied with my own affairs (he would have forgiven that too). I don't think he ever guessed how much I had feared him.

So, yes, dear friend, I have a great debt to pay off. Let me start by talking some more about your poetry.

Joachim composed four different collections whilst he was in Rome: the satirical sonnets I have spoken of, some rustic poems simple and spontaneous, with a smell of the earth about them, and sensual Latin love lyrics for the Italian courtesan, Faustine. Yes, despite our commitment to the French language, Joachim made a wager on immortality by writing occasionally in Latin (whilst I continue to stake my life's work on the hope that French will survive as a language and speak to as many future generations as Latin has to past ones). This wager – was it a betrayal? For reasons I have already gone into, it is not I who has the right to judge; I have betrayed too much myself to condemn others.

Above all, Joachim found his great theme, the fragility of earthly things. Before he set out for Rome, he had told us: 'Everything that nature, art and destiny are capable of, went to make ancient Rome great. There was nothing, no compass or ruler, that could measure the greatness of that city. From its seven proud hills it spread its dominion over the whole of the ancient world. It is that spirit of ancient Rome I'm going looking for.' He returned declaring he had found nothing of Rome in Rome. 'The ruins have been eaten away by time, the temples plundered by hordes of modern barbarians.' Rome's aspirations had offended the gods; its downfall resounded like a thunderclap across the ancient world. Only the shadow of its glory lives on in dusty manuscripts, in the pale spirits of its poets and in its sickly, diseased descendant, the Roman Catholic Church.

Picking his way through the rubble of the proudest city ever built by man, Joachim was filled with melancholy. In his insecurity, he fled the horrors of modern Rome to rebuild the ancient city stone by stone in his poems. He woke the Caesars with the music of his lyre and hauled those old Romans from their dusty tombs. He tried to make time stay still in his poetry, to give his fragile, fleeting life the stuff of immortality. His verses poured out in a waterfall of crystal; he distilled the stiff sonnet form into the heady wine of poetry. He had found his voice.

Aha! I saw you trying to stifle a yawn. Why am I dwelling so long on poetry? Why isn't there any action? Because, because – don't you see? – he was a prophet. It was all to happen again, in

France, and very soon. Poisonous pus was coming to a head in the cities and towns of our country and all our hopes for France's glory were about to turn to dust. Yes! The ancient saying is true that only a dying man can predict the future accurately. Panurge was right to visit the poet Raminagrobis on his death-bed to learn what the future held. Joachim read the signs before any of us. Only, he spoke in parables and no one understood until it was too late.

His parable went like this: once upon a time all the world was Rome and Rome was all the world. Only Rome could conquer Rome. Things seemed safe enough. But then cracks began to appear in the empire. Romans plunged their swords into the stomachs of their fellow countrymen. It was civil war, not surprising perhaps in a city built on a fratricide. People began to realize that destiny had been against Rome from the start, old sins lurked at its origins.

There were lessons here for France, if only we could have seen them, but Joachim's words fell on deaf ears and it was not till long afterwards that people remembered (and borrowed from his poems to describe the situation in France).

Chapter 13

Joachim appeared at the French court like some Old Testament prophet, condemning the corruption he saw all around him, the lack of respect for learning, the fawning of the nobles.

'If the King said he had seen the moon at midday, they would nod their heads in agreement,' he grumbled.

Poetry was his consolation; like the lotus flower it made him oblivious to pain, to his longing for that other world from which he felt himself an exile. I, meanwhile (yes, it's time to speak of myself again), was learning to employ the Muses for my own ends. I was becoming adept at plotting my moves.

The year 1557 was a miserable one both for France (our disastrous defeat by the English and Spanish at St Quentin) and for me (I had no patron). Henri waged war ceaselessly on foreign powers; in Italy, against the Pope, against the Spanish Emperor. And then, at the beginning of the New Year, Henri's big dream: Calais was captured from the English. It marked the turning-point in my own fortunes as well as my country's. My poetry went public. I followed the King's army to Amiens, where the Spanish were waiting to do battle with us. Whilst cannons vomited smoke and trumpets sounded (even I can hear those), I sat down in my tent to urge the French to join battle. But war never came; instead, peace negotiations got under way. That didn't worry me; I wrote a poem in support of peace.

'You're becoming a pawn in the King's game,' warned Joachim. I ignored him.

It was my friend the Cardinal of Lorraine with the silver-edged tongue who led the negotiations on the French side. I praised him, of course, but, like Simonides, all I got was a box full of empty promises. (My father was right: the benefits of poetry are as invisible as dust in the wind.)

Henri, eager to seize on the triumph at Calais to draw a veil over the St Quentin disaster, ordered celebrations to honour the Duc de Guise, who had led the French to victory. Étienne Jodelle was put in charge. Ever since the success of his tragedy, *Cleopatra*, Étienne had been riding on the crest of a wave at court, becoming increasingly arrogant and self-satisfied. He saw poetry as a means of earning a reputation for himself.

'Poetry has nothing to do with popular acclaim,' Joachim warned him. 'It must be loved for itself.'

Étienne did not listen to him any more than I had. He strutted around the court dressed in a crimson cloak and expensive velvet doublets. He was the best dressed of any of us (it was a mystery where he got the money – we teased him about having a rich mistress hidden away). Étienne's masquerade celebrating the taking of Calais was to be the culmination of his ambitions. He wrote new verses for it and ordered special music to be composed. The theme was Jason and the Argonauts and their voyage to find the Golden Fleece. Étienne was to act the part of Jason.

It poured with rain the day of the performance, but nevertheless the whole court turned out as ordered. The room in which the masquerade was to take place had been hung with tapestries. There was a banquet beforehand but the caterers ran out of food (I remember not getting a bite to eat all night). After the 'meal', the chairs were turned round to face the makeshift stage.

In the front row sat the large athletic figure of Henri. On one side, his sallow-faced Médicis wife, Catherine, run to fat through bearing his ten children. On the other, the King's mistress Diane de Poitiers, as tall and beautiful at fifty as in the days when she had been François I's mistress. Chaste Diane, huntress and protector of kings, descendant of warriors and crusadors. (Heartless bitch! she was another one who never responded to my pleas for patronage. I shall suppress all my poems to her. Yes, a nice little revenge. There! Gone, in a puff of smoke.) It was Diane who ruled the court. Her face, which she kept unlined by washing daily in cold water and using no make-up, was hard as stone. There was no greater contrast with the homely and superstitious Médicis woman, the shopkeeper's daughter who, it was rumoured, had had recourse to magic to provide heirs for the French throne.

With the royal party sat the victorious Duc de Guise, and beside him, in cardinal's red, Charles of Lorraine, his brother. They were now in the ascendant at court; one had conquered the English with his sword, the other with his tongue. Their niece, Mary Stuart, charming and cultured daughter of the 'Red Fox', James V, was to be married to the French heir, François. She went scattering brightness like the dawn over the French court (and now she is shut up in a dark hole by that English witch, her cousin Elizabeth). The Guises were skilful opportunists. With Diane they ruled France in the King's stead. Only in our poems could the King play the leading part.

Étienne's masquerade . . . the actors were under-rehearsed and forgot their lines. Étienne came on stage as Jason and stood before the King, opening and shutting his mouth like a fish, struck dumb by stage fright. The scene changes took place at the wrong times. One of the stage-hands had misread 'clocks' for 'rocks' and in a scene where Neptune was supposed to rise from the rocky sea-bed an enormous grandfather clock appeared on stage. The court tittered nervously, then anxiously craned their necks to check the King's (or, more precisely, Diane's) reactions. She was watching the stage in amazement. Then her pale lips parted and she threw back her head in laughter. A second later the King joined in. Relieved, the court laughed with them.

After the 'performance' we went backstage, but Étienne had fled to his patron's residence in the country. Some months later he published a long, self-pitying prose work in his defence. It was entirely unnecessary, since by then the fickle court had found other things to gossip about.

I might have learned from Étienne's experience, but no, I have never troubled to alter my character by reason or discipline. If one part failed, I rushed on to another. My former opponent, Saint-Gelais, died, and I succeeded him in the post of almoner to the King. I received a salary and, in return, I had to attend court three months out of every year. I had become a churchman. When I was on duty I would go early to the palace and wait for the King to rise and dress. I handed him the velvet cushion on which he knelt for prayers. I took his orders for mass and transmitted them to a chapel clerk waiting in the antechamber. At mass it was my job to give Henri his prayer-book and hold his gloves. When we left the chapel, it was I who distributed the King's alms amongst the waiting beggars. (I know what you are thinking. You think, that's why I became a defender of the faith, to keep my job. No, it wasn't quite like that, though you are not alone in making this assumption. I was shortly to make quite a number of spiteful enemies.)

Joachim accused me of selling my soul. 'Your poetry will suffer,' he said, 'for poetry is the natural sound a soul makes and therefore that soul must be kept pure by prayer and fasting.'

But I continued to slip, eel-like, in and out of the intrigues at court. I never said no to life then. Everything was pleasurable – a conversation, a good dinner, the sight of a pretty woman walking amongst the jasmine in the Tuileries. I enjoyed my growing importance. If there was a wedding to be celebrated, or a death to be mourned, it was my verses that were requested. I had never felt so confident, so sure of my power as a writer. Oh yes, Aquinas was right, pleasure clouds the mind. For I had become at last what I had always despised, a court poet, as elegant and polished – and simple – as Marot (you didn't think I would admit it, did you? Well, only between these four walls).

I made many trips to the Louvre to see the Cardinal Châtillon, my patron. I learned to watch men's faces to see if they were sickening and if there might soon be a vacant post. The King had still given me nothing for my epic – it was architects and fools who got the abbeys. Italian refugees under the Queen's protection flourished overnight like mushrooms. Whilst I, a poet, was forced to write begging letters.

The Cardinal of Lorraine invited me to his newly renovated château at Meudon to compose poems for the celebrations of his cousin's marriage to one of the King's daughters. It was there I made fauns and dryads and satyrs dance in my verse and published the first bucolic poem in the French language. Well, Antoine Baif will tell you that he was the first to write that kind of thing – and I did give him the credit for a while, but now I have decided I might as well have the glory myself; after all, he was not the first into print and that is what matters (fortunately for me). I should not really be telling you this; there are some things best kept to oneself. It is old ground. No need to go over it again. Old ground. No one will know.

So I went, gathering scraps of pleasure where I could, as a bee collects pollen. Joachim, meanwhile, was increasingly convinced there was no peace for him in this life. The family quarrels over his nephew's succession rights continued – his brother-in-law had taken advantage of his absence in Rome to seize the family property. Joachim had to spend more and more time with lawyers. He was involved, too, in his uncle's financial affairs, negotiating with international bankers to arrange payment of the Cardinal's debts. Knowing that he was so highly placed, people continually solicited him for ecclesiastical posts. This in turn made the clergy at Paris jealous of Joachim's influence in Church matters. Amidst this chaos of worldly affairs, with fever gnawing at his bones, Joachim set his face resolutely towards that other world from which he felt himself excluded. Once, listening to a reading of Horace, he sprang up from his seat shouting, 'Poetry is all I live for.' Another time, he said, 'Only poetry has the power to suspend doubt and shape the fragments of life into a meaningful pattern.'

But he was like a bird caught in lime; his struggles to be free served only to entangle him further.

And I was no help to him. No, I was too busy with my own affairs to take notice of his problems. It is only now, as I sit staring into the face of death myself, that I begin to glimpse what he was trying to do in his great poems on the downfall of Rome. It was his own death he was practising, turning it over in his hands, tasting it, taming it.

Yes, that is what he was doing, getting used to the idea of his death. But whilst he wrote poetry to learn how to live and how to die, I wrote it to be famous. Cicero says the whole of our life should be a meditation on death, but in those days I didn't understand. I always put life first. Death was merely the end, not the goal, of life. And now that end seems perilously close, Lord have mercy upon me. Why am I so afraid to die? I have already passed through so many deaths – death of the child, the boy, the adolescent soldier. Yesterday dies in today and today will die in tomorrow. Nothing stays the same. And I long sometimes, as he must have longed, for time to stand still, to opt out of the relentless flow and surge of life, to shelter for a while in God's calm embrace.

Come come, cheer up. You can't expect any readers if you pile on the gloom like this. Let's talk of youth instead, for it was about this time that I acquired a young disciple named Jacques Grévin. I can see you think this has nothing to do with my role as defender of the faith, which I'm supposed to be describing, but there is a connection, an intimate one. Just sit back and relax. I have to tell this story in my own way.

Grévin had studied literature at the Boncourt under my old friend Professor Muret and had then transferred to study medicine at the University of Paris. He called one day with a manuscript of some love poems he had written.

I groaned as I opened the door and spied the bundle under his arm. 'No, no, I can't,' I said, waving my hands at him. 'I'm far too busy to read your poems, if that's what you've come for.'

I made to shut the door. He stuck his foot in the gap.

'They're very good. You'll like them.'

My eyes widened. I looked this blond-haired youth up and down. He was dressed, a trifle melodramatically, in black doublet and hose.

'Professor Muret sent me. I'm a great admirer of yours. There are lots of echoes of your work in these poems. Just let me leave them with you and see what you think.'

No one is more self-confident than a bad poet, I thought. I opened the door just wide enough to allow him to pass the sheaf of papers to me. 'Come back in three days' time,' I said, sternly. 'I might not have found time to read them, mind.'

He grinned. 'I'm sure you will have.' And he turned on his heel. The young man certainly had a gift for self-promotion. I looked down at the bundle in my hand and noticed that the top poem had already been published. It was a hymn celebrating the marriage of Mary Stuart with the Dauphin of France. I raised an eyebrow. Quite ambitious to attempt to imitate my hymns; they are difficult poetry, not for beginners. I read the poem through, standing in the hallway. It wasn't bad at all. I noted that he had put me at the head of his list of favourite authors. I smiled wryly to myself. This young man would go far.

Three days later there was a knock at the door. I had been waiting for it, but I feigned surprise. 'Oh, it's you,' I said, opening the door. 'Well, well, come in.'

I was pleased to note that after all there was a trace of anxiety in his eyes. I led him through to my study.

'Sit down.' I indicated a chair. 'I have read your poems.'

'And?' He sat forward on the edge of the chair, his hands closed tightly around the arms. It would do this young man no harm to go through a few anxious moments.

'Well, it's always difficult,' I began and was suddenly overtaken by a fit of coughing. He remained fixed to the chair. Out of the corner of my eye I saw that his knuckles had gone white. Time to put him out of his misery. I broke into a smile. 'In my opinion, these are some of the best love lyrics I have seen by a poet of your age.'

He relaxed back into his chair with a sigh. 'Do you really think so?'

'But surely you already know that.' I couldn't resist teasing him a little. 'You told me yourself they were good.'

He looked slightly abashed and spread out his hands, suddenly tongue-tied.

'I know, I know, you had to get past the front door. Well, listen, I'll write a prefatory poem for this volume – it will make it easier for you to find a publisher.' I waved away his thanks. 'I might get some of my friends to write a few lines as well. Have you met Joachim Du Bellay and Rémy Belleau?' He shook his head. 'I'll introduce you to them some time. I'm not doing this for you, but for poetry,' I said sharply as he rushed over and kissed my hand. 'We all need help at the beginning.' (All the same, I was touched.) 'Now take your poems and be off with you.'

We began to include the young poet in our discussions. This blond-haired Apollo seemed able to turn his hand to anything – poetry, medicine, the occult. Under Muret's encouragement he had begun to write a play about Julius Caesar. We had high hopes of him. He would be the leading poet of the next generation. We thought his many gifts seemed to fit him to write philosophical poetry.

'The philosophical poet must unite all things in himself,' I told him. 'He must know how to be priest, prophet, lover, doctor, lawyer and herbalist. He must tame the winds, charm the thunder, know all the properties of herbs and stones.'

'Such poets are like the alchemists,' said Joachim. 'They need spiritual perception to penetrate the invisible, to see beneath the surface of things to essences. Remember, poetry was the first language of the gods.'

'It's said the old alchemists were able to bring plants and animals to life again,' put in Grévin.

'And that's what you must do in your poetry,' I added.

'There's one difference, though,' said Joachim. 'The alchemist seeks a state of absolute perfection, and there is no absolute perfection in art.'

He sighed and I recognized beneath these words the old agonizing struggle between his poetry and his faith. At times like this his soul was tormented by the paganism of his art, seeing in it only a self-indulgent distraction from praising God.

Whilst we discussed poetry, events were marching on. France had made peace with Spain at last. All the court gathered in Paris for the double marriage celebrations for the King's sister and daughter. The marriages were political, intended to cement France's newly formed alliance with Spain. We poets were called upon to compose verses in commemoration. Our beloved Marguerite, who had defended us in the beginning from our enemies, was going to live in Savoy with her new husband. May it always be springtime in your country, my princess, and may meadows burst into flower beneath your steps. No, no, what am I talking about? She is dead, like all the rest. Buried in foreign soil.

Henri insisted on showing off his prowess in jousting to the Spanish. In the midday heat, just as Nostradamus had predicted, the tip of his opponent's lance pierced the King's left eye. He was brought to bed and the doctors were summoned. Confused and contradictory remedies were prescribed. The court was flung into panic. As the King prepared himself for death, Diane tried desperately to hold on to the remnants of her power. People looked the other way when they saw her coming. The political manoeuvring had begun. Whilst her husband was alive, Catherine promised faithfully that his mistress would keep her place at court. On 10th July Henri died. The next day Diane found herself on the way to exile at her château in Anet. The woman Catherine had tolerated throughout the long years of marriage suddenly found herself without friends or power.

The frail, blue-eyed Dauphin François was crowned at Rheims and France had a Scottish queen. With his niece on the throne, my schoolfriend Charles looked set for a period of unlimited power. And all the time, waiting in the wings, was the King's mother Catherine – but no one took account of her, she was only good for producing heirs. We had reckoned without the Médicis blood which flowed in this stout widow's veins.

1st January, 1560. A new decade. The old year had shed its skin, the new had scarcely begun when Joachim finally left us, in the most peaceful manner possible, in the middle of the night whilst working on a poem. In death as in life he remained a poet. All poets would die that way if they could. Joachim's death far overshadowed for me the death of the King. With him my youth finally passed away. By the time of his death the struggle to establish a reputation was over. My words were listened to at court. I was already beginning to form a new role for myself. But such things cannot be expressed in public. I chose to remain silent.

May the earth lie light on your body, dear friend. Your song can never die. As long as there is poetry in this world, the music of your flute shall be heard.

Chapter 14

My life was surging on like a great river, like my native Loire. The first collected edition of my poems was out. My songs were scattering like seed all over France. There had been a certain pleasure in ordering and revising the work of the last ten years. It set me first in rank amongst my friends. With its variety of forms and themes, the collection fulfilled most of the programme we had outlined all those years ago in *The Defence of the French Language*. Odes, songs, epitaphs, sonnets, elegies and eclogues; it ranged from simple rustic themes to grand philosophical poetry. And always, always, the doomed search for perfection.

The publication of a collected edition gave people the idea my creativity was at an end. 'He has run out of subjects,' they said. I knew it wasn't true. Nevertheless, at thirty-seven, it was time to stop singing of nature, love and wine. I had become a grand old man of letters. It was time to act the part. I looked round for a subject that would match my age and reputation. In this I was helped by external events.

There was one, however, who had preceded me into the public arena. Jacques Grévin had passed his medical exams and was a fully qualified doctor. His volume of love poems had been published, preparing the ground for a successful career at court. And then suddenly he had to flee to England. He had done what many of us wanted to do, but none of us dared: he had published a poem criticizing the Cardinal of Lorraine (my schoolfriend, Charles) for his influence over the young King François and calling him a warmonger and debauchee. The publisher of this poem was caught and hanged. Grévin escaped only just in time.

He did not have to stay in exile for long. The sickly François died at the end of the year, finishing Charles's power and leaving Mary Stuart a young widow. In her long white robes of mourning she glided around the court like a widowed dove. Some months later she left France for good to rule over her cold, grey kingdom. The court without her was dull as a picture without colours, a sky without stars. (She is in prison now, poor Queen, in England. That Tudor bitch!)

France had a new king, François's brother Charles. He was nine years old. If ever the law of hereditary succession has led to absurdities, it was then. He was rumoured to be fond of poetry, however. I sniffed unforeseen possibilities hovering in the air.

Jacques Grévin returned from England in time to see his tragedy on Caesar performed. He was working on a second volume of poetry and at the same tudor had resumed his medical studies, hoping to get a postgraduate degree. He lent me a book on antimony, a drug that contains mercury. He was angry at its over-prescription by the medical profession and had begun a campaign to have it banned (I never knew such a man for taking up causes). 'Read it,' he said, tapping the leather cover. 'See what poisons they stuff into people's bodies.'

I calmed him down and put the book away on a shelf, promising to read it when I had time. In fact I never did, for reasons which I shall now outline and which are entirely to do with history.

Until Charles reached his majority, his mother Catherine was Regent of France. The Médicis woman had come into her own at last after all those years of waiting. But the country she had inherited was a troubled one. For several years France had been beset by a growing number of adherents to the ideas of Luther and Calvin. Bearded men with furrowed brows and wildly staring eyes (in imitation of John Calvin) filled the streets. Grim and pale-faced, they never let a swear-word pass their lips. Many died at the stake, but this only increased their number of supporters. Calvinism crept up on France till one morning she woke to find that half her inhabitants belonged to a faith other than the official one. Nostradamus predicted disaster for the country.

The Calvinists caused an upheaval in our country comparable to an earthquake. They made cracks appear in people's beliefs throughout the Western world; they forced every single one of us to re-examine the basis of our faith, and reason became swept up in a whirlpool of opinion. A company of men had risen out of the earth's belly, like the army that sprang from the dragon's teeth Jason sowed at Thebes, to make war on each other in France. They rampaged through the countryside in their long coats, spreading their doctrines by steel and gunpowder. They brought foreigners, German mercenaries, into our country. Shops stood empty, fields lay unploughed. Death stalked our land like a great black beast.

Henri II had sworn to make the streets of France run red with Protestant blood. My beloved patron, Cardinal Châtillon, turned Protestant and fled to England, but wicked men may preach the truth and a good man may follow a false doctrine. The Queen Mother, however, was inclined to tolerance. She was moved less by concern for religion (can the religious impulse ever touch the politic mind of a Médicis?) than by the awareness that the monarchy was in a dangerously weak position. Until her son grew older and had heirs, she must watch over his authority. The Calvinists were too numerous to suppress by force, she reasoned. They must be won over and learn to trust the monarch as a friend. She even invited Protestants to preach at court.

Here the Queen Mother and I parted company. True, there were many aspects of our Church that displeased me: the bribery, the jockeying for posts, the ignorance of the clergy who acted as if they were mere administrators. Good Catholics had been pointing these things out for years. The Calvinists behave as if they were the first to demand reform, but Joachim said it in his Roman poems: the Church of God had been sold out by the priests. Yet I believed – believe still – that Calvinism would be the ruin of all we had worked for.

Do not misunderstand me. I know that there is something clean and bare and pure about a religion cleansed of its superstitions, its relics, its bargains. I recognized that a long time ago in Germany, listening to John Calvin. The call for services to be performed in French, the language of the people, fits in well with our programme for literature in French. Yes, there are faults on both sides. But it is not a comfortable religion for an artist. Calvin fills his city with spies and forbids any kind of art except that which fits in with his dogma. For instance, all drama is banned from Geneva. Such narrow and cramping views do a great deal of damage to the arts. What great work of literature has come out of Geneva since John Calvin took up his reign there? No, dogma and art do not mix.

Not only that, they limit God's power to work freely through the artist. My friends and I had made people respect the poet's profession. The revival of Plato through the translations and commentaries of the Italian scholar, Marsilio Ficino, has given music, poetry and scholarship a status they have never before enjoyed in France. Even if its praise often goes to the wrong writers, to Desportes rather than . . . others, the court now recognizes that the poet has a right to his independence. That he is a craftsman with an aura of priesthood about him, not a performing monkey to be fed and encouraged to do tricks. I was afraid that if France turned Calvinist (and that is still a possibility), all we had worked and planned for would be destroyed and the poet robbed for ever of his freedom and his claim to be God's mouthpiece. Already our poetry was under attack in Geneva, for being 'frivolously pagan', and yet Joachim was the most religious man I have known.

At that time in France the Protestants had all the best writers on their side; their cause was bad but they defended it well. 'The Reformation began with books and must be combated with books,' I said. Whilst the court under Catherine teetered on the brink of Calvinism, I took up my pen to save France for the Catholics. I appealed to my fellow countrymen to shake off their apathy and defend their freedom against tyranny from Geneva. In a flourish of rhetoric I urged the young King Charles to uphold the Catholic faith of his ancestors. I manacled my poetry to history. My verses would mirror, or even determine, our nation's fate. It was my most glorious role yet.

Glorious, yes indeed, but sincere? There seems such a mixture of motives, such a tangle of half-truths. Perhaps I am exaggerating my part in things? I gather up my memories, turning them over in my hand. They are as fragile as pollen; if I blow on them they will fly away and be lost for ever. Nothing is real, nothing is certain. This much I know: I had a genuine concern for my country's unity and a need to find a new style of writing in order to consolidate my position as chief poet at the French court. I saw a way in which the two could combine to allow my poetry to break through the personal into a universal moral vision (this can happen, I think, only when an artist has so mastered his art that he is able to transmit a moral message through his chosen medium without descending into the didactic). It is not enough for poetry to be beautiful, I argued, it must go beyond the purely aesthetic to be a moral force, a force for good in the world. The first poets were priests and prophets, law-makers and founders of cities; poetry arranged treaties, pronounced oracles and announced wars. . . . Every poet at one time or another sees himself as a prophet with a mission. My mission was to explain and comment on events, as they happened, to the ordinary man in the street. And behind all this, a thin, wavering flame of faith.

Up to this point, the doctrines of the Catholic Church had played no great part in my life. I had been content to leave those to the theologians. I had quickly grown out of the simple soldier faith of my father, and my acquaintance with the absurd rituals at Navarre College had provided no substitute. Religion took on a social aspect and became somehow linked in my mind with the King of France and political stability. I performed my scanty duties as a cleric conscientiously but without enthusiasm. Whilst I was at court I paid priests to carry out my duties in the curacies in my charge, as is the custom. I attended mass regularly, but it was no more to me than washing and dressing, part of the routine to be got through before the day could begin. I was angry with God on account of my deafness.

'You can't be angry for ever,' Joachim warned me. 'One day He will force you to forgive Him.'

There were times when He did seem near – in the countryside, for instance. Christ, too, was a poet of nature. Our physicians try to harness natural forces in order to heal disease.

'Healing is a process of co-operation with nature,' Jacques Grévin told me, 'and therefore a doctor must learn all about the workings of nature. He has to study the physical sciences, astronomy and alchemy. He has to know what influence the stars have on disease.'

My friend, Jacques Gohory, a lawyer and doctor, had been performing alchemical experiments at his home in Paris, finding them useful for his medical studies. I became interested in the strange quest of the alchemists to uncover the power of God in matter, which some say is also a spiritual journey. They pore over numbers and signs, using the same symbols as we poets in their endless search for the secret elixir.

The science of numbers also contains divine mysteries.

'Our century is in search of a pure mathematics,' Peletier explained (you see, I promised he would turn up again), 'which, like poetry, will trace the path to the heavenly spheres, where harmony reigns.'

'Music too,' interrupted Antoine. 'By listening to music the soul is awakened from its earthly torpor and aligns itself with the cosmic harmonies.'

Yes, if I had any genuine religious spark in my soul, it was nourished by these men, Peletier, Grévin, Gohory, the polymaths of our age who groped after the divine hand at work in the universe. Music, magic, mathematics – all these different paths to penetrate the mystery of the divine. And the Calvinists offered only one in return: the doctrine of their master set out in that noxious little book, *The Institutes of the Christian Religion*.

I have been called the great Catholic champion of France. 'His poems have done more to keep France Catholic than all the tracts and sermons of bishops,' they say. But I am no theologian. It was poetry I was defending (of course, fear came into it too – I dislike change in a state). The Calvinists sing psalms in the kitchen and debate theology in the fields. The Bible is left open amongst the recipe books and gets covered in flour. Their God is vulgar and familiar. Our God is awesome and full of mystery. And there are many ways to Him.

The Calvinists believe that, because they have translated the Bible into French, they have solved the mysteries of the Christian religion. Their religion is a religion of the schoolroom with everything made clear. There is no poetry in it, and without poetry, religion no longer holds sway over people's hearts.

The Calvinists deny that God paved a way for Christ's coming in the hearts of pagans and would therefore do away with all the works of pagan writers. Do they not see the divine in Homer? In Virgil? When the pagan magician Hermes Trismegistus met Moses in Egypt, he was granted a revelation that has passed down to us through the books of Ovid, Virgil and Plato. A secret, esoteric knowledge, known only to a few initiates, like the cabbala of the Jews. That madman, Guillaume Postel, studies these mysteries in his asylum at St Martin-des-Champs. (I saw him once in the Louvre with a white beard down to his waist. They let him out from time to time to speak with the King.) Postel wants to find a law that will unite all the different religions which are cracking our world (perhaps he is not so mad after all).

The Calvinists have torn down these ancient mysteries that men have revered in their hearts for centuries and declared God's Church to be in the wrong. They have created a new religion, one which has neither unity nor holiness nor the apostolic tradition. Their doctrine is like a beggar's coat, held together by scraps from here and there (there is no possibility that the Jews and Turks will convert now, when even Christians reject their heritage and change their minds over dogma). Their religion began in Saxony and divided itself into sects – Zwinglian, Lutheran, Anabaptist, Calvinist, Puritan – in order to spread war across Europe. Christ brought miracles, but Luther brings the sword. I have seen Bèze go to preach in Paris with a sword hidden under his long coat and accompanied to the pulpit by a gang of armed soldiers. They have brought foreigners into France, violated women and children. If this new religion they have invented has not made them live better, what use is it?

Meanwhile Calvin has stayed safely in Geneva, directing youths to their death, and his followers have desecrated God's altar by their questioning of the divine mysteries. Even Plato and Socrates were forbidden to speak on matters entrusted to the Delphic priests; but these people prattle on, mingling the divine and the everyday till all respect for the divine is lost and atheism begins to creep into men's hearts. They think heaven is open only for them – oh yes, they will tell you so in all seriousness (just the same, there must be some little corner in heaven for Catholics).

See how impossible it is, even for a poet, to escape the pressure of events. I had hoped to write the biography of a private person and here I am, shackled to history. Poetry, for me at any rate, has never been free of the march of events and never more so than at this time when I was deliberately going public. Hum, I know better now. Shhh, I have an idea. Let us step outside history for a moment and speak of private life. Now now, no objections. I am in control – and I need an interlude. Private life is best (and interesting things were going on, I assure you, oh yes). I shall return to the public later.

You see, I had fallen in love again. Love makes everything worthwhile; I cannot do without love any more than I can do without the sun for long periods. Rémy's diamond had been no protection against Genèvre; Genèvre, whose voice was as sweet as a nightingale's. It was about six in the evening. I had been working all afternoon at the stone table in my garden in Paris. Money from the publication of my collected edition had enabled me to buy a house on Ste Geneviève hill in the university quarter. The garden had a mulberry tree under which I used to write on hot days. Even so, that evening I felt hot and sticky and in need of a swim. I put down my pen and strolled out into the narrow streets, which smelled of spices and dung in the heat.

I made my way down to the river, stripped off, leaving my clothes in a pile by the path, and plunged into the Seine. After the heat of the sun, the cold water took my breath away and I had to swim vigorously for a few minutes. I floated on my stomach, watching the water ripple around my arms. Water has always fascinated me with its pattern of continuity and transience, like life.

As I turned over on to my back I caught sight of a lawyer acquaintance of mine strolling along the river path. I used to bump into him now and again in the Louvre, and I raised my hand to acknowledge his wave, when my eye was caught by the woman beside him. She had half turned to see whom her husband was waving to. Her hair tumbled down in two yellow tresses on to her full breasts. I swam to the bank and clambered out, naked as I was. Raising my head, I found myself looking into a pair of twinkling brown eyes.

'May I introduce my wife,' said the lawyer. 'Genèvre, meet Pierre Ronsard.'

She held out her smooth, cool hand.

'I have read your poems, of course,' she said, smiling.

We stayed chatting for a few minutes. 'You're shivering,' she said suddenly. 'Come, Blaise, we must not keep Monsieur Ronsard from his swim any longer.'

I bowed and plunged back into the water.

I returned home, but I was too excited to work and prowled restlessly around the garden for an hour. I decided I needed some company. I saddled my horse and rode over to St Germain-en-Laye, where the court was residing. I had a meal, spoke distractedly to a few friends, and retired to bed late. It was impossible for me to sleep. At dawn I pulled on my boots and went for an early morning walk round the grounds of the château. I stood on the terrace and watched the sun rise in a golden mist over Paris. Somewhere down there was a pair of wonderful, fiery eyes. I foresaw all sorts of complications – her husband, for a start (I had no wish to act out a medieval farce). But those eyes. . . .

I arrived back in the city at sunset and went straight round to Rémy's house to bully him into giving me Blaise's address. He guessed what I wanted it for and shook his head. 'Be careful. The old lawyer has a temper.' I shrugged. Love is a game of chance. I can never resist throwing the dice.

As it turned out, Blaise also lived in the Latin quarter. It was the easiest thing in the world to stroll casually by his house later that evening and find Genèvre sitting in the doorway, sewing. We smiled.

'How strange to come across you again so soon,' I remarked, 'but then perhaps it's stranger that we haven't met before, since we live in the same quarter.' (It is sometimes useful to have spent one's life constructing fictions.)

She was bright, lively, much too spirited for her crabbed old scholar husband. She began calling on me on her way home from market or from church and we would sit together under the mulberry tree. At first she was reticent, rather sad. Then one day she told me why.

'I had a lover, a marvellous, sweet man. He died six months ago. His illness was long. He got thinner and thinner and coughed blood all the time. It was awful,' she shivered.

There was a silence. She twisted one of her blonde plaits round and round in her fingers.

'There's something on your mind, Genèvre. Tell me what it is.'

'You are a poet, you are used to dealing in love and death. Can you explain to me why he kept insisting I take another lover after he was gone? He said it over and over again. I could not understand it. The only condition he laid down was that the lover should be someone worthy to follow him.'

'He must have been a very brave and honest man,' I said softly. 'Most people like to imagine they are irreplaceable and will go on being mourned for ever.'

'I know, I could not understand it – that he would not want me to remember him always and remain faithful.'

I took her hand. 'He was very wise, I think. You see, he knew that endless fidelity to a dead love is unnatural. We have to go along with the flow of life, however cruel it seems. We have no power to keep the past alive.'

'What do you mean?'

I thought for a moment.

'Love is amoral, like nature. It is we humans who try to twist it into something moral. The Church fathers, for instance, invented the rule that love outside marriage is a sin, but nothing in nature can be sinful. The Greeks revered the love instinct as a manifestation of the divine, to make love was for them an act of piety. Think of their cult of Priapus. Those pagans knew more about love than we, who have betrayed nature by adding on conventional notions of morality which have no place in love – in marriage perhaps, but not in love.'

I told her about the great Latin poet Tibullus, who loved two women, Nemesis and Delia, at the same time. 'For Tibullus, love was an overwhelming force against which reason, society, convention stood powerless.'

'I wish you could have met my lover. I think you two would have understood each other.'

She turned to look at me. I touched her face. Her skin was as smooth as a pearl. I kissed her and caressed her blue-veined breasts. Our coming together was like the twining of an ivy about an elm.

Whilst the troubles raged in France, Genèvre visited my house many times that year. She was one of the most intelligent women I have met, one of the few who knew how to read a poem. She would pronounce the lines slowly, rolling them over her tongue, savouring their salt and honey taste. She was as warm and loving as a woman can be. And grief had made her wise. More so than that dusty old scholar of a husband to whom I was still nodding in the Louvre.

'Loving you', she laughed, 'is a beautiful game of tennis. Only the present exists. You are a poet without ties or responsibilities.'

She, though, was not free. What? You dare to ask me to unpeel my memories? You do not know what you are asking. Off comes the bandage, slowly, slowly. As I thought, still the red scar. Well, it makes company for the others. Always in a hurry, to prepare a meal, to meet her husband in the Tuileries. She would enter the house in a rush – we had half an hour when she was supposedly buying material for a dress. Undoing my shirt and kissing me at the same time, she would push me towards the bedroom. Afterwards she would rearrange her hair, give me a final hug, and dash off.

One day the inevitable happened. One of my many enemies at court saw Genèvre leaving my house. He informed her husband who, being the man he was, his head filled with history books and romances, challenged me to a duel. Of course I had to accept. Genèvre was distraught (she had been forbidden to leave the house) and I felt ridiculous. He would have been a wiser man if he had let the whole thing drop instead of making such a fuss – his undoubted virtue would have stifled the gossips. Besides, who hasn't been cuckolded: Caesar, Pompey, Cato kept quiet and were not the less respected for it. But no, we were to meet on Tuesday at the quai de Tournelle. I had to busy myself finding a second. In my opinion, duels are a cowardly and selfish way of fighting. They are killing off the best of our nobility. I wouldn't include myself in this group, but still, in principle, I'm opposed to the practice.

At the eleventh hour, mutual friends intervened and soothed the injured husband's feelings. He made Genèvre promise never to see me again. She did call, the next day, at some danger to herself (though by then her husband was back in the library). We agreed it would be better not to see each other. She was strong and brave – I hope that mad husband of hers values her sweetness. It was a long time before I could forget my companion under the mulberry tree. Her softness, like the morning dew, had penetrated my very skin. Passion did not have time to dull into indifference, which is perhaps why her memory remains, sharper than the rest. Genèvre – juniper tree, whose leaves are prickly and make you bleed.

Chapter 15

Back to public life, then. I have got a bit behind on events, but that's the way it is: we are all egotists of some form or other. Anyway, one can have enough of history. A little bit of love livens up the tale, like colour in a picture.

In September I attended the colloquy of Poissy, arranged by Catherine to get Catholics and Protestants to debate their differences in the King's presence. The conference took place in a Dominican convent, three miles west of St Germain. On 9th September we all trooped into the refectory. I stood at the back amongst the spectators. The young King Charles, standing on a wooden box so that he could be seen over the heads of the bishops, opened the proceedings with a call for peace and reconciliation amongst his subjects.

'By the time you leave this room, it is our wish that all differences between you will have been resolved.'

'Some hope,' muttered Antoine, raising his eyes to the ceiling.

Théodore de Bèze stood up to speak, dressed in a long black coat under which, I suspect, there lurked a sword. Bèze is Calvin's second-in-command in Geneva. He fled to Geneva after publishing a volume of erotic poetry. Quite good verse (I have sometimes borrowed a line or two from him). Of course Calvin shook all that kind of thing out of him and he is considerably embarrassed now by this book – we remind him of it from time to time when his attacks on our 'pagan' poetry become too tiresome.

Bèze began diplomatically enough, but somewhere along the line he put forward the unfortunate suggestion that 'Christ's body is as far removed from the bread and wine of

Communion as heaven is from earth'. There was uproar in the room. Conservative Catholics immediately pounced on this direct denial of the doctrine of transubstantiation. Perched on his throne piled high with cushions, King Charles scowled down at his quarrelsome subjects. Order was restored. The Cardinal of Lorraine got up to reply. Like Bèze, he took a conciliatory tone at the beginning. He was prepared, he said, to consider the marriage of priests, allowing the laity the cup and introducing a simpler liturgy into the churches. However, as is the way with these things, the forces of moderation were soon shouted down by the extremists. The ten-year-old King yawned and fell asleep on his throne. I nudged Antoine and we slipped out of the overheated room.

As we wandered out into the gardens, Antoine grabbed me by the arm. 'Come, I want to introduce you to a nun.'

Despite my protests that I had just left the room to get away from clergy, he led me on to a gravel path. We came up behind a woman dressed in the robes of a Dominican. He tapped her on the shoulder.

'Anne de Marquets, mystic and poet. Meet Pierre Ronsard.'

Antoine gave a low bow and hurried off. I found myself looking at a pale-faced young nun with huge brown eyes.

'A poet', I said, 'and a mystic? Why aren't you inside listening to the theologians?'

She smiled slightly. 'There are levels of religious truth where the dogmas of theologians can never penetrate.'

'True,' I replied, jerking my thumb towards the refectory. 'It seems as if they have turned their backs in there on love and charity in order to disagree over doctrine.'

We started walking along the path. Her movements were graceful, calm and unhurried.

'All religions contain some part of the truth,' she began. 'At the highest level, the differences between Protestant and Catholic are reconcilable. They are merely different halves of the same truth, don't you agree?'

She turned to look at me. Her voice was low and rich and had such an extraordinary power that for a moment I was almost persuaded. Then I shook my head. 'On this point, I agree with Bèze. Tolerance simply allows each man to go to hell his own way. We must stick to the religion of our ancestors.'

She waved her hands impatiently. 'Submission to Church authority – whichever Church, yes, of course – but after that, higher than that, is . . . love.'

There was a silence.

'I have never felt that kind of love,' I said.

'Because you have never been open.' She leaned forward eagerly.

'Because I have never been sure', I replied firmly, 'that God is not just playing with me.'

She looked shocked. 'You are a poet. Poetry and music are supposed to open up the heart to the divine.'

'I know but. . . .' How could I explain to this young Dominican that my faith was faith in the ancient gods of Greece, in Apollo and Bacchus and the Muses? 'I once had a friend – he's dead now – I think he would have understood the love you are speaking of.'

The gentle nun looked sad. She showed me some of her poems, mystical sonnets on divine love. I brought a copy of them back to Paris. They sat on my shelf, looking reproachfully at me as I renewed my verbal assault on the Calvinists.

Tolerance was promised to the Calvinists by Catherine in the January edict. But in March twenty-three of their number were massacred during a church service at Vassy by François de Guise's troops. Louis Condé withdrew from court and began organizing the Reformers into an army. They took Orleans, Angers, Tours, Blois and Lyons. Seeing that war could no longer be averted, Catherine gradually banished Protestant preachers from court and threw the weight of the monarchy cautiously behind its Catholic subjects. At the time I naïvely believed that she did so because of the persuasive power of my words. Now I know that no one sways politicians from pursuing their interests. She had recognized that the monarchy could no longer be neutral. Under pressure, it had always to be Catholic.

In Paris huge bonfires of Calvin's books were burned daily on Notre-Dame bridge. People suspected of heresy were drowned in the river or stripped and dragged naked through the streets by their neighbours. The Seine overflowed in the middle of June. Everywhere there were food shortages. God was angry with France. The workers left their shops and ploughs to rush off to hear preachers. They were bewitched by talk of freedom. Freedom! Their Christ wears a helmet and carries a smoking pistol in his hand. In September the ultimate betrayal – Coligny sold Calais to the English in return for troops.

I stayed inside my house. My poems had made me into one of the most hated targets of the Calvinists (I once ventured out and was shot at five times by someone firing an arquebus from a window). Nor had the Calvinists been slow to attack me in their poetry. For the most part they were young poets, poets even who had once been my disciples (I noticed bitterly that Bèze himself did not deign to step into the arena). They accused me of avarice, debauchery and atheism. Like rebellious pupils they plundered my work to use it against me. They must have written at least twenty separate attacks on me.

But the worst blow was the betrayal of Jacques Grévin. You didn't expect that, did you? Nor did I. He published a scurrilous poem directed against me, describing a temple built in honour of St Ronsard, the atheist. Very bad taste, I thought. He had gone carefully through my poems, picking out lines to use at my expense. He called me a homosexual, arrogant, greedy. He accused me of having venereal disease and of eating meat during Lent. He alluded to my affair with Genèvre. And if that were not enough, he said I was ugly and my teeth were rotting (well, they were, but only a little). Yes, I can laugh about it now (through clenched jaws), but I was pretty devastated, I can tell you. The others did not matter, but I had watched over Grévin's career as a father over a son. I had guided his poems into print, smoothed the way for him at court, and this was how he repaid me!

The worst of it was that he had never seemed bothered one way or the other about religion. True, he had spoken out against corruption in the Catholic Church (who hasn't?), but he had never, so far as I knew, committed himself to the Calvinists – all his poetry proves that. He uses pagan myth just like a Catholic and writes on erotic subjects. He would have been highly disapproved of in Geneva. Besides, he openly admits he has no interest in religion. And so I was forced to conclude that he had attacked me as an easy way of achieving fame. He was the kind of person who changes religion as a chameleon changes its colour, according to the country he is in. Grévin's god was profit and self-advancement. I was struck by a sickening thought: was that why he had declared himself an imitator of mine in the first place – to increase his own reputation?

'That's the last time I help anyone,' I said angrily, scrubbing out his name from my poems. I took down the book on antimony he had lent me (now you see why I never read it) and tried to scratch out his signature with a knife. I wanted to make him vanish completely from my life.

I had written many poems on the fickleness of women, but it was not till that moment that I experienced for myself what I had been trying to describe in verse, and I realized that a reader who had been hurt by a woman's betrayal might well have been insulted by the lightness of my tone. Never mind, too late to alter them. All the same, it was a dirty trick, not only on my friendship, but on the Muses too. I could not help feeling he had stained them by his attack on me.

But no one can stay angry for ever, of course. Poor Grévin, little good did his poem do him. His life in Paris became a series of quarrels with the medical faculty. He died abroad some years ago, long forgotten by his countrymen. If I had not asked young Claude Binet to commemorate his death in a poem, there would have been nothing at all to remember him by.

The fighting and my poems continued for a year. Men and women were tortured, their fingers crushed, the soles of their feet burned, their eyes popped out of their head by a cord pulled tight around their forehead. There was no end to man's ingenuity in devising methods of inflicting the most excruciating pain on others. Wars breed vices: as Seneca said, no vice is self-contained. The fighting made men frenzied, beside themselves.

Then the Protestant leader Condé was captured and the Peace of Amboise was agreed upon, allowing Protestant nobles to worship freely outside towns. The peasantry complained of a sell-out by Condé, as well they might. But the treaty called a halt to the fighting for the time being, and in July the nation united sufficiently to take Le Havre from the English. In September a royal edict forbade the publication of hostile pamphlets between Catholic and Protestant Frenchmen. Catherine was once again playing off one side against the other, like the brilliant politician she is. My poems had become an embarrassment to her. I obeyed the edict and retired as defender of the faith.

I was already beginning to tire of my role. I had been fighting for freedom, but in that atmosphere of bigotry all my words had done was to fan the flames of hatred. In such circumstances it is better for the poet to keep quiet. As a friend of mine once said: 'The more you talk about God, the less people believe in Him.' Words have a magical power to curse or to heal, they must not be abused – and especially not by a poet. The nun had been right: poetry should not enforce but should heal divisions. My poems had become stained with the blood of my countrymen.

Social responsibility had placed too great a burden on my writing; I had begun even to cease to deserve the name of poet. 'It is time to do away with metaphor and simile, people are dying,' I had said, forgetting that metaphor and simile are the nerves and tissue of poetry. And I had written bad poetry, poetry that could be understood by fools.

You see, the poet's task is to transform the bread and butter of daily life. A good poem is one in which the meaning is unravelled bit by bit. I had turned into another Lucretius, speaking of dogma and doctrines. Whereas a true poet rarely calls things by their proper name – he creates beauty and mystery by means of more or less convincing fictions. Years ago Dorat had taught me that truth must be veiled in images so that the ignorant could not mock the sacred mysteries. Now I had laid them all bare, tossed them into the air like a bouquet of flowers for their perfume to be carried away by the wind.

It was time to stop before I lost the right to the name of poet. I wanted to speak of blood no longer, but of love and rose-petals, dreams and leaves. Violence was unnatural. I retired to the country and let the war continue without me. I consoled myself by publishing a collection of light-hearted poems in which myth became a protection against the wars and I created my own world again, of gods and goddesses, love and beauty. Like Icarus I had flown too high and singed my wings, but I am always ready to glue my wings back on and try again, oh yes. Don't make the mistake of thinking a king's decree can't be got round. Read between the lines of my hymn to winter for a snipe at the Protestants. Myth can hide a multitude of.... No, I shan't explain it to you. Work it out for yourself.

So I could not avoid the violence altogether. No one could. On one of my visits to my church at Evaillé au Maine we were attacked by a band of Protestants. It was during the celebration of mass, attended by a handful of monks and a few peasants from the village. A hoard of half-mad bandits broke down the door and set upon us with staves and poles. I defended myself as well as I could with my sword, but they managed to tear down the altar and make off with the silver chalice. They left several of the congregation badly injured from blows around the head and genitals. They dragged off two of the women, raped them repeatedly, and then cut off their breasts. Just another of the incidents in these long, long wars.

The fifth civil war has just ended as I write and there is no sign that it will be the last. Thick clouds of dust hang over our land every summer. A generation of Frenchmen has grown up knowing only war, guarding their speech in front of strangers and sometimes even with their own family. There are spies everywhere. It is no longer safe to venture out of doors. You need a passport to move around and your luggage might be seized at any moment. The wars prevent the free flow of trade between towns, so farmers cannot get their crops to market, nor an artisan his wares. These civil wars are very far from the glory I imagined in my youth. Soldiers surely cannot think it is religion they fight for as they plunder villages, stealing from the peasants and raping the women. There are no military funerals. Soldiers' bodies are left where they fall, for wolves, crows and stray dogs.

Children's minds have been poisoned with hatred for the other side. Our country is full of wandering prophets dressed in filthy rags, with yellow eyes and unkempt beards, shouting their predictions in the market-places to idiots who stand around gaping. The wars have distorted our language. We need speech made honest again, language purified through precision. Erasmus says that language is what separates us from the beasts. I have often wondered whether the deeper one's understanding of the language, the further one penetrates one's humanity. Brutal language and the behaviour of beasts go hand in hand in these wars.

Lives have been broken in two by the violence. Peasants are burned alive for theological subtleties they will never understand. Luther had a dream of a Church purified of burden and superstition. The dream underestimated the masses' need for authority and ritual. He threw them back on their own resources and realized too late that they have none. Instead they projected their fear and confusion into a war which has spread across the whole of Europe. Perhaps, in centuries to come, religion will be a matter for private conscience, but not now, not as our people are, stupid and selfish and fearful. Polemicists of both sides have lit a fire impossible to put out. I regret my part in fanning the flames.

In the brief intervals of peace, our King Henri leads his subjects on penitential pilgrimages. Wearing only a robe of rough sackcloth, he goes barefoot through the towns of France with ashes on his head. His followers scourge themselves till the blood runs down their backs. Yes, our religion has become drenched in blood. He organizes festivals and balls in an attempt to forget that chaos is come and his kingdom is collapsing around him. When things get difficult and he is pressed by both Catholics and Protestants for a statement, he goes hunting at Vincennes to avoid having to commit himself to either side. In this way he preserves the balance of power whilst France weeps for her children.

What can a poor poet do in the face of such a monumental unleashing of the powers of darkness? Simply go on singing, soothing his fears by the music of the word, and hope that one day the darkness will lift and his songs will be heard again. On a personal level, at least, the war roused me from my apathy. Joachim had been right. I could not be angry with God for ever. He had allowed me to fight a battle, different from the ones I had dreamed of in my youth, but one that had its own kind of glory. I felt the invisible tug of the thread drawing me back into grace.

Yes, out of all my roles, perhaps this is the one from which I shall be able to salvage something.

But it is time to speak of my last and most disastrous part. Shall I? Do I have the strength? No matter, something is at my shoulder hurrying me on. Is it death?

PART FIVE

THE COURTIER

Chapter 16

Cold, cold. I lie under the scarlet wool coverlet at Croixval and I feel so cold and sick. Perhaps I am in hell; in Dante the farthest point of hell is icy. The air in the room is over-scented with burning spices and sickly sweet pomanders to ward off infection. Amadis has put me on a strict diet of milk to reduce the fever that is shaking my bones. But the black threads of my life are unravelling and there is nothing he can do to stop them. Death in old age is natural. Illness must take its natural course, as my father said. All the same, I wish Denise the witch was here now with some charm, or better still, a woman to warm these old limbs.

There is a knock. Amadis puts his head round the door.

'You have a visitor, from Paris. Don't stay too long now,' he says to an unseen person.

The person steps into the room. She is dressed in grey. Two heavy braids frame her pale face. I am touched that she has made the long journey from the city to see me.

'Come and sit here,' I say, patting the side of my bed.

She prefers to wander round the room, fingering a jar here, arranging a glass there. She stops in front of a phial of my blood. 'Ugh! How black it is! It's as if you were dead already.'

Even her best friend would not call Hélène a cheerful sort of person. I am not sure I shall feel the better for her visit.

'Have you the Argus in tow?' I whisper, referring to the elderly chaperone who dogs our footsteps and seems to have a thousand eyes trained to spot the slightest impropriety.

'She's outside in the carriage,' Hélène whispers back.

I smile, wryly. I suppose she thinks I am harmless now,

being so ill. Hélène sits down by my bed and tells me the latest gossip from court.

'The King has gone on another pilgrimage to pray for an heir. The Queen Mother has approved new plans for the extension to the Louvre . . .'

'Whilst her subjects starve.'

'The building will benefit the whole nation. Its construction will provide jobs for people who are currently out of work. Besides, a great monarch needs a suitable palace, do you not agree?'

Hélène is one of Catherine's ladies-in-waiting and very loyal. She plucks solemnly at the coverlet on my bed. I guess what is to come.

'The whole court is waiting for the publication of this new edition. They are dying to see the poems you have written for me. Some people are saying they might even rival Desportes.'

I sigh. This woman, who is supposed to be my Muse, knows nothing about poetry. She continually (and quite unknowingly) pours cold water on my work.

'My poems for you will be greater than anything Desportes has ever written,' I say firmly.

'Oh.' She lowers her eyes. Obviously this is going too far. 'I am just hoping there will be nothing too, well, you know. . . .'

Her eyes remain lowered.

'Nothing too suggestive, you mean?' I say, with raised eyebrows.

'Yes. You have written some terribly indecent stuff in the past and Desportes writes so chastely.'

A glare from me and she senses she is on the wrong track. She hurries on.

'I mean, I have all kinds of rivals at court just waiting to ruin my good name. I honestly do believe Plato was right and the spiritual kind of love is best. And you know that there has never been anything else between us.'

Not with you so frigid, ma'am, and I so impotent.

'Well, well,' I pat her thin hand, 'you need not worry. It will be a perfectly proper collection, I assure you.'

She is visibly relieved. I wonder after all, should I be so touched by her visit? The court breeds self-interest. Who knows what goes on in the frozen landscapes of Hélène's soul? I suspect her self-image feeds off my poetry like a devouring harpy. She talks for a while longer. In my mind a poem is slowly ripening. Under its impulse I become impatient of her chatter and wish her to go. She senses my withdrawal and rises to take her leave.

'I mustn't tire you or Amadis will never forgive me. By the way, don't you think his poems are good?'

'Like singing water.'

I am always eager for praise of those I have helped in some way.

'I'll send you the cuttings from Paris and you can tell me the names of the plants.'

'Of course. . . . Ask Jacques to give you some fruit and eggs from the garden,' I call after her.

When she has gone, I sit up in bed. The thought of a poem to write gives me enough strength to get up and limp over to my table. There Amadis finds me an hour later, pen in hand, and scolds me roundly.

'There is no point producing a collection of poems to outdo Desportes if you are not there to see it published.'

'Men's lives unfold like waves against a bank,' I say, leaning on his arm as he leads me back to bed. As always after completing a poem I feel sadness coming over me, filling up the gap left by the outflowing of creative energy. 'Even you, Amadis, cannot prolong my life against nature's will.'

'No, but there are some ways that are quicker to death than others,' he replies, pulling the coverlet over me.

Dear Amadis! He has been like a son to me (a feeling I had thought was gone for ever after Grévin's betrayal). Amadis won me over, a lively, agile boy with the fragile bloom of a narcissus, rushing to fetch the wine cooling under the hawthorn hedge, sitting cross-legged, drinking in our conversations about poetry. Noticing his remarkable powers of concentration, I sent him to Paris to study under Dorat. He showed a great eagerness for learning and a special bent for history. He returned to act as my secretary and keep out intruders. He became acquainted with all my tastes, chose my wines, learned not to order meat in summer. He wrote letters for me and copied out my poems in his beautiful round hand, even adding explanatory notes for the reader. My enemies, the Calvinists, accused me of having homosexual relations with him – are there no depths to which these people will not sink?

Amadis was with me the day the King himself came to visit me at St Côme. But wait now, I am getting ahead of myself. As I have said, my poems attacking the Calvinists became an embarrassment to the Queen Mother when peace was made. (I was not the only one in disgrace, if you'll excuse a diversion for a moment: the wily Cardinal of Lorraine pushed his luck too far when he flew in the face of Catherine's new liberal policy by supporting Catholic extremists. He had played the system once too often. As for me, I could hardly avoid a smile. I had washed my hands of him several years ago, since it became increasingly obvious that I should never get a penny out of him – can you credit it, after all those poems?)

To redeem myself in the Queen Mother's eyes and fall in with her schemes for reconciling the two sides, I composed some poems in honour of a relation of hers, Isabeau de Limeuil, who also happened to be the Protestant leader's mistress. That blonde-haired, blue-eyed whore – high-spirited they called her (more likely, oversexed). The hunch-back Condé plied her with jewels, dresses and expensively bound books. He became a prisoner of her charms. God knows how many abortions she had before she finally got her claws into that greasy Italian banker she has married. 'The Lady Isabeau has taken a little trip to the country' – the Queen Mother is skilled in these matters (she keeps paid quacks in attendance especially for this purpose). Anyway, I suppose she thought she owed it to the Lady Isabeau, for it was Catherine who had encouraged her kinswoman to become Condé's mistress in order that she would be kept informed of his plans (though we were supposed to be at peace). In this way the Queen Mother, like a true Machiavellian, keeps a close watch on all potential conspirators.

She has other ways of keeping control. In order to bring the two sides closer together and unite them in obedience to the monarchy, Catherine organized a huge carnival at

Fontainebleau to take place just before Lent. There were to be ballets, concerts and mock battles in which both Catholics and Protestants would take part. I was commissioned to write some songs and masquerades. Catherine used these kinds of festivals to provide a ritual exorcizing of political enmities, a purging of violence through acting it out in mock warfare between Catholics and Protestants (we had just made peace with the English, which was an additional cause for celebration).

On Shrove Tuesday six companies, each made up of twelve Catholic knights, had to attack a tower defended by the Protestant leader Condé and his troops. The Catholics' task was to rescue two 'prisoners', which they did, and then came the highlight of the carnival as the tower exploded into flames. The day before there had been an outdoor concert given by Catherine's ladies-in-waiting with singing by a castrato. Nymphs in green costumes danced over the lawns. The festivities included the performance of a tragicomedy (tragedy being forbidden on account of the political situation – Catherine wanted only happy endings). I composed some poems to be sung during the intervals. The play was called *La Belle Genièvre*, which stirred certain happy memories.

The Queen Mother's idea, you see, was to impose order on her country. Encouraged by magicians at court, she believed she could draw down magic powers to aid the French monarchy, and by means of music and poetry effect a change in people's hearts and bring about a spirit of peace and reconciliation. This suited us. We had always claimed that poetry and music calm the soul. Did not David cure Saul's rages with his songs? And Orpheus quieten the wild beasts with his lyre? If there were people who hoped to reform the world through education, religion or the occult, we saw change as being brought about by words and music. Listening to music, the soul, we argued, comes into harmony with the singing spheres. Through music we wanted to unite France and drive out the discordant chants of the violent. Our philosopher, Pontus de Tyard, wrote a book about the effect of music on the soul. Antoine had even greater plans – like the ancients, he wanted to match the syllables of poetry to the notes in music in a quest to recapture the dance of the planets and calm the passions that were tearing our country apart. But more about that later. . . .

The star of Fontainebleau was Françoise d'Estrées, one of seven sisters nicknamed the seven mortal sins for their teasing beauty. She took part in the festival wearing a sumptuous costume decorated with agates, rubies, pearls and diamonds (though her beauty needed no ornament). Her blonde hair spread around her shoulders like a flight of birds. The captain of the Guards' regiment, Béranger du Gast, fell in love with her and asked me to compose some poems for her. I naturally obliged. (I also wrote a poem for that pair of lesbians, Anne and Diane.)

The festivities at Fontainebleau lasted ten days. After that we moved on to Bar-le-Duc for the baptism of Catherine's first grandson (more verses). Then I returned to Paris. Loath to waste any of my work, I collected all these poems together and had them published with a dedication to Elizabeth I of England – at that time it was proposed to marry our young King Charles off to the old hag. Paris was alive with rumours: that the Calvinists were preparing to take up arms again, that the Germans would invade France, and that Catholics of all countries were about to make war on Geneva. It was said that the Turks were getting ready to overrun Europe (an old one that), that all the Church's property would be turned over to the State (worrying for clerics like me). I wrote Catherine a long epistle keeping her informed of the situation. And so I went, showering nectar on princes, being controlled by events when I thought I was controlling them.

All these little moves put me on very good terms with the royal family. I had shown I was not arrogant enough to continue pursuing a political line that had fallen out of favour; I was prepared to bend with the prevailing wind. 'Very sensible,' said the Queen Mother, giving me my first (and only) abbey. So I became the King's official poet at court, and in his pay along with his doctors, his astrologers and his furniture makers.

To promote her policy of peace and reconciliation, Catherine took her son on a two-year tour of the provinces. It was during this time that they visited Amadis and me at St

Côme. I had just moved in, I remember, and was busy reorganizing things. I had promised the monks that repairs would be carried out on the buildings and I reallocated money my brother had earmarked for food and vintage wines to the building project. In my spare time I was working on the garden, which had been grossly neglected and was overgrown with brambles and thistles. It had taken shape enough to enable me to present the King with some of the first melons. He thanked me shyly, with eyes lowered. He was a pimply, red-eyed adolescent, too much under his mother's thumb.

'I believe you have a magnificent view from your balcony, Monsieur Ronsard, is that not so?' said Catherine in her thick Italian accent. 'I should like to see it.'

So Amadis and I took them up to the first floor of the priory, where there is a vista over three valleys. Autumn had painted the trees brown. We drank in the sudden flowering of oranges, dull yellows and gold, that unrolled before us.

'You are interested in poetry, I think, sire?' I said, turning to the King, hoping to draw him out.

'Oh yes,' interposed his mother, 'Charles has read all the old French poets. He even writes verse himself. You should compare notes.'

'Oh, Mother,' said the King, shifting uncomfortably from foot to foot, 'they are only scribbles. Monsieur Ronsard would not be interested in those.'

I felt sorry for this trembling adolescent.

'A true Frenchman', said his mother, firmly, 'will always be interested in anything his King writes, isn't that so?' She turned to me and I caught a whiff of sour breath.

'Of course,' I murmured. 'I should be delighted to see the King's poems, if he would deign to honour me.'

The heavy chin jerked up and down several times in approval. As I followed the stout figure in widow's weeds down the stairs, I dared not meet Amadis's eye. I knew I should see irony in it. I shrugged inwardly. Servility and fame, or freedom and obscurity, these were the choices. I had a duty to my poetry to remain submissive. I did not realize then that the promises of kings are as bubbles in water.

Yes, we were all very polite, the royal party and I, but they still had not handed over all the payment they had promised for my poems. That should have warned me if anything could. But I was becoming beguiled by the court sirens who sit combing out their dark-blue hair, offering gold and fame to poor sailors who do not notice the rocks on which they are sure to founder.

I wrote poems for the ladies at court, commissioned by their admirers. Nobles always want such long poems! If I had been writing for myself, these verses would have been much shorter, but nobles always demand oceans of words. My songs were sung before the King by the renowned castrato Estienne Le Roy. The King and I even began exchanging poems (you see how bad things can get!). On wet days he would summon Antoine, Dorat and me to his wood-panelled study and there, whilst huge fires roared at either end of the room and sleepy dogs kept watch, he would have us read to him. Sitting in a tall, carved chair, Charles would listen, head bent, to our poems. The present King Henri looks you straight in the eye. He is the better actor.

Then our turn would come to beg the privilege of hearing the King's own poems and we would suspend all judgement in order to praise them. We were very careful not to appear his rivals – the tyrant Dionysius condemned Philoxenus to hard labour because his poetry outdid his own. In truth, Charles had few enough pleasures for a king. Timid and jealous of his younger brother Henri who had all their mother's love, he was ill at ease in his own court. Scarcely out of boyhood, he was alarmed by the number of women ready to step into his bed. He fled the giggles of his mother's ladies-in-waiting for the cool of the forest. The virgin goddess Diana was more to his taste than the complicated machinery of love-making at court. In this he had my sympathy.

At other times, he retreated to his forge to watch weapons being made and coins minted. Sometimes he participated himself. And whilst Charles rolled up his sleeves like a blacksmith and Frenchmen starved, Catherine poured huge sums of money into extensions for the Louvre. The royal architects became rich overnight and bought themselves titles and Church posts. Catherine handed France over to the Italians – the Strozzis, the Sardinis, the Gondis, the Biragos. The nation was overrun by Italian financiers, Italian bankers, Italian lawyers and Italian tax-collectors (who were always inventing new taxes for the French to pay). Whilst Italians lined their pockets at Frenchmen's expense, the country was going steadily bankrupt.

The King sought desperately for a way to escape the problems that had been laid on his too frail shoulders. He re-arranged council sessions to take place during the night so that he could go hunting in the daytime. A simple enough solution to his own problems, if not to his country's. Sometimes I went with him and watched as he drove his thin, bent body to the point of exhaustion. This even battle between man and beast suited him far better than the subtleties of court diplomacy. His horses were no flatterers – they were as likely to throw a king as a tradesman. He delighted in feeling cold and hunger, simple needs he could satisfy. Meat cooked out of doors over a fire pleased him more than all the heavy sauces and spices he was forced to swallow at court banquets. He had no pity for the creatures he caught. I have watched him grin with delight at the sight of an animal lying in its own steaming guts. He generally slit the animal's throat himself, and I have seen him lick his lips and salivate as the blood gushed out. Our noble King of France was a true primitive.

He could be crude too. 'Poets are like horses,' I heard him say once. 'If you feed them too much, they become full of wind and just fart around.'

There was no danger of that. I should often have starved to death if I had relied on the promises of kings.

One day I was summoned to his study. He was standing by one of the fireplaces, looking pensive.

'We were thinking, Ronsard . . .' – I groaned inwardly, it is always a bad sign when kings start to think – 'that it would be a good thing if France were to have an epic poem glorifying the nation's history. Greece had Homer after all, and Rome had Virgil. Every great imperialist power needs an epic to commemorate her achievements, and her kings.'

I remembered my barely started poem about Francus.

'Sire, there is perhaps a subject in the son of Aeneas, Francus, who, legend has it, escaped the fall of Troy and founded our nation. I wrote a few lines on this theme when your father was alive.'

And never got paid.

'Excellent, excellent,' he said, looking at his toes.

There was a pause.

'An epic poem takes years to write, sire. It would mean abandoning all my other projects . . .'

'Yes, yes, I will see that you are amply rewarded for your trouble.'

'Thank you, sire.' I swept my hat to the ground.

'There is one other thing – a small matter. I have been thinking it over and have decided that our national epic should be written in lines of ten syllables.'

His words hit my ear like a stone.

'The decasyllabic metre, sire?' I could sense the panic rising in my voice. 'But that's totally out of date. We poets, as you yourself know, sire, prefer the alexandrine metre nowadays. And the twelve-syllable line would be so much more suited to heroic subject matter. Decasyllables are for love poetry.'

'No, I have thought about it a good deal. The alexandrine is a new invention. I want our epic to contain all that is best in French tradition. The decasyllabic metre was good enough for our forefathers. I think I know a little about such matters?'

He looked at me with raised eyebrows, a trick he had copied from his mother. I began to see the disadvantages of having a king who took an interest in poetry.

I struggled and struggled with that wretched poem. It hung around my neck like a dead albatross for years. Wrestling with the decasyllabic metre I became more and more entangled in a cobweb of rhymes as I tried to stuff battles, crimes, births and deaths into lines too short to hold them.

'Of course,' said the King on another occasion, 'I must have all my ancestors included, good and bad alike.'

What? A dynastic history, no less! There were nights when my head reeled from delving back into the past through the long list of France's kings. Sixty-three monarchs weighed my shoulders down as I searched the history books in an effort to find something about them to praise. Amadis helped by ferreting out facts about their lives. On my suggestion he had begun translating *The Iliad* into French. As he worked his way through, he made a list of Homer's images for me. I needed to know all kinds of things – about weapons, anatomy, politics, daily life. I was becoming a damned encyclopedia of information about early France. But it didn't help my poem. Malicious rivals would ask how it was going. 'Has Francus set sail yet?' they would say, with a snigger. 'Friends' predicted its success in their poems. Everyone climbed on the bandwagon.

Amadis and I worked at St Côme separately during the day and in the evening we showed each other our labours. He advised me on history, I advised him on style. From time to time there was light relief in the form of visits from ladies who lived in the neighbourhood. Amadis had fallen in love with a young woman who lived with her husband in a château by the Loire. He wrote endless love poems to her. I teased him about his sentimentality but stopped when I saw the look of hurt in his eyes. It was truly like having a son of my own. I would have protected him from such pain if it had been in my power to do so. Instead I offered to help him with his poetry. I was flattered to see that he had adopted a style similar to my own. A slightly clumsy modulation on the strings of a famous lute, he called it.

Is it prejudice on my part that makes me think he has become a lesser poet since he left me? This new fashion for sweetness and sophistication seems to have robbed his verses of their naturalness. He listens less often to the spontaneous promptings of his heart. Yet he is fêted in all the salons of Paris for his dancing lines. He has somehow managed to make the leap across into this new Italianate poetry practised by Desportes. He has been young enough to adapt. Prejudice – yes, it must be. Fathers must know how to let go of their sons. All the same, is it wrong of me to hope that one day he may wake up and smell the stench of corruption at court?

Four years, can nothing really happen for four years? I plodded on, writing history rather than poetry, becoming a slave to rhyme. There were times when I felt like a beast in a net, hunted down by the King's literary ambitions. I became accomplished at making excuses for my delay ('I have to read up on the history of France', 'Some prince has asked me to write a funeral elegy for a relation', 'I wouldn't like to show you anything unpolished, Your Majesty'). Mind you, I had not been paid.

Pottering around the garden had become more pleasurable than writing poetry. I spent less and less time at my desk.

'The country life, splendid!' I told Amadis. 'No need to think of ambition or making money. I'm too lazy and deaf for court life.' He raised an unbelieving eyebrow.

But of course the Muses had their revenge. I fell ill twice, the second time with malaria. My body felt as if it had been pumped full of shot, like one of the King's boars. The monks at St Côme despaired of my life. In Paris the rumour went round that I was dead (it was eagerly encouraged by my good friends the Calvinists). Some people even published epitaphs for me (it's not surprising they killed me off in their verses, since it is these that are killing poetry).

Eventually, Amadis's skill with herbs, together with my own knowledge of my body's strengths and weaknesses, brought me through. Remembering my father's advice, I rejected all medicine except the herbs Amadis picked for me at specified hours of the day (verbena for the blood, the leaves and roots of the artemisia plant for a tonic) and certain peasant remedies such as strong wine mixed with saffron and spice. These home-made remedies act more gently on the body than the drugs prescribed by doctors. Nevertheless, my health has remained permanently weakened by this attack. For the first time I felt darkening evening closing around my life.

I had had omens, oh yes. The laurel I had planted at Croixval suddenly and inexplicably died. One of my servants had his head kicked in by a horse and died with my name on his lips (an especially bad sign). One morning I had woken up to find a cat on my bed – 'sign of a long illness', my mother used to say (how I hate cats). The peasants say that God gives us all kinds of warnings through animals; for instance, if you sight a crane, it means you will go on a journey, whilst a tortoise means you will have misfortunes. But I was not wise enough to heed these warnings. I was too busy avoiding the pages of my unfinished epic which lay, like a threat, on my table.

My illness limited my life for months to a small room in the monastery. So I had plenty of time to think over my failure to complete my epic. I came to the conclusion that the battle had been lost before I began: French is not a language suited to the epic form. Oh, in translation, yes – Amadis's translation was coming along quite well, its lines flowed gracefully with, here and there, glimpses of the soul of Homer. Of course, he had no restrictions and had sensibly adopted the twelve-syllable line, which allowed Homer's verses to glitter like jewels under his pen. But even if I had not been constrained by the royal preference for the decasyllable, I still would have failed and it would not have been my fault. You see, it is impossible to compose a Homeric epic for modern France; the times are simply not right for heroic poetry (besides, Homer is the first and last of epic poets – he made epic poetry in its infancy mature and perfect and left no imitators). There are no heroes any more. My Francus was shipwrecked as soon as he set sail, becoming stranded on the sandbanks of a non-heroic age.

And whilst we are on this subject, the faithful Jean Galland has sent me a new volume by the young poet Du Bartas. A Calvinist, Du Bartas has decided to attempt the task at which I failed, namely to write an epic poem. He says he wants to unravel the universe in his poem and give it a new shape – but all he has done is create chaotic verse. What is worrying, however, is that he claims to be imitating my early style. He claims, as I did then, to be divinely inspired. Good God, did I really write in such an inflated way? In panic I rush to take a look at my early poems. Perhaps they are a little overdone, a little pretentious in their claims (we were terribly serious young men), but surely . . . surely they are better than the formless stuff Du Bartas has managed to produce?

I close the book. Damn him! He brings me into disrepute by claiming to be an imitator of mine. It's true I did endorse Horace's notion of divine inspiration. Well, for one thing, it gives the poet the freedom to write on any subject he chooses without fearing censorship (who would dare censor the gods – clever, eh?). Yes, but it does sound pretentious all right. And yet there is a sense in which I am inspired when I write. Poets need madness, a holy madness possible only by the intervention of grace. Writing demands an intense concentration of all the faculties, a kind of spiritual drunkenness, in order to penetrate the level of conscious perception – in specially favoured moments, I project images from my mind on to the page in a state of trance. My soul strives to leave the body, to get outside itself, possessed by rapture. I can see this is putting you off; all right, forget it then. All the same, you should pay attention, those of you who would judge my life by my poems, for in such a state I am carried along (by inspiration?) and say even more than I intended.

Yes, it is very difficult to explain all this to the outsider without sounding ridiculous. When I see some of our imitators croaking like open-mouthed frogs, I wonder if we were right to talk so much about our art. Poetry is a gift, it cannot be forced. And Du Bartas will get us laughed at. He lacks all taste and judgement, all sense of proportion. Ah, these young poets – goodness knows, I have tried to help them: our country is not yet so rich that it can afford to crush new writers. I try to awaken vocations where I can, but this . . . his poems resemble the pigs' bladders children blow up to play football with; they are full of wind and if you press them they shrivel up.

Chapter 17

I recuperated and kept out of the way of the war that was waging again in France (Louis Condé had seized Blois and was besieging Chartres) by devoting my time to gardening and repairs at St Côme. We led a simple life – roasts by the fire, accompanied by a local wine. On fine days I put on a thick topcoat and a big hat to protect me from the sun and we went for picnics by the fountain. Amadis prepared wild strawberries and cream, apricots and melons (I never eat meat in the summer). I began to take an interest in cooking myself (though I have never been a gourmet like my brother). I liked gathering herbs for salad, washing them in the fountain, salting them and putting olive-oil on them (not walnut-oil, by the way, which is bad for the stomach). Amadis scolded me that salads were not good for an invalid. 'Nor is poetry,' he added. My illness had made me think nostalgically and gratefully of all that poetry had given me. I abandoned the epic, for reasons I have already explained, and instead wrote poems for my friends: for Antoine, in memory of our early days together; for Belot, with whom I once stayed and who presented me with a beautiful lyre. Yes, poetry distracted me from my illness, took me out of myself, and as for salad, well, it's healthy and light on the stomach and tastes of sunlight and all the good things in nature. It can't be any worse than the broths and gruels prescribed by the doctors.

It was during this period that I actively began to enjoy my duties as prior. The monks and I went visiting the poor of the neighbourhood, trying to relieve in whatever way we could the ravages of civil war. We saw fields set alight, villages wrecked by hordes of starving soldiers and we walked amongst the smoking ruins of cottages. Bands of homeless peasants wandered the roads, their eyes dazed with fear; ragged women went begging from door to door with their children. It was sights such as these that awakened my admiration for the loyal courage of the peasants. The way that, after each bout of violence, they set to work to rebuild their homes and heal the land. I became godfather to their children. I took up the Fortin case I told you about (and had to dedicate my next book of poems to the lawyer in charge of the case, Pierre du Lac, in lieu of fees).

On one of these visits I met Cassandra – yes, it was incredible. She was now a plump, stately matron of forty with a daughter. She complained about her tenants and described, with a gleam in her eye, various schemes for making money. She had become penny-pinching, a true Salviati. She must have been alarmed at my appearance, for my body had shrunk and my eyes were now as red-rimmed as the King's. But she made no comment and our relationship threatened to end, as it had begun, on a note of polite formality. Then something, a movement of her arm, a light in her eyes, brought back the beautiful young girl of my poems. The past broke through the years and youth and beauty trembled before me. I remembered a certain ball at Blois where a black-eyed girl had danced like a bird to the sob of violins. In the air around I could feel them sobbing still – for the loss of love, of youth, of joy.

Despite my illness I continued to plot my moves at court and when peace returned to the provinces I went back to Paris. I gave an elaborate supper to mark my return. I wanted to let people know I was back, fighting for my position. Imagine my horror then when I found that a certain handsome young poet with curly hair and a sensual mouth had taken advantage of my absence to make a name for himself at court with his dainty verses. Philippe Desportes had come back from a visit to Italy determined to establish a career for himself by introducing the Italian style of love poetry to France (not indeed a particularly difficult task at a court where all the most important posts are held by Italians!) To my dismay, I found that his poems for Diane were beginning to make people forget the names of Cassandra and Marie. Something had to be done.

Desperate to cling to my position at court, I flung myself

whole-heartedly into preparations for the King's marriage. Overcoming his fear of women, Charles had chosen as his wife Elizabeth of Austria, granddaughter of France's former enemy, Charles V. It was a political match, of course, intended to cement the alliance between two great imperial nations, France and Spain. But this sweet, pious girl who spoke only Spanish, had captured our King's shy heart and it became a love match. Dorat and I were put in charge of the celebrations (for a fee).

We chose as our theme peaceful imperialism, with the Queen Mother as Juno, arranger of marriages, presiding over the union of two empires. I took the opportunity to work into my verses passages from my still unpublished (and unfinished) epic poem. It is always a good idea to whet the public's appetite (little did they know how few lines of this marvellous epic had actually been written). Amadis also composed three sonnets for the occasion. I had brought him to Paris with me to get a taste of literary life in the capital. Dorat and I advised the painters and architects on the visual presentation of themes from our poems. They constructed a statue of Francus at Porte St Denis and inscribed my verses over a triumphal arch at Pont Notre-Dame. Our verses were all over Paris. What glory!

Music was provided by Antoine and his newly founded Academy of Poetry and Music. Bitter at the public's rejection of his songs of love and springtime (in which birds whisper through the trees and the earth makes love to the sky), Antoine had turned to exploring the relationship between music and words. He and the musician Thibault de Courville had founded an academy for the purpose of producing music and poetry based on classical musical theory. As usual when anyone attempts something new in this country, they encountered stiff opposition from the growling dogs at the Sorbonne. But with the help of the King, who was interested in their project, the professors were silenced. And now the house at Fossés St Victor rings from morning to evening with the sound of music (they say), and every Sunday afternoon a concert is held there.

Music, painting, costumes, architecture and poetry – we planned the marriage celebrations as a total spectacle, where everything would hold together and have a place. There was dancing too, for dancing, like music, is a way of escaping from human limits through its ancient rhythmical patterns, which imitate the flight of the planets through the sky. The celebrations were an attempt at total expression in all the arts, where the insufficiencies of one art would be remedied by another and where everything was guided and governed by our poems.

But it was not enough. Philippe Desportes's name was on everyone's lips, its syllables fell one by one on my aching ears. The King, anxious to know how my epic was progressing, summoned Amadis and me to Blois for a private reading. Great consternation! However, Amadis had just finished making a copy of Book Four, and this is what he read to the King. In return, Charles showed me a manuscript of his book on hunting. His prose was better than his poetry. He urged me to publish my epic as soon as possible. I urged him to publish his treatise on hunting. We parted on the best of terms.

And still thudding against my ears came Desportes's name, beating, beating on my brain. I woke up at night in a cold sweat. I would not be defeated. But what could I do? The court was partial to his verse. And then it came to me, white-haired as I was: I would have to compete with him on his own ground, with love poetry. What an idea for a man of my age! All the same, I kept an eye out for a suitable subject. I had written some poems for Sinope, one of the Queen Mother's ladies-in-waiting (no, I shan't name her, she is too well known). When I met her she was sixteen years old and trembling on the edge of womanhood, childish and a flirt at the same time. She made no secret of the fact that she was on the look-out for a rich husband at court.

I teased her about the horrors of marriage. 'You'd be much better off with a cleric,' I said. 'They are free to have affairs and they have no wife to spend their money on.'

She laughed and whispered all sorts of wicked suggestions in my ear.

But a young girl could not be the subject of an old man's love poems – as Ovid said, old men are as out of place in bed as in war. I would be the laughing stock of the whole court. Yet I wanted to write of love. How could I do so without looking ridiculous? It was a problem.

In the end, it was the Queen Mother herself who found me my subject. I was talking to her one day at a reception in the salon of Claude-Catherine de Retz, in the faubourg du St Honoré. The Maréchale de Retz is a very cultured lady – they call her 'the tenth Muse' because she knows Greek and Hebrew and likes to surround herself with scholars and literary folk. Leaning on her cane, the Médicis widow pointed to a young woman dressed in grey sitting soberly in a corner talking to a friend.

'What about our Minerva, as we call her? Hélène de Surgères. She would be just the thing for you.' She wheezed garlic over me. 'Learned, virtuous, always with a book in her hand. She speaks several languages, you know. And she has recently lost her fiancé, poor soul. He was a soldier . . . these terrible wars, killing off all our young men!'

The old Queen's eyes misted over. She was off on her favourite subject and my poetry was forgotten, but one can't argue with queens.

As soon as I decently could, I made an excuse and went over to the two women in the corner and introduced myself. (Of course I knew I needed no introduction, but one has to preserve the form, for modesty's sake, at least.)

'You were speaking of Plato just now, I believe?' I said, by way of starting up the conversation.

'Oh yes,' cried Hélène's companion, Jeanne de Brissac. 'Don't you think he's just the most divine author you've ever come across?'

'One can't live by him, of course,' I replied, intending to provoke. Plato was going through an irritating revival in the ladies' salons. He has never been my favourite writer. 'For a start, his idea of love is so ethereal that the human race would have died out by now if we had followed his notions. Women, in my opinion, should be like Pythagoras' daughter-in-law, leaving their shame off with their underclothes and putting it on again with their bodices.' I was really warming to the subject.

Hélène turned her head away. Jeanne blushed, 'Oh, Monsieur Ronsard, how you tease one,' she said, but there was laughter in her eyes.

I could enjoy the part of a dirty old man if I hadn't my

reputation to consider. I suppose I should not get very far, which is some consolation; there is a craze at court for despising all bodily functions so that what's natural becomes cloaked in hypocrisy and riddled with shame. These ladies of the court seem to want to be all spirit, and that is going against nature, which created us body and spirit equally.

'What's your opinion, Mademoiselle Surgères?' I asked, forcing Hélène to turn her head back again.

'I think Plato is a very fine writer,' she replied, coolly, 'especially in the original Greek.'

I swallowed. 'You read Greek fluently, then? Very impressive. What other languages do you have?'

'Spanish – I am Spanish by birth.'

It was heavy weather, making conversation with Hélène. She answered my questions so soberly and quietly that I thought she must still be grieving for her dead fiancé. Now I know that lifelessness is the permanent condition of her soul. The philosophers say there are two attitudes to the human condition, to laugh like Democritus or weep like Heraclitus. Hélène wept – continually.

When I spoke to her about my plans to write a cycle of love poems, however, she became animated for a second, and the glint in her eye showed me that this pale Minerva was not immune to the temptations of fame.

After that I began to invite her out to walk with me in the Tuileries or take a boat down the Seine. As we strolled through the gardens laid out with rosemary, box and privet, I was subjected to hours of talk about Platonic love. She proved to me that my instincts had been right – Plato's theories of ideal beauty render life, and therefore art, sterile. Encouraged by Plato Hélène yearned for an impossible perfection and despised the humans she met for failing to achieve it. She had learned to set herself above nature.

'Poetry', I said one day, as we ambled among the elms and sycamores in the Tuileries, 'aspires to the perfection of a rose.'

'Is that all?' she said, disappointed. 'No higher than that?'

'What can be higher than nature? For me, art is inseparable from the chaos and disarray of life. It has little to do with the search for the absolute.' (I was exaggerating.)

God keep me from a woman who knows Greek and Latin!

Her inability to be simple, her prizing of the intellect above all else, chilled me. We took rides in a carriage, always with the elderly, Argus-eyed chaperone in a carriage two paces behind our own. We went to the home of the Secretary of State, Villeroy, who owned a house at Conflans, an island in the middle of the Seine. He had a marvellously rich library and generously allowed Amadis and me to work there sometimes. During our breaks Hélène would join us as we strolled along the sandy paths between the lawns, where the heady perfume of the orange trees sent my head spinning. But their scent was lost on Hélène.

'All knowledge comes to us through the senses,' I said, and quoted the paradox of Democritus. 'Nothing is in the intellect without first being in the senses.'

'Loving the intellect without loving the body is like preferring a picture which has no colour,' I said on another occasion. (I did rather lecture her, poor girl, but then I was partly working out the cycle of poetry through our conversation.) 'It's the flesh, the senses which give colour to life.' (I should have remembered, she likes pictures only in black and white.)

It was no use.

'I should like to live in a convent,' she said one day, leaning on the window-ledge, looking out from the Louvre over the fields to Montmartre.

I sighed. 'The only perfect love is fleshly, Mademoiselle. Against such a powerful god, prayers and fasting are of no avail.'

Her soul was like ice. Her joyless approach to life had merely been strengthened by the death of her fiancé. Her cult of death was frightening. One day she wept unrestrainedly at the tomb of an old friend.

'Nothing is prized by you unless it is dead,' I grumbled.

That is probably why there is so much humour in my poems to her, to counteract the general air of depression she scatters behind her (of course, *she* reads only sad poetry). Yes, she is more at home with ghosts than with the living. I am sure that, if I were dead, she would love me better.

Nevertheless, her reputation for learning, her apparently inexhaustible virtue (I know, I laid siege to it once, in a weak moment) and, above all, her name, the classical symbol of beauty, make her an eminently suitable choice for an old man's love poems. 'Her name, concentrate on her name,' I would repeat to myself after a particularly trying session.

Yet I pitied her too, pitied her proud and lonely spinsterhood. (The Queen Mother was right, our wars are condemning our women to celibacy.) With her two heavy braids looped up and framing her pale face, she will never be famous for her beauty, poor woman. Always dressed in a grey, high-collared dress with billowing sleeves, Hélène is one of the plainer of Catherine's ladies-in-waiting.

A special breed of women these are, the two hundred or so noble ladies the Queen Mother keeps around her. Ostensibly their role is to adorn the French court and make it the most elegant and cultured in Europe. Their job is to civilize the noblemen who have spent years fighting in the wars and return with manners more suited to the barracks than to court. These ladies exchange scented notes, act in comedies and ballets, play the lute and encourage their gallants to write verse for them. They are present on all royal occasions. With lowered eyes they participate in Good Friday processions. But they deceive no one; whenever they are around, the air is thick with sexuality. There have been one or two cases of lesbianism, and on one embarrassing occasion a search for pistols in the Louvre turned up four large phalluses hidden in a lady's trunk. They have a more sinister purpose, too, these ladies-in-waiting. Like Isabeau de Limeuil, they are there to divert the nobles from rebellion, to entice them into their beds, and then report back political secrets to the Queen Mother.

But I am sure that Hélène in her lofty rooms at the top of the palace (how often have I panted up those stairs to take her out!) has no time for such sexual intrigue. With her parchment-coloured skin she is hardly fitted by nature for such a task; the Queen Mother keeps her on for her learning, not her looks (she should be grateful, thin and plain as she is, that I have transformed her into a beauty through my poetry). And yet there were times when I suspected she wanted something more from me (sometimes a poet's insight can be a curse). 'You are free to love anyone you choose,' she said stiffly one day. Of course I was, why mention it unless. . . ? In her letters, too, there's a hint of looking for a husband. But she was never open with me. I felt her calculations. Since she could not have love, she was betting on fame. She is no saint, my Hélène. She recoils from the world, but her values are still its values and her judgements its judgements. There is a sort of spiritual dampness about her.

Well, she shall have her fame. My poems for her strike a new note in love poetry, I am sure of it, a note of irony and disillusion perhaps even with love itself. No sentiment, tenderness or convention has been allowed to creep into these poems. It is a purely professional collection, eked out with an old man's memories. It shall be an indiscreet trampling on the conventions of love poetry. Perhaps my Muse is freeing herself at last. But what will the court think? Ah, that's the problem.

Chapter 18

I am pouring myself a glass of wine as I approach the end of my story. Yes, it is almost time to finish. The new edition of my poems is nearly completed too. I shall soon be off to Paris to see the printers. Meanwhile . . .

Hélène's loyalty to Plato remained absolute (which is just as well, since I had become as impotent as Attis). The wars continued. The Queen Mother went on building a new Louvre on top of the old, paying out huge sums of money to foreign architects whilst her country starved. Then, suddenly, a truce was called and Catherine, always hopeful that the magic of love would unite the two factions, arranged a marriage between her daughter Marguerite and the Protestant prince, her cousin, Henri of Navarre. Her lively, black-eyed daughter (who scandalizes the court with her low-cut dresses and golden wigs) sulked at this plan, being in love with another nobleman. But Catherine's mind was made up, she would try every way to peace. All the Protestant leaders gathered in Paris for the marriage celebrations. There was duelling and jousting, and there were mock battles and other festivities in which both sides took part, Catholic with Protestant, in an attempt to exorcize political hatreds by acting them out in war-games.

But peace was a garment too frequently patched by the Queen Mother. It was splitting, coming away at the seams. Beneath the celebrations the atmosphere was tense and brooding. The city was crammed full of people. Swiss guards surrounded the Louvre. But the conspirators were inside the palace, not outside. The plot was hatched amongst extremist Catholics. The Protestant leader Coligny was fired at by a hired assassin as he walked past the palace. Badly injured, he was taken to his house and the news was brought to the King as he was playing tennis. Flinging down his racket, Charles yelled hysterically, 'Will I never have any peace?' But worse was to come. On the night of 23rd August, a bunch of Catholic extremists broke into Coligny's house and murdered him as he lay sick in bed.

The whole city was thrown into uproar. And then the horror – the massacre of three-quarters of the Protestant population in one night, under a sky as black as grapes. St Bartholomew – my tongue sticks in my mouth at the very name. The great stalking beast that had always been at my back, had finally caught up with me. Fires came out of the earth, as out of some giant's belly, and devoured our people.

The houses of Protestants were sacked. They were robbed, stripped and thrown into the Seine. Family quarrels and old scores were settled under the cloak of religion. At midday on the Monday a hawthorn flowered in the cemetery of the Innocents. Crowds flocked to see it, believing it was a sign from God that He approved the massacres. So they continued. Violence broke out in imitation in Rouen, Lyons and Orleans.

The King's ministers, taken aback by the violence, hastily tried to take control and argued that the massacres were necessary for the peace of the nation. But I knew, going through the mud and smoke, bending over the shattered bones of children, that peace bought at this price was worthless. Others wrote verses in support of the King (for he now pretended that the spontaneous unleashing of violence had been planned policy). I confess I tried but could not do so. The words would not come. 'But you have written such verse before,' they said. I shook my head. The extent of the horror had choked my imagination. They stayed for their pieces of gold. I threw the papers into the fire – and the pen I had used – and I took my horse and fled to the country. There, at least, the air would be pure.

But the red roses blooming in my garden were drops of blood shed during that night of terror. Dismembered corpses strewed their guts across my garden path and the fields were drenched in blood. My tranquil, friendly Loir seemed as threatening as the Seine which I had last seen filled with bodies, their torn limbs sticking up out of the black waters. The very moon was spattered with blood. I woke in the night, hearing the cries of women torn and bleeding from some soldier's lust. Children screamed. Soldiers grunted as they satisfied themselves and speared their prey. Licking their lips and salivating over the corpses, their faces became the face of the King. One by one, bodies fell with a thud on the cobbles. And then, at last, I thanked God I was not a soldier.

I could write no more verse for this King. I had finally found a horror so great that it burned out my hereditary instinct for self-preservation. I placated Charles with a few extracts from the ill-fated epic, but he was beyond all help on this earth. He was no longer a king, but a poor frightened boy pushed around by his mother and a handful of Catholic extremists. He, too, woke screaming at night, red-eyed and spitting blood. Twenty-one months later he died at his fortress in Vincennes, a sinister place haunted by crows and owls.

As Nostradamus predicted, Catherine lived to see her favourite son on the French throne. The year before Charles died, his younger brother Henri was elected King of Poland. The Polish ambassadors entered Paris in August, and Catherine, continuing her policy of using State occasions to make people forget the wars, gave a magnificent ball at the Tuileries. Ladies-in-waiting danced by candlelight to the music of Roland Lassus (a musician who seems indeed to have stolen his harmonies from the heavens to delight us here on earth). There was a ballet on the theme of France's beauty: sixteen ladies dressed in costumes representing the sixteen provinces of France. The horror of St Bartholomew's Day seemed on the surface to be forgotten. Henri set off for his icy kingdom, accompanied, I was glad to see, by Philippe Desportes.

With Desportes out of the way I found renewed enthusiasm for my Hélène cycle. I read through some of Joachim's poems again and borrowed his technique of satire and puns. Has it taken me all these years to achieve his skill in handling the sonnet form, to be able, finally, to adapt it to any emotion I choose? No, no, scrub out those lines. I am giving too much away again. The facts: after the publication of passages from my epic, Amadis, his job done, finally left my side to establish himself as a court poet. He had been anxious to go for a long time. I had kept putting off his departure, begging him to stay awhile longer with me. A selfish old man trying to pin down a gaily coloured butterfly.

And then, after Charles died, Desportes was back again. Henri had given his Polish subjects the slip and galloped half-way across Europe to claim his throne. He brought with him his band of young men, dressed in their starched ruffs, short cloaks and velvet bonnets such as prostitutes wear. Hélène went south with the court to welcome him. She sent me oranges from Avignon, I remember. Almost immediately upon his arrival in France Henri's mistress died and the court was plunged into extravagant mourning. The King led a funeral procession by night, wearing her cross around his neck and her ear-rings. Even I wrote poems lamenting her death, in which, I fancy, something of the King's hysteria is captured (I was told they practically had to stop him getting into the tomb with her).

It's no use, the court always wins in the end; we poets cannot live without her. I tried again with the new King. Oh yes, I don't give in that easily. I may be an old war-horse, but there is vigour in me yet. I wrote poems greeting Henri as the new ruler of France, poems even when he was in Poland (to prepare the ground). I gave him advice on how to govern – well, I have seen a few kings in my time. Pay your debts, I said, don't be extravagant (huh, that's funny), avoid flatterers, bring peace to your country. I asked permission to write satire. I did not always want to be writing about love, you see, I wanted to write on more serious topics (let someone else speak of arrows and tears and sighs). I outlined the themes – the decadence of the clergy, the clothes and extravagance of the courtiers. Not a peep out of him. You realize now why the Hélène poems are so important: *the King will read only love poetry*.

So a new tone was set at court. Philippe Desportes, charmer of ladies and spinner of light-hearted verses, had now firmly established himself. 'Ronsard is finished,' they began to say. 'Desportes is the leading French poet.' My poems for Hélène will prove them wrong. (Naturally I dropped the epic like a hot cake when Charles died. I never got paid for it anyway – and now in this collected edition there is no place for it. It doesn't fit. I shall have to tack it on at the end, like an afterbirth.)

Well, I am at St Côme, healed once again by Amadis's herbs and working on my fifth collected edition. (But still a trembling ghost of a man, sitting by the fire without sight or hearing or taste.) Meanwhile, Henri summons comedians from Italy to entertain the court and holds balls where men and women swap clothes and dance during Lent. His followers fight amongst themselves and kill each other off in duels. France needs a strong leader, I cry, and good councillors. She needs to pay off her debts and help the unemployed by giving jobs to Frenchmen rather than foreigners. The King ignores me.

Well, he won't be able to ignore Hélène's poems, oh no. These poems have something new in love poetry, a tone of irony that accords well with an old man (though I am not sure it will please Hélène). She still pursues me with letters full of Plato, demanding that the collection should do nothing to damage her good name. But there is little of the passionless Hélène in these poems. I have mingled in poems and memories from earlier, happier times. A golden vase that belonged to the Salviatis, a masked ball at which Marie executed her first steps, weaving in and out of the dancers like a spiral of smoke, delighting my heart . . . there is a lot of Marie in them. Like a sorcerer I go stirring up the ashes of lost loves and mix my memories according to a secret recipe in order to create the magic potion.

Yes, Hélène is a difficult person to write for. She gives off a chill that numbs my fingers whenever I take up my pen. There is a colour of ash about her. Why does she anticipate death so? Is it not possible for her to reach out and grab the slightest occasion of pleasure? No, her poems are not perfect. I am too old, she too cold. Nevertheless, they are the best I have written for a woman. Ironic, really.

It is almost time to set off for Paris to see this edition through the press. It is rumoured the King wears necklaces now and wanders around his apartments dressed in his wife's clothes. You see what I have to contend with. I wonder, shall I find a court full of women?

EPILOGUE

Once more I heave my pack of aching bones into the cushions and set off on the long journey to the capital. I deliver the manuscript to the printers and prepare myself to spend the next few weeks hanging around at court, biting my nails in anxiety. I have gambled everything on this edition. I nod distantly to Desportes. That man never seems to leave the King's side. Ah well, death will be the end of both of us, the years will swallow up our work. Everyone at court is wearing necklaces, but thankfully no one parades openly in clothes of the opposite sex – yet. The King's wife, Louise, drifts past like a pale lily, unspotted by the corruption around her, carrying out her many works of charity but unable to produce an heir.

On Sunday I visit Antoine at the house in the Fossés St Victor. The inscriptions from Homer are still painted on the façade, though their splendour is slightly faded now. His mistress opens the door and shows me into the study where Antoine is on his knees playing with his son Guillaume. The scene is of such domestic calm that I catch my breath in envy. Guillaume runs up to put his arms around me. At eight he reminds me so much of the little boy who stood on the doorstep, solemnly reciting Greek verse. He has the same high forehead as his father.

I remind Antoine of that first meeting. He laughs.

'I was dying to go with you to Germany. I was so jealous of you. Oh yes,' he says, as I look surprised, 'your reputation as an athlete had preceded you, and I had never been good at games. I had heard my father speak contemptuously of the education at the Stables, so I was determined to prove my superiority, at least in that regard.'

'And I thought you were an arrogant little runt.'

We laugh. Antoine pours out some wine.

'How far we've come,' he says, as we sit by the fire, two old men suddenly overwhelmed by memories. The child squats cross-legged by his father's chair, listening, amazed perhaps, that we could once have been young.

'Would we go through all that again, I wonder, if we had known in the beginning what it would cost us?'

'The meanness of kings.'

'The ignorance of the people.'

'The indifference of the court.'

We fall silent.

'I think we would,' I say.

'I think so too,' he murmurs, watching the flames crackle and leap in the hearth.

'After all, don't forget we have raised the standard of French poetry to a level never before attained,' I say, quoting one flattering review.

'Created a new language for poetry,' he adds, joining in the game.

'Reformed spelling.'

'Made people take poetry seriously.'

'Experimented with new forms and metres.'

'Supported royal policies.'

We grimace at each other.

He shakes his head, 'What does anyone care now? And do they even remember?'

'They will,' I reply, slapping my knee. 'They will, when this edition of mine is published. Then people will remember that our poetry is worth more than all Desportes's sugary love lyrics – and they'll persuade the King to support us again.'

He looks at me sadly. 'I hope you're right, Pierre. I hope you're right.'

Preparations are beginning for the Sunday afternoon concert. I take my leave. A deaf man has no place where music is being performed.

Riding back to Boncourt College in my carriage, I think over our conversation. Is it true that we would do it all over again, knowing what we know now? Poetry has been a bitter gift to many of us: to Antoine, who has soldiered on in the face of public indifference and neglect; to Joachim, for whom the world was an intrusion on his poetry; to Grévin, dying alone and unremembered in exile; to Peletier, whose efforts to reform our spelling have been constantly ridiculed. . . . And then there's Étiènne Jodelle. He died in poverty, a bitterly disappointed man. Jealous of others' success, he had refused to publish his poems or accept advice. When his posthumous edition came out, it was a great disappointment; many of the poems were mediocre and some bordered on the unintelligible. If only he had published them earlier, he could perhaps have improved them. But he refused to accept criticism.

Of all of us, perhaps only gentle Rémy Belleau found poetry a joy, but then he was made for sweetness. Lacking all ambition for himself, he saw it as his task to go on creating things of beauty in a world that values only the vulgar and the utilitarian. In the country, where for years he was tutor to a nobleman's family, Rémy struggled against a backcloth of violence and destruction, blackened villages and smoking fields to paint the delicate things – butterflies' wings, glowworms and oysters. He once showed me his collection of mounted stones – diamonds, rubies, opals and agates – and, lying amongst them, an odd-shaped pebble or a brightly coloured rock, which he valued just as much.

Rémy died last year in Paris. Antoine, Amadis and I carried the body of this gentle, friendly poet to its final resting-place. His life had been a blaze of beauty in the dark and stormy skies of our century. Is it enough to redeem us, I wonder, one creative spirit in an age of destruction? He once sent me an amethyst, the colour of wine, with a note, 'To protect you against drunkenness!' No, I can't get used to their trick of disappearing from my life. So many friends dead and I alone remain, a solitary monument to our hopes.

The moment has come, the moment I have been waiting for since this story began. My poems are out.
   'What sort of love poetry is this?' mocks the court.
   'He speaks of old age and death. Where is the passion, where the tenderness?'
   'He has no faith in love.'

'Give us back Desportes.'

That's it, then, my last great part has failed and my career as a courtier has finally come to an end. There is no room for me here amongst this powdered, perfumed younger generation that places Desportes above Ronsard. This court of homosexuals and transvestites, led by a sallow neurasthenic. At every turn I am thwarted. These curled and made-up courtiers have never done a day's work in their lives. They belch over my verses when they're bleary-eyed with too much wine and red meat. I am out of step with the times.

I return, defeated in my last great public battle, to private life in the country. There I find a letter from Hélène waiting for me. She lists her complaints. Item, I sometimes made her hair blonde in the poems – did I think she was a whore to dye her hair! Item, many of the incidents described in the poems never happened at all. She never said she was in love with me. Item, I must write a preface stating clearly that we had never been lovers, that our relationship had been conducted strictly according to the rules of Plato. Item . . . I throw the letter on the fire. Lovers! The wretched woman has only to take a look at herself in the mirror. I am a poet, for God's sake, not an historian. Poetry is concerned with the possible, not with facts. I am not obliged to tell the truth.

What is left for me now but death, the final part? Crippled by arthritis and plagued by gout, I am hardly a human being at all. I have a fever in my head and kidneys, not to mention other disgusting side-effects of old age which I would rather not go into here. I take opiates to make me sleep. Amadis can do nothing further for me, death is a goddess without eyes or heart.

Outside this room the wars continue. Bloody hail and sulphurous thunders fill our land. Red rain drenches the fields and roses weep tears of blood. The forces of evil are closing in around us; even poetry cannot save the world now. The barbarians are coming again.

And still the King refuses to pay his soldiers, spending all his money on clothes and dogs. The Crown is bankrupt and even the Queen Mother despairs of her favourite son. He goes barefoot in sackcloth and ashes to plead with God for an heir, whilst all wise men pray he will be childless. The kingdom will be handed over to a Protestant, but no matter. France needs new blood – that which runs in the veins of the Valois has become very thin and cold. They and I, who tried to serve them and failed, are going down together.

How grim these lines sound, how exceedingly cheerless. Yet in between the bouts of sickness I carry on visiting the poor, tending my marigolds, my foxgloves and my beans. Nature makes a very good alternative to 'civilization'. . . . Last night I burned all Marie's trinkets, her gloves, the lock of hair – and then, to cheer myself up, I burned Hélène's letters.

All this to distract myself from yet another failure. Yes, you may not be surprised to hear that my plan for self-knowledge has failed. When I look back over my life, I see no sense in it, no single purpose. Memories ebb and flow, some covered for ever by the waters of oblivion. I have played many roles, none of them with success. My self has gone changing shape in the wind, one part of my life is not consistent with another. It is futile to try to fix it, to portion it out into neat compartments. The more I try to understand my life, the more elusive it becomes, like holding water in your hand – the more you squeeze it, the more it flows out between your fingers. I was born and will die. These two certainties bound my life. I have no others.

Yet throughout it all, like the steady thrum of a lyre, my poetry. Yes, in the end I am brought back to this – this will be my last will and testament. My self, it seems to me, is empty, I belong entirely to my poetry. Well, it is too late to alter things now: a habit has become a way of life. Maybe it is true after all that an artist has no self, no personal ends. I feel that I have merely been the instrument through which my art has realized its purposes. I almost begin to think that the personal life of an artist is an irrelevance. What is man's life anyway – an autumn leaf that falls with the first strong breeze, a tiny sliver of foam on the water. Only my poetry will remain. This is not how I wanted to end . . .

The final portrait that I leave for posterity, however it will look, will not be my true self. I know that now. The portrait has become for ever distorted by the mask of fiction. I don't myself believe all that I have written here, why should anyone else? For instance, it is probable I was more in love with

Cassandra than I have admitted, more hurt by Marie's rejection than I have acknowledged. And there are mistakes over dates, small things, but worrying all the same. How much else has slipped from me? And even if I am speaking the truth, who cares in this unpoetic age? For poetry has become the image of the world for me, the sum total of my memories. And it is trivialities the reader wants.

Well, what does it matter? Here I sit looking out on to the land where I first learned to sing, where my poetry was born amongst the honeysuckle and the vine. How lucky I have been to spend my life with language and the lyre, moving even the hearts of stones. I have found poetry everywhere, in rocks and fountains, forests and meadows, found mysteries in the humblest flower. Since the century is corrupt, I must rely on my own judgement of myself as artist – yes, and my poems have been a plea for beauty in a world full of ugliness, a search for harmony in a world become more and more chaotic. I have tried to transform the mud of daily life into the pure spun gold of poetry. As long as there are still books in the world, my poems will be heard. And after that? Ah! My imagination does not stretch that far.

And now the smell of death lingers in my nostrils, it is my own death . . . am I ready for it? No, of course not; who can bear to look death in the face? No one, not even Socrates. And I have been a greater sinner than most men; I have allowed myself to be lured by the charms of the senses, I have more often lived by beauty than by truth. I am a maker of books, nothing else. In them lies any value my life has had, certainly not in my relations with others. I have, I admit it, been callous with women, envious of rivals, ambitious at court, a flatterer of princes (in short, a bit of a hypocrite). All this for the sake of my poetry, and therefore if I have been a bad poet, I deserve to be judged all the more severely. Shall I be damned? The Bible nowhere speaks of an artist saved by his art. Is Homer one of the damned then, and Virgil? Nevertheless, though salvation may not lie in literature, yet there has been, as Petrarch says, a way to salvation there for many. I am one of those. My poems are the best part of me, my life stands or falls by them.

A toast then to the Muses! Death itself cannot be more painful than this weighing of sorrows: let us leave this matter of self-knowledge for wiser men. It is time for me to seek out the black-eyed goddesses again, the only women who have ever really mattered. I wonder, old man as I am, can I catch them in their moonlit dance? I am playing a game against time now; it is just the two of us, jousting together. An unequal game, of course, time always wins in the end. But it can't be helped. I shall go on writing poetry till my last breath. I was wrong to doubt – the machinery was set in motion a long time ago, on that night when I first looked out of my window and saw the planets rolling in the heavens and nature as a mysterious poem. Yes, it was all set in action then. I have no choice but to continue.